THEOCLEA
(The Delphic Oracle)
and
PYTHAGORAS
in
ELEUSIS AND ATLANTIS

PanOrpheus

PanOrpheus Press
Thorndale, Pa. 19372
Theoclea (The Delphic Oracle) and Pythagoras in Eleusis and Atlantis
by Panorpheus

Copyright © 2013 by PanOrpheus

ISBN: 1482052229
ISBN-13: 9781482052220

All rights reserved. No part of this book may be reproduced by any mechanical, photographic, or electronic process, or in the form of a phonographic recording, nor may it be stored in a retrieval system, transmitted, or otherwise be copied for public or private use – other than for "fair use" as brief quotations embodied in articles and reviews – without prior written permission of the publisher.

The intent of the author is only to offer information of a general nature to help you in your quest for Spiritual Growth. In the event you use any of the information in this book for yourself, which is your constitutional right, the author and the publisher assume no responsibility for your actions.

Certain Characters in this book may have had real lives, however, events portrayed in this book are fictitious. Other characters are simply products of the author's imagination.

To a friend—

When she finally visited Eleusis, she said—"What happens next? I want more! There's got to be more!"

"There is more," I said, "there's Atlantis!"

PanOrpheus

Thanks and Appreciation

To Carl Kerenyi, Dr. Robert Schoch, Arysio Santos, Ignatius Donnelly, Edgar Cayce, Madame Blavatsky, and so many others who taught me, entertained me, and made me wonder about The Mysteries of Eleusis and Atlantis...and other Mysteries of our past and our ancestors.

The quote:
> "Twas on the plain, Eleusis
> where they met,
> mother and child; and all tearful regret
> was wiped away between them, as they sang
> and held each other,
> and the high world rang!"

...is from a poem by Edward Carpenter

The 'Invocations' mentioned in one of the opening chapters of the book are my own shortened versions of invocations from Thomas Taylor's book first published in the 1790's—'The Hymns of Orpheus'.

Parts of Theoclea's speech are paraphrases from the works of Dante. Chapter 25 in the 'Atlantis'
Section is my interpretation of Dante's voyage in the 'Paradiso—the third book of Dante's 'Divine Comedy'

Contents

Thanks and Appreciation v
Foreword xi

Book One...Eleusis

1. Three Children 1
2. On the Plain of Eleusis 9
3. The Invocations 17
4. Morain and Panelle 25
5. The KeyRose. 29
6. On the Island 43
7. The Sybil. 49
8. Pythagoras and Vorios 57
9. The Dancer. 69
10. The Dance 81
11. The Elements enter 93
12. Before the Speech 101
13. The Speech. 113
Epilogue 131

Book Two...Atlantis

1. More Whispers 137
2. The KeyRose Reading 143
3. The Vision 151

4. Pythagoras Arrives 159
5. Vorios and Theoclea 165
6. The Planning 171
7. The Stone and the Merchant 177
8. Pythagoras and Vorios 187
9. The Workshop 199
10. The Hanged Man 207
11. The Meeting 217
12. The Bonding 223
13. The First Ritual 237
14. The Sixth Day 251
15. Theoclea Bound 255
16. Theoclea Returns 271
17. The Attack 275
18. Another Dream 287
19. Theoclea, Morain, and Panelle 293
20. The Discussion 299
21. The Next Dream 305
22. On Atlantis 311
23. The Plain of Atlantis 323
24. The Grandfather 329
25. The Gryphon 337
26. Aurora 347
27. The Lady in White 357
28. The Guardian 365
29. Theoclea Returns 377
30. Theoclea Healed 379
31. 'Seeing' and 'Knowing' 383

The KeyRose Pieces mentioned in this book 401
Two Poems of Prophecy 426

*Take a look at our new website
www.delphic-oracle-books.com.
My facebook page is Pan Orpheus

My books can be ordered through createspace, and both the paperback and kindle versions are on Amazon.
To order from createspace go to the website above to get discount codes, then search PanOrpheus, and/or Oracle, and the paperback versions of the books will appear.

To order from Amazon.com, go to books and put in the appropriate search words:
www.amazon.com

There is also a Facebook group site called Delphic Oracle Mystical Magical Fact and Fiction that you can join.

Other books in the series are:
Theoclea (The Delphic Oracle) and Pythagoras in Egypt Phoebe (The Delphic Oracle) takes Nikola Tesla to Peru...and other stories by PanOrpheus Phoebe (The Delphic Oracle) and the Medallion of Gaia

Watch for the new book 'Songs and Stories from Tesla's Tower', coming out in the Fall of 2013

*Author's Note—If you have enjoyed this book, please leave a review. Reviews can be given at:
http://**www.amazon.com/heoclea-Pythagoras-Eleusis-Atlantis/product-reviews/1482052229/**
Just click on the 'Create a review' button.

Foreword

Regarding the Mysteries of Eleusis, I can say virtually nothing. For well over a thousand years there was a death penalty that applied to anyone who wrote or spoke about what occurred during the Mysteries held at the end of September in Greece! Carl Kerenyi and others have broken new ground, so I suppose that in 2013, we may now apply some conjecture to what happened. Perhaps the drink 'kykeon' put the pilgrims into some kind of a psychotropic state. Perhaps the Mysteries had something to do with the myth of Persephone as shown on the vases that were sold in the area where the Mysteries occurred. Perhaps fiction is the only way to imagine some answers, and in this book Theoclea's speech before the Mysteries are about to begin only provides more questions, and perhaps a few answers. Remember... this is a fictional ancient Greece...an alternative history in the metaphysical/fantasy genre.

The subject of Atlantis is another matter. There have been frequent catastrophic events in the history of our planet. Asteroids and large meteors have hit the

Earth, bursts of radiation...and other horrible events have resulted in earthquakes and tsunamis. Recently, Dr. Robert Schoch has suggested that there may have been a mega plasma blast from the sun in 9600 BC that may have triggered all kinds of catastrophic events on the Earth. He also postulates that this event may occur every 10,000 to 12,000 years! I will deal with that idea in my future books, so watch out...the Sun may not be as benevolent as we seem to think that it is!

I've been very impressed by Prof. Arysio Santos' theories about Atlantis. He has clearly established his belief that there was an enormous eruption of Krakatoa, and possibly one or more other volcanoes at around 9600 B.C. That is in accordance with Plato's dating of Atlantis' destruction in his Timaeus and Critias—the first writings on Atlantis in a modern language. At the same time, the ice was melting, an ending to the last Ice Age was occurring and the catastrophic explosion of Krakatoa may have had more than ten times the power of the entire nuclear arsenal of our time. The result is that the sea near the Malay peninsula, where we now see Java and Sumatra and other islands, rose by as much as 130 meters in a very short amount of time. A great deal of ash was created, and the atmosphere was no longer conducive to humans and animals. Many millions may have died in a matter of days.

It has been said that perhaps 30-40% of the species of animals and even one or two other species of human beings became extinct at that time. The religious books written near that time and afterward, especially those of the region, written perhaps in ancient writings similar to Sanskrit and Dravida, all mention a great catastrophe. If you look at the area of Java and Sumatra today and lower the sea level by 130 metres you get a continent "the size of Libya and Asia combined", according to Plato. It would have extended down much closer to Australia.

Also—please remember this—The Greeks of Plato's day knew nothing of the existence of North and South America. Maps of Plato's time show one continent that includes Libya (North Africa), Europe, and the whole of the middle East well into Asia (Asia Minor) and beyond to the shores of the Eastern sea. The British Isles are shown, as well as an Island called Taprobane in Indonesia...assumed by some today to be Sumatra. The one continent and the islands are surrounded by the Great Sea, or Outer Ocean. The terms 'Atlantic Ocean', 'Pacific Ocean' and other subdivisions of the 'Outer Ocean' of the Greeks are relatively modern terms from *our time*...those terms were unknown to the Greeks. A map might have shown the ocean around Taprobane (Sumatra) as being 'the Ocean of Atlantis'...where the Twin Pillars of Atlas existed.

'Twin Pillars' are mentioned by Plato in his description of Atlantis in the Timaeus and Critias, and Dr. Santos' interpretation of the works. Gibraltar comes to mind, of course when thinking of 'twin pillars'. If one were to move eastward from the Mediterranean sea, there were other places where one might see rocky places similar to Gibraltar that would resemble the 'twin pillars' suggested by Prof. Santos. The idea that Krakatoa and another volcano formed the "Twin Pillars" of Atlas, and that they were somehow a mirror of the Twin Pillars of Hercules (Herakles) is open to conjecture. There was a phrase that the Greeks used—'The Sun rose between the Pillars of Atlas (in the east) and set between the Pillars of Hercules (in the west—Gibraltar).

Dr. Santos'choice for the location of Atlantis is a part of the world that is the most unstable part... called "the fire belt" of the earth...there are simply more volcanoes, a history of destructive Tsunamis, and other catastrophic activites in and around Java and Sumatra...a proven history of the unstable nature of that part of the world.

So what does all of this have to do with our Oracle—Theoclea, and the Spiritual world that she lives in. In this novel, I've combined Carl Kerenyi's ideas on Eleusis, Edgar Cayce's views of Atlantis, Madame Blavatsky's occult writings on Atlantis, other sources too numerous to mention, and combined them with the latest scientific theories of Prof. Santos. Through imagination and conjecture I've created a backround for an idea.

Theoclea is the ultimate *'Seer'*. She can *see* an event of the past or future...but she doesn't always *know* the 'why', 'where', or 'when' of the vision. Her position as the Oracle of the Temple of Delphi demands that she interpret a question given to her...she must always choose her words carefully. In this book...a work of fiction...I have chosen to present her in that way.

Theoclea is surrounded by counselors...one of whom is Pythagoras. He's the ultimate person in my fiction who *knows*. His *knowing* is composed of what he carefully calls suppositions; theories; legends; myths; possibilities, and other somewhat vague terms...he *knows*, but often is uncertain about how much to reveal. *The final confrontation of the 'seeing' and 'knowing' are ultimately what this novel is about.*

So, once again I must say that you are about to enter a world that is not Ancient Greece, but simply a world that "resembles" Ancient Greece in many ways. A dream, a vision, populated with people with enormous powers. Sometimes some of them use these powers against others. Theoclea, The Delphic Oracle seeks to balance all of this, for she feels that balance is the answer to our unspoken question. In the end, it is up to all of us to decide if she succeeds.

Book One-
Eleusis

"Midway
In the journey
of this life,
I found myself
in a dark wood,
for I had
lost
the right path"

Dante...The Inferno

Chapter One...
Three Children

The bright scattered sunlight was diffused by the leaves of the trees, creating a multitude of changing patterns in an ancient forest.

"Look—do you *see* that cloud in the sky?" Theoclea said. "It's pointing to the magic grove! There's the Pan statue, in the grass! Now I *know* that we're on the right path!"

Theoclea carefully led the way to a stand of trees; the others followed behind her. They were children, they were different, and they viewed the world with a heightened sense of wonder. They passed an empty donation urn, and peered into it.

"I've been told to stay away from these urns, and never to touch one. They have spells on them!" Theoclea said.

It was a beautiful spring day and there were moss-covered rocks on the ground. Theoclea picked up one of the rocks, put it in a fabric bag, and said,

"I have a new saying—if you if pick up a rock, you must return and place three rocks on the same spot!"

"Theoclea—you're going to be a writer, the cards have told me that," said Troyana. Finally they entered a clearing ringed with pine trees. They approached the center, and Theoclea pointed ahead.

"Do you see that big standing stone? That's another marker...we're getting closer! There's the treasure chest!" Theoclea said excitedly. She pointed to an old chest that was in the middle of the grove, and hanging from the gold lock on the chest was a large red key.

"That red key opens the chest," Theoclea said. "I opened it this morning and it was full of papers with pictures and symbols on them." Carefully, she took the red key, and inserted it into the lock. The lock opened and she lifted up the top of the chest, as the two other girls looked on in wonder.

"The papers are gone! It's full of clothing and other things. We can all dress up for the ritual!"

Chapter One...Three Children

"Why do we have to dress up?" said Anka, "It's always hard to find the right things to wear when we do this."

"We have to dress up so that we can BE the Goddesses, you know that! Now today, Anka, you'll be Artemis! There's a bow and arrows in the trunk! Here's a white tunic that you can wear, too."

"Why can't I be Aphrodite, Theoclea, you always get the best part!"

"Alright, Anka, I know what you want, so let's let the stones decide!"

"Yes, the stones," Anka said, taking some stones of various colors out of her pocket. Bending down, the others joined her. She rolled the stones on the ground, and shrieked with delight. "You see, the stones are saying that I shall be Aphrodite today, and you shall be Artemis!"

Troyana watched them, shaking her red hair.

"When will the two of you ever learn to stop fighting over these things? I have the best way." She took out some cards from her pocket with strange symbols that she had drawn on them.

"You may think that I drew these yesterday, but you're wrong," she said in a low mysterious voice.

She motioned to Theoclea and Anka to be seated. They all sat down on the mossy-cool ground. Continuing in a low voice, Troyana said, "these are the cards of a Sybil, and only I know what they mean! The symbols come from Egypt, and they're very old!"

"Oh Troyana, we know that you drew these cards yourself," Anka said.

"Hush, little ones, these cards can read the past, present and future! I know this to be true!"

Theoclea thought for a moment. "I think that maybe we can use the cards in our ritual! Yes," Theoclea continued, "that's the spell we can work on, seeing into the future…Here's the chant, we have to practice it. Over and over we can say 'It's starting, it's starting, it's starting'. We shall begin, of course with all of the proper things, just like they do at the Temple. The purification of the members, the dark invocations, the directions, and, well you know, all of that silly stuff! Then we'll dance and chant round and round, and THEN we'll look at the cards!"

"They don't do that at the Temple," said Troyana.

"How do YOU know?" said Theoclea. "Do you see them in the clouds, like I do? Do you hear their whispers?"

Chapter One...Three Children

"Here she goes," said Anka. "Calm down Theoclea, it's only pretending."

"Pretending, you say, pretending, well how 'bout this, is this pretending?"

She stared at the stones on the ground intently, and nothing happened. Troyana looked doubtfully at Anka. Suddenly, Theoclea looked up and saw her friends as if they were frozen in time, as if an old crystal film projector like the kind they had on Atlantis had stopped, and only one frame of a black and white film could be seen. She looked around and it seemed as if the daylight had disappeared, as if it were night. There was no breeze. She was sitting on the ground, with her friends, but they were frozen on the spot, looking at each other doubtfully. She looked around again, and knew that something was wrong. A loud cracking sound broke the silence. She faced the direction of the sound and saw a tree, and in an instant she *knew* that it was about to fall.

She looked at the others, frozen in the frame of black and white. She looked at the tree—it was frozen as well, but she had heard the sound and she *knew* that the tree would injure them. She *saw* the direction of its fall. She looked up and there were vague crystal lanterns against a black sky. In an instant the light came back, and she grabbed both of her friends and screamed at them, pushing them away as hard as she could, and throwing all of her weight at them. The tree fell with a loud crack, and she blacked out. All was blackness, except for the amorphous light-shapes.

Suddenly the amorphous lights took shape and she saw that she was in the subterranean room where the Oracle gave her prophecies. The room was cloudy. She was sitting on the chair, the one at the Temple, where the Oracle sat. She smelled the funny smell that came from the chamber, and she wore the Red Key on a thong around her neck. She saw faces, she heard whispers. Then all was darkness. For a brief moment she saw a gate with white crystal lights flowing away from it it. A man was standing near the gate. She touched the gate, then held her right arm out in a "come hither" gesture, her palm up. She brought her left hand forward, and placed it directly over her right hand so that the thumb and all fingers touched. She folded over the middle fingers, so that only the thumbs, forefingers and little fingers were touching. Quickly, she brought both hands to an upright position, the hands still clasped, the fingers and the thumbs pointing upward. The sign looked like the gate. She then parted her hands, palms up, mimicking the flowing strands of white crystal light that flowed away from the gate. Then all was blackness. Slowly a small circle of light appeared in the darkness. The light grew, until she heard familiar voices, and saw familiar faces. The light brightened, and the clouds parted.

"Theoclea, are you all right?" Anka said.

"Theoclea, you saved us, then you fainted. What happened?" Troyana said. Tears appeared in Theoclea's eyes, and she started to cry.

"Yes Theoclea," Anka said, "What did you see, you saved us from the falling of the tree." She pointed at the tree that rested only a few feet away from them.

"What happened, Theoclea?" Troyana said once more.

Theoclea tried to hold back the tears, and when she finally calmed back down a bit, the crying stopped. She looked at both of her friends as if *seeing* and *knowing* them for the first time. Then she said,

"There was a tree, then…strange crystal lights in the sky…there was a room with the Oracle's chair in it. Then I saw…a gate with lights on it. A man was standing near the gate." She paused as if trying to remember.

"I touched the gate, and…I…did something with my hands…I think that I saw…the…the…

FUTURE!"

Chapter Two...
On the Plain Of Eleusis

The sky was a deep blue without even a wisp of a cloud, and sunlight flooded the plain. If you looked directly over your right shoulder, you would have seen a low tree line. If you moved your gaze slowly to the left, the tree line arched up slowly, then dropped slowly, leveled off, then arched slowly up again, and dropped slowly once more to meet the horizon directly over your left shoulder. It was a breathtaking panoramic view of a mountain. The shape was repeated on the plain of Eleusis where a large gate was being erected made of poles and white crystal lights. The gate itself was a reflection of the shape of the mountain.

Demetrios surveyed the field in front of the stage where the rehearsals and event would be held. A stage was being built especially for the appearance of Theoclea, the Delphic Oracle.

"Sephera," he said to a gray haired woman, in her mid-fifties, next to him, "the preparations for the Festival and the Mysteries are going well." The woman, Sephera had a confident smile and a commanding presence.

"Good," she said. "Demetrios, this is very important, have the Priests and Priestesses of the Mysteries had the Oracle's wishes made known to them?"

"Yes, Sephera, they have, and there are no problems there." Sephera looked at the mountains and then at the Festival Gate. The workmen were lifting strings of crystal lights up on the poles.

"Demetrios, Theoclea wants you to use certain invocations of Orpheus in the Opening Ritual of festival week. She has shortened the invocations, and made certain changes in them, are you aware of that?"

"Yes, Sephera, although I would prefer to use something more modern."

"No," Sephera said, "everything is to be done according to Theoclea's wishes. I see that the gate to the plain of Eleusis is being erected with white lights, according to her design."

Chapter Two…On the Plain Of Eleusis

"Yes, the gate will look exactly like the drawing that I was given."

"Demetrios, the gate is being made to look like the headdress of a Sumerian Goddess, Inanna, but that is to be kept secret, no one is to know the source of the design, no one, Demetrios, that's a direct order from Theoclea!"

Demetrios looked at the gate, and then at the plain of Eleusis that spread out in front of it. He hummed a tune as he surveyed the scene.

"What are you humming, Demetrios?" Sephera said.

"Oh, I'm working on a song about Persephone," he replied. "I've got everything but the last few lines. I've rehearsed it with my musicians, but I just can't get the lyrics right at the end of the song." His attention was brought back to the discussion.

"Have you ever met Theoclea?" Demetrios said.

"Yes, I met Theoclea a year ago when I was summoned to Delphi to discuss the possible plans for this event."

"Well, what's Theoclea like?" Demetrios said. "She's been sequestered in that old Temple for so long, is she aware of the happenings in the modern world?"

Sephera paused a moment and then said—

"She's...different, no doubt of that. She has dark hair and an innocent, almost child-like smile. When I asked her if she wanted to see the Mysteries herself, she told me that there was no need for her to attend. She said that she had envisioned the Mysteries of Eleusis in her mind last year! She felt oath bound to secrecy, like all of the other pilgrims. She wanted the same Invocations of Orpheus that were said last year to be spoken by you, Demetrios, at the opening ritual of festival week, before the Mysteries! She indicated to me the changes that she had made to the invocations so that her oath of secrecy would not be broken. It's hard to believe that she could have envisioned the Mysteries in her mind, but then how would she have known which Invocations were chosen last year for the Mysteries?"

Demetrios became emphatic—"The Temple of Delphi is the richest Temple in Greece! The presence of the Oracle keeps the money and the gifts flowing. You'll see, before Theoclea speaks on the last night, the Delphi crowd will put out those stone donation urns. The urns will be all over the plain of Eleusis. Panelle's Guardian Unit will carefully guard them and empty them quickly. The Temple of Delphi will

Chapter Two...On the Plain Of Eleusis

leave here with lots of donations to fill their coffers. Theoclea is their treasure! It's rumored that they have informants everywhere. If a wealthy nobleman, or politician seeks a prophecy, you can be sure that certain people at the Temple of Delphi know the intimate details of the person's life, before anyone offers a question to Theoclea. I have my doubts about all of it," Demetrios said.

"Have you read her book, Demetrios?" Sephera said.

"You mean '*WHISPERS*'? Of course I've read it! Almost everyone that I know has either read it, or had it read to them! Some of the sayings contain wisdom, I have to admit. There's no doubt in my mind that she's a brilliant gifted woman, probably the greatest of all the Delphic Oracles."

Sephera paused for a moment, then said, "She's certainly the most beloved of all the Pythian Priestesses. The people call her 'dear one'."

Dementrios was still adamant.

"That doesn't change my doubtful attitude toward the others at the Temple, or my suspicions about past practices of her predecessors. I know that one of her teachers was Pythagoras, and I admire him, and have respect for his work, but what about Vorios, and the

Magicians at the Temple? Her closest friends, that woman on the island, and the Sybil, are diviners as well. I wouldn't trust them. I suppose that the Priests and Priestesses at the Temple are okay. Why is she always protected by Morain and Panelle? It's all suspect as far as I'm concerned. Who knows what trickery Theoclea herself uses."

"Let's get back to the planning. Theoclea requested that you, Demetrios, provide music for the opening and closing excercises. She requested a certain song that she said you were working on. She told me that she had heard your musicians and your music!"

Demetrios shook his head. "We've never performed at Delphi, or anywhere near Delphi, that's impossible!"

"She told me to give you this parchment." Sephera handed him a rolled parchment tied with a red ribbon. He untied the ribbon and looked at the words on the parchment.

> "Twas on the Plain Eleusis
> where they met
> Mother and child;
> and all tearful with regret…"

Chapter Two...On the Plain Of Eleusis

He gasped, and stammered out—

"My God, the lyrics, how is this possible? They must have informers everywhere! These are the lyrics to that song that I've been working on, the Persephone song. I've rehearsed it with the musicians. I've got most of it finished, this is the last part. How could she have gotten the lyrics? See what I told you? They have informers everywhere. Why...even one of my musicians could have been contacted, they're always in need of money!"

His attention wandered to the Gate and the Plain again.

> "Twas on the plain Eleusis
> where they met
> Mother and child;
> and all tearful with regret..."

"If I take a word or two out, and add...let's see... perhaps..."

> Twas on the plain, Eleusis
> where they met,
> mother and child; and all tearful regret
> was wiped away between them, as they sang

and held each other,
and the high world rang.

"That's it, Sephera, the end of my Persephone song!" he cried. Then bursting out in song he sang the words again.

"Twas on the plain, Eleusis
where they met,
mother and child; and all tearful regret
was wiped away between them, as they sang
and held each other,
and the high world rang!"

He looked at Sephera. "Perfect! One never knows when an inspiration can come!" She smiled a somewhat doubtful smile back at him, and gazed at the plain of Eleusis.

"I had forgotten… this is where Demeter was reunited with Persephone…how could I have forgotten that?" she said.

Chapter Three...
The Invocations

Sephera went on to describe the Oracle. As she spoke, Demetrios listened, with renewed interest.

"As I was saying before...she's different...but when I got to know her a little better, I found Theoclea to be delightful and gracious," Sephera said. "Her black hair is cut in the way that a child's hair would be cut. She also has an immediately endearing quality to her. Theoclea has a lovely child-like smile. She asked me about myself, as if it were the most important thing of the moment to know all of the facts of my life. She said something to me that I shall always remember."

'I like to know all about the people that I see, Sephera. It's like my visions—I just don't like to see half of the picture, I want to know—all of it.'

"I had the feeling that she was seeing far more than anyone I was ever likely to meet. I wound up telling her many of the details of my life. She did so as well and there was this feeling of our being confidants immediately. After we'd told each other about ourselves, I became aware that I had forgotten the formalities and started to rattle off a series of her accomplishments, her titles, and more. After I was finished, she looked at me like a child and whispered to me as if we were childhood friends,

'I have the Red Key, and the Rose Medallion, the Token of Inanna' and like a child wanting to show a secret gift, she said, *'would you like to see them?'"*

"She reached into a pouch and took them out. She placed the Red Key around her neck, and looked at me with a sly smile. The medallion was made of red clay, about three inches wide. On one side was the face of a Goddess, the other side was blank. She gave it to me and asked me to stare at the face side, then turn to the blank side. I did what she asked me to do, and Theoclea asked me if I saw any writing or pictures on the blank side. I tried hard, but I saw nothing.

She looked at me curiously, and stared at the face side of the medallion. After a short time had passed, Theoclea turned the medallion over, stared at the

Chapter Three...The Invocations

blank side and a wide grin appeared on her face, tinged with excitement. She looked back at me, and then at the Medallion, and said *'Sephera, it's starting, it's starting!'* She looked up at the sky and shouted loudly—

IT'S STARTING!"

"It's starting?" Demetrios said. "Is that all that she said? It's starting?"

"Yes," sighed Sephera, "that's what she said."

"It's starting." Demetrios paused, deep in thought. He shook his head. "I'm afraid that we're all in for it, definitely in for it!" Sephera looked at Demetrios, and shook her head in agreement.

"That's what her Counselor Morain, and her Protector Panelle said to me, when I met them 'We're ALL in for it!'" Sephera and Demetrios looked up at the sky. A flight of Geese could be seen flying from East to West.

"Geese flying west, is this their season?" he mused. "It's starting, that's what she said, not even, perhaps one or two words after that?"

"No, that was it."

"Oh, yes, Demetrios, there is one more thing. Here are the four Invocations that Theoclea wants you to say at the Opening Ritual on the first day of the week-long festival prior to the Mysteries." He looked at the invocations.

"Okay, Apollo, Dionysus, I can understand that, they're her patron Gods, but why the Moon, and the Stars? I think that two invocations always are proper, don't you Sephera? Four invocations, it seems odd. Well, she's shortened them and made changes, thank the Gods and the Goddesses."

THE INVOCATIONS...

THE MOON

"Hear, Goddess Queen, diffusing silver light
Bull horn'd and wand'ring
through the gloom of night,
With stars surrounded,
and with circuit wide
Night's torch extending
Thro' the heavens you ride

Female and Male
with borrowed rays you shine,
now full orb'd, now tending to decline,
Mother of ages, fruit producing moon,

Chapter Three...The Invocations

whose Amber orb makes Night's reflected noon

Come blessed Goddess, prudent, starry, bright
Come Moony Lamp with chaste and splendid light
Shine on these sacred rites
with prosperous rays, and please accept the Pilgrim's mystic praise.

THE STARS...

With Holy Voice I call the Stars on high,
pure sacred lights and genii of the sky.
Celestial stars, the progeny of Night,
in whirling circles beaming far your light

Powerful rays around the heav'ns you throw,
eternal fires, the source of all below.
With flames significant of Fate ye shine,
and light a path for all mankind!

Hail twinkling, joyful, ever wakeful fires!
With Hope, shine on all our just desires.
Give these sacred rites life giving rays,
and end our works devoted to your praise!

To Apollo....the Light

Theoclea (The Delphic Oracle) and Pythagoras in Eleusus and Atlantis

"Oh, Apollo,
whose light producing eye
views all within
and all beneath the sky.
'Tis thee all Nature's Music to inspire
with various sounds and harmonious lyre.
With the right hand the source
of morning light, and with the left
The Father of the Night.
Immortal Apollo, all-searching,
bearing light,
source of sustenance, pure and fiery bright.
Great eye of nature
and the Starry Skies,
doom'd with immortal flames to set and rise.
Propitious on these Mystic Labors shine, and
bless these Pilgrims with a life divine.

To Dionysos….the Dark

I call upon loud-roaring and Night reveling Dionysos,
primeval, two-natured, thrice-born, Bacchic lord,
dark, secretive, two-horned and two-shaped.
Ivy-covered

Chapter Three...The Invocations

Spirit of the midnight revels, wrapt in foliage, decked with grape clusters.
Resourceful Dionysos, immortal god sired by Zeus When he mated with Persephone in unspeakable union.
Hearken to my voice, O blessed one, and with your dark wine and madness
breathe on me a spirit that creates Balance and Union, for one cannot achieve perfect truth until The Light and The Dark are balanced

Chapter Four...
Morain and Panelle

"Morain, is it true? I've heard a rumor that I can hardly believe. Does she really want to go there?"

Morain sighed,

"Yes, what you've heard is true, Panelle, she insists on going. She has her heart set on it."

"But Morain, how can I protect her? The crowds, the revelry, anything can happen!"

"You'll have to protect her with all of the magic that you can summon up. You'll have to use all of your gifts. The plan is for both of us to be with her constantly."

"But what if she goes into a trance? There are times when she's scarcely lucid!"

Morain thought for a moment. "Panelle, you're her Protector, her Guardian, and I'm her Counselor, her closest advisor. We'll have to be constantly looking at the crowds as well as attending to her well-being and balance. Panelle, the only time that she's allowed to be out of my sight is when she seeks the advice of trusted friends or advisors. For instance, when she travels to the island of Hydros, to see her old friend, Anka, or when she visits Troyana, the Sybil."

"I know," said Panelle. "For four days I have to wait on the shore for her return from Hydros. Morain, I know that she meets Anka on the island, but what is it that she does when she's there?"

Morain shrugged her shoulders, and ran her fingers through her short jet black hair.

"I have little to tell you. She goes there to see her childhood friend, Anka, the Queen of Hydros. All of the inhabitants of the island walk about in the nude. Anka never leaves the island and considers nudity to be a way of life. She's a skilled practitioner of Hunaos, divination using stones. You do know that Theoclea, Anka, and Troyana, the Sybil, were friends that played together and grew up together, don't you Panelle? Anka is a beautiful woman with short gray hair—she's probably a little older than Theoclea. As a young

Chapter Four...Morain and Panelle

woman, Anka was drawn to Hydros and its lifestyle and has been there ever since. As I said before, she never leaves the island. Panelle, all of this is common knowledge."

"I know," said Panelle, "but I was hoping that you could tell me more."

"My oath of secrecy forbids it," Morain said, "and I'm not allowed to be present at the conversations that go on between them. She refers to Anka as her first mentor. Now let's start planning for the trip to Eleusis. I'm worried, she insists on visiting the tent city. She wants to see the entertainment, and visit the market. She wants to attend the rituals, and she definitely wants to meet the pilgrims."

"My God," Panelle said, "does she realize what she might see?"

"Yes, replied Morain, "I've told her that for most of her life she's seen near perfect rituals, rituals in which the circle is always cast and opened properly, rituals in which the elements and directions are greeted and said farewell to properly, with the most noble language."

"Even the followers of Dionysus know the proprieties of the Temple. She knows that she might see the Gods and Goddesses invoked through chanting and dance, and that nudity is practiced in many of the pilgrims' rituals."

Panelle shook her head and then said—

"Does she know that sometimes they don't bother to open the circle—say farewell to the directions—say farewell to the Gods and Goddesses? Why they simply drink themselves into a stupor, dance all night, and then fall asleep at the fire."

"Yes," Morain said, running her fingers through her hair once again, "but she keeps telling me that many of the pilgrims come from places where the customs are different. Ecstatic dancing, chanting, all different kinds of music…she says that she has seen parts of the rituals in the clouds that coalesce in her mind. She wants to experience them. She claims that they're magnificent in their own way. She also wants to visit the merchants, and perhaps buy some gifts. She keeps on saying that she wants to 'see it all'."

Panelle put her palm on her forehead and said, "She wants to 'see it all'. We're in for it, we're definitely in for it!"

"Yes," sighed Morain, and in a dark tone of voice she replied, "no doubt about it, Panelle, we're definitely in for it."

Chapter Five...
The KeyRose

She was the Delphic Oracle, the Pythian Priestess, the Pythia, the Dragon Priestess of the Earth. The Gods and Goddesses had inspired her, and she had achieved a great deal. Her name, Theoclea meant 'The Glory of the Gods and Goddesses'. She had written a book of wisdom widely read by the Greek people called 'Whispers', and her Prophecies were widely credited with having brought back a sense of pride that the Greek people had in the institution of the Oracle, although there were still many who were suspicious of The Temple and its' inhabitants.

One night, she lay on her bed and thought back to her initiation as the Oracle many years before. Theoclea had been initiated, and three days later,

Theoclea (The Delphic Oracle) and Pythagoras in Eleusus and Atlantis

Pythagoras, one of her teachers had departed. She had no idea of whether she would see him again. They shared a secret that might be revealed some time in the future. Her powers of prophecy were not yet strong enough to know when. She sat in her bedchamber and reviewed some of the events that had occurred in the training that she had received prior to her initiation—and her thoughts lapsed into daydreams.

A few months before her initiation as the Delphic Oracle, Theoclea was given the Treasure Chest of Orpheus. It was to be given to the Oracle who was brave enough to become both Priestess of Apollo and Dionysus. She was the first one in 700 years to have been strong and confident enough to receive the training that Orpheus had described in his writings. The Temple of Delphi had two doors and two altar rooms for both of the Gods, but the Priests and Priestesses who conducted the rituals seemed to be from one group or the other. Theoclea was determined to realize one of Orpheus' dreams, unification.

When the Treasure chest was given to her, she had already had sufficient training in control of her breathing. She was ready to assume the duties of the Oracle, entering the subterranean chamber two days a month, and sitting on the Tripod chair, above the cracks in the earth that emitted the trance-inducing fumes. The spot was called the 'Hearth at the Navel of the Earth', and had been known for thousands of years for the gases that produced states of euphoria and trance. She was trained to use the dream state to commune with the God Apollo, and answer questions. Breath control and concentration were taught and practiced by the Priests and Priestesses, and they passed on all of their knowledge to her. She was also taught the wisdom that Pythagoras thought would be helpful to her in her new position and responsibilities.

Months before her initiation, when she opened up the Treasure chest of Orpheus, it had not been opened in seven hundred years. No one else was allowed to be in the room, for those were Orpheus' wishes. She carefully took out the items that were described. There was a Medallion with the face of a Goddess that she was later to identify as Inanna, an ancient Sumerian Goddess whose symbol was *The Rose*. It was on a leather thong, and she carefully placed it around her neck. She read about the suggestions for its use. There was a Red Key, a Black Key, and a Gold Key, and she read Orpheus' description of the history of the keys. There were other things, too numerous to mention. Finally, there was a box with a drawing of the Red Key on the top of the box.

She carefully read the instructions from Orpheus.

"You will have to practice with this, it will take time for you to learn how to use it, but it may become one of the most valuable divination tools that you will have. It is to be used with another object called The Pentacle and the Rose. The symbol of the Pentacle and the Rose must be used to give it more power." She read more. She knew that her initiation was to happen in a few months, and she practiced with the box each day. The treasure chest also had a drawing of a gold colored basket with a dark metal star in it, and four roughly drawn roses at four of the points. She had no idea that three days after her initiation Pythagoras would enter the subterranean chamber…and present her with a fully charged Pentacle and Rose. Her mind went back to the last time that she had seen Pythagoras…

She was sitting in the subterranean chamber on the Tripod Chair, three days after her initiation. Pythagoras entered the chamber and revealed to her that he had a gift for her, and would be leaving Delphi. The gift was the Pentacle and Rose divination tool that he had been given during the eleven years that he had studied to be a Priest in Egypt. He explained to her that he was told that the time would come when he would have to give it to another, and that he would know who that person was and immediately know whether they were worthy of it.

He told her that he had learned to use it, but it had ceased to work for him. He attributed this to his studies of logic and reason, and that he had neglected the instinctual, imaginative side of his mind.

Pythagoras gazed into her trance-laden eyes, and pointedly said, "I think that I may have lost part of it during my travels during the last few years." Then he waited for her to respond. He gave her the Pentacle and Rose–a gold-colored basket with a dark metal star in it, and four fresh roses that were arranged at four points, with the fifth space at the bottom being empty.

Theoclea stared at the gift. He waited patiently for her response. Theoclea immediately knew that the KeyRose box, one of the divination tools that was found in the Treasure box of Orpheus was indeed the missing part, for the Pentacle and Rose was described in the parchment of Orpheus' that was in the box.

Theoclea had decided to keep the KeyRose box behind the Tripod chair for she knew that it would prove to be helpful in some of her divination work.

She sat on the Tripod chair in the subterranean Chamber below the Temple of Delphi. The fumes were rising. The Oomphalos stone that also emitted the gases stood about 10 feet away. She looked at the basket, the metal star and the roses, and then said:

"Thank you, Pythagoras." Then she reached down through the smoke and gases that surrounded the chair, and produced the KeyRose box.

"This is the missing part Pythagoras," she said.

"Yes," he smiled, *"You are truly worthy of this gift."*

Her daydream ended...she shook her head and realized that she had something to do before going to sleep. Theoclea rose from the bed, and looked out the window that was beside the bed. Geese were flying in front a cloud that obscured the moon. She took the KeyRose Box off of its shelf and sat down at the writing desk in her chamber. She held the box in her hand, and fondly touched the drawing of the Red Key on the top of the box.

She opened the box and placed all of the pieces inside on a black cloth on the desk. She smiled as she handled the thirty images, like seeing old friends. The images were on small gold-colored thick pieces of fine paper. The warm radiance of a crystal lantern illuminated the black cloth and the pieces.

One by one she placed them on the right side of the cloth, making sure that all of the images could be seen. She left the blank pieces in the box.

She looked down at all of the familiar pieces on the right side of the cloth. The Ancient Mother; the

Chapter Five...The KeyRose

Large shell; The Horn; the Dancers; The Pentacle-Man; The Rose, and the other pieces. She also looked at the pieces that she had added to the original set that had been handed down to her- The Storm Cloud; The Lightning flash; The Knife; the Red Key; The Rose Medallion; Magic in the Air, and others.

She liked using the KeyRose because it allowed her to add images to the blank pieces, making this set her own personal set. Anka had her stones, Troyana had her cards, but Theoclea had been given the original KeyRose Box (The box of possibilities), as a legacy from Orpheus. She turned on the musical chimes set, that was powered by a crystal lantern. The tune that it played was composed by Pythagoras just for this purpose of use in Meditation. Her hand slowly passed over the images. One of them seemed to be singing to her. It was called The *Dance*—one of the original 30 pieces...she recalled the poem that she had written about that piece:

The Dance

As we grow old,
the dance lives on-
'tis the same ancient dance that met the dawn
in a time when all of the maidens and men

would dance with abandon in some
shade-laden glen,
then run with each other to lie in the field
in the soft-dewy grass
where all wounds are healed.
Yes, they danced with each other
for they didn't know
that their dance would end
in the soft-falling snow
and the wint'ry cold
would chill every hearth
So, with age and change
The dancers would part

Now, as we grow old
the dance lives on—
'tis the
same ancient dance that met the dawn
in a time when all the women and men
would dance with each other in some
shade-laden glen.

Now the glen in its gladness sheds its
win'try-silver moon,
and the stilless is broken by the

Chapter Five...The KeyRose

song of a loon.
The midnight is fading,
The Rose awaits the morn,
the dawn is rising, and no longer forlorn,
The Dancers return,
But 'tis not them!
'Tis their children,
who'll start the dance
once again.

She placed *The Dance* in the center of the cloth. She allowed her hand to hover once again over the pieces. Another piece was calling to her, and it seemed to want to sing with the first piece- it was *The Fingerprint,* another one of the original thirty pieces. She remembered the poem that she had written in response to *The Fingerprint-*

The Fingerprint

She left a fingerprint
on the Gate,
it took so long to get so near.
Now YOU are here
why hesitate?

> For most of us the path is clear.
> Now why stand still
> When you've come so far?
> Your strength and will
> tell us who you are.

> Ah yes, this Gate may be your last,
> And you are filled with fear, of course.
> **<u>GO THROUGH!</u>**
> The stones have all been cast,
> This gate will lead you to The Source!

She placed it in the center of the cloth. As she moved her hand, she felt that two other pieces were calling to her- *The Guardian*, and *The Bullseye*, so she placed them in the center as well. They were also two of the original pieces. Most people had an aversion to the first piece, seeing a warrior, but Theoclea imagined him as a *Guardian* of some kind. She placed both pieces below *The Dance*, and *The Fingerprint* in the center of the cloth.

She remembered the poem that she had written... In her book, *Whispers*—the poem that went with the pieces.

The Guardian and The Bullseye

"What are you aiming for?"
(The Guardian seeks an answer)
...and I reply
"A truer arm,
a steady gaze
with no alarm.
A focused mind, a fuller heart,
protection from life's
chance-laden dart.
The Guardian thinks,
And then replies,
"I see the truth, it's in your eyes-
Your heart is good,
You seek the cause,
To be yourself,
Obey YOUR laws,
To be complete,
Your task to meet."
(Then I reply)
"I seek an answer to this question,
how can this be done?"

(He thinks a moment
then reflects)
"To reach the Gate before life's end,
to see the reborn You
'tis better to miss
again and again
in the end your aim will be true!

Was there another piece that beckoned, a piece that wanted to be with the others in the center of the cloth?

Nothing came to her, so she let her hand do the picking, for the hand itself often knows which images to seek. Her hand picked *The Lightning Flash*, one of her own pieces, not part of the original set. It was on the cover of her *Whispers* book. '*An odd combination of pieces so far*', she thought briefly.

She looked at all of the pieces that she had placed in the center of the cloth. Usually two or three pieces called to her in a reading. It was unusual so far, that so many pieces were singing and dancing with each other. Something was still missing, yet she didn't feel the need to add an image on a blank piece. Next, she had to pick the piece that she would never choose. As usual, she picked *The Rigid Structure*, the piece with the dot on the inside of a rectangular structure.

Chapter Five...The KeyRose

Something about this piece never appealed to her. She placed it on the left side of the cloth.

Theoclea closed her eyes and visually looked at the remaining pieces in her mind. They floated about, falling here and there like snowflakes falling through a cloud of whispers. The chimes gently played. She opened her eyes and looked at the remaining pieces on the right side of the cloth. Quickly she turned them all over so that she couldn't see the image sides.

She placed her hand on the Pentacle and Rose that Pythagoras had given to her. It looked like an ordinary gold-colored basket with a black metal star in it, the gift that Pythagoras had given her. It was highly charged. The symbols of Apollo and Dionysus joined together to form a Pentacle. The light and the dark joined, and yet, the four Roses at four of the inside points hinted at the presence of Goddesses bringing a kind of balance to the symbol.

Theoclea placed her hand in the center of the star and felt its power surging through her. She then took her hand and placed it over the remaining pieces on the right that had all been turned over. Three of the pieces felt warm to her touch. Usually, one piece was being offered to her, one random piece from the Macrocosm, or Universe. Today, three pieces felt warm to her touch. She picked up the pieces, and slowly, one by one she turned them over.

The first piece was one of the pieces that she had added. It showed a hand sign that she had known since her first vision of the future, when she was a child, and saved herself and her friends from the falling of a tree. She always called the sign *The Gate of Eleusis*. She hesitated before she turned over the two remaining pieces. The next piece was another piece that she had added. It was a bird—she called it *The Phoenix*.

She held the last piece, and heard a voice in her mind "it's starting, It's Starting, IT"S STARTING!" She turned it over. It was another piece that she had added- *The Rose Medallion*, The Token of Inanna, one the pieces that she had personally added to the set. The Pentacle and the Rose and the KeyRose (The box of possibilities) had spoken.

She put the pieces back in the box, and put the cloth away. The box was put back in its' special place on a shelf. She touched the crystal lantern and the light dimmed and went off. Briefly she wondered about what made the lanterns work—some kind of lost magic, she had always assumed, the wisdom of the past that had somehow been lost. She lay down on her bed, and sleep quickly enveloped her.

Chapter Six...
On the Island

Theoclea sat at the fire and stared up at the wide expanse of clear sky. The view was spectacular, the stars could be seen clearly, as well as the central mist of the Milky Way. She briefly wondered whether the stars could be moved to form other patterns. Suddenly, there was a shooting star that crossed the heavens. Nearby, there was a tent that was lit with white crystal lights, and she studied the lights carefully. She turned to Anka who sat near her.

"You know that I'm going, and nothing will stop me. I want to go there, meet the pilgrims and speak to them. I have things that have to be said."

Anka smiled a wide toothy smile. She had exotic eyes, short gray hair, and a hearty laugh.

"You'll never change. You're the same serious girl that I knew when we were children." She shook her head.

"Dear One, your head was always in the clouds. If it were me, of course, I would never go to Eleusis. I never leave this island. Everything that I need is here—look at that clear sky! I never have to wear clothes! Nudity is practiced by everyone on this island. Some of the inhabitants of the island leave every once in a while, and visit other places. When they leave, the fashion is for them to be adorned all over with magical henna tattoos. The magic in the henna makes them practically invisible when they want to be. The henna is applied so skillfully that they blend into the background. Some of my people have the ability to apply the magical henna to others, making them invisible as well."

The island provides us with everything that we need. Listen—there are birds everywhere that make music for us, and the plants provide food and medicine for us. I know every stone on this island. I know what they're made of, I can speak to them. They listen to me, and then, they tell me of many things. I've learned to work with them, to feel their magic and

Chapter Six...On the Island

direct it. They will do things for me if I ask them in the right way."

"I was always respectful of the stones," Theoclea said. Her eyes welled with tears. Anka saw this and stopped.

"Let me look at you, Theoclea. She paused a moment as she surveyed Theoclea's face. She reached out and put her hands on Theoclea's hair, slid her hands down to Theoclea's cheeks, and gazed deeply into her eyes.

"Are you unhappy, Theoclea?" Theoclea said nothing.

"Theoclea, you've done so much. Orpheus predicted that someone like you would come. He would have been so proud of your accomplishments. You're bringing back the Golden Age. Your prophecies have saved lives that would have been lost in foolish wars. Your book, that wonderful little book...'*WHISPERS*'... so many have read it and been inspired by your sayings. Troyana and I knew that you were destined for more than we could ever dream of. Even the inhabitants of this island know of you. Dear One, I always looked out for you. Troyana and I owe our very lives to you. I was always worried when you had those fits, when your eyes glazed over, and you started whispering. Why give up the safety of Delphi to walk among the pilgrims?"

Theoclea composed herself, looked away into the distance and sighed.

"There's so much that I have to say to them. Do you remember when we played together and pretended to have rituals? I always wanted to lead the chant.

I always wanted all of us to see more. I knew that there was magic! There's something in the air, Anka, I know it, I feel it. The pilgrims have to know it and hear it, see it, feel it. My head spins when I think about it! It's glorious Anka, it's glorious! I have to be strong when I speak to the pilgrims!"

Theoclea stopped, and stared up at the stars. Heat lightning flashed across the sky. A lone tear appeared in one of her eyes. In the center of the sky there was a lone cloud. Theoclea and Anka were silent for a few minutes.

"Dear one," Anka said, as she took the stones out of her pouch. "You have a question for the stones, I sense it." She handed Theoclea a clear stone, and then a number of colored stones. Theoclea held them in the palm of her hand. She looked at Anka, and said—

Chapter Six...On the Island

"Anka, all of the other Oracles had their own symbols, they designed them so that the symbol was unique to them. Others knew of the symbol, and immediately associated the symbol with the Oracle. It can't be a sigil, or a glyph, but a simple design that can appear in many guises. I haven't done this. My question is: What of me? What is Theoclea's symbol to be?"

"Throw the stones, Theoclea, but...there is more, am I right?" Anka looked puzzled, and waited silently for Theoclea's reply. Theoclea held the stones in her palm, her hand was shaking.

"There is more. I've been told that I must not do it, that people would not understand, that it would disrupt things, that it would be blasphemous, but I want to. I want to wear it...I want to wear the Rose Medallion, the Token of Inanna, when I speak to the pilgrims."

Anka remained silent. Theoclea threw the stones.

Anka drew a diagram of two jagged lines in the sand, and then roughed up the sand above the crossing of the two lines.

"You see, Theoclea, the stones are saying that the design could look something like this...a jagged line like a lightning flash, then another one, and above the spot where the lines intersect, the cloudy part." Theoclea looked at the sand, and then up at the sky.

"Yes, Anka, I see it! That would be perfect!"

Then Anka looked troubled and peered down at the stones for a minute more. She drew some symbols in the sand where the stones had fallen, measured the distance between one stone and another, then made more measurements between the stones. The distances were all compared to a clear stone that seemed to be more important than the others. Finally, she stared at the stones.

"The stones are saying that you MUST wear the Rose Medallion when you speak to the pilgrims! You already knew that, didn't you, Theoclea?" Anka slowly looked up at Theoclea. Theoclea smiled at her old friend.

"Yes," she sighed, "I suppose that I already knew the answer to that part. A KeyRose reading told me that." She looked up at the sky once more. "Anka," she said with a growing realization, "the symbol...the two jagged lines with the cloud above the place where they intersect... it's perfect! It looks like the cracks in the floor under the Tripod Chair, and the cloud could be the smoke that comes from the cracks...the Dragon's breath that helps me to go into a trance!"

Chapter Seven...
The Sybil

The tent was dimly lit by a three candles of red, gold, and black, that Troyana had placed on a low table. She sat on one side, in a chair, while Theoclea reclined on a cushion on the other side. A pack of cards was on the table. Theoclea had chosen three cards at random from the deck, and the cards were in the middle of the table. Troyana studied the cards that had been chosen for a few minutes, and then looked up at Theoclea.

"The first card, Theoclea, represents the past, it shows a chair with a Treasure Box to the side of it. There is a Magician looking at the box. A wand is on the ground. The box is like the treasure chest that we used to play with. There is a window to the right of the chair, and in the distance there is a crowd of people with their backs to us, walking away. The second card shows the present. There are many objects here, as you can see. It shows decay, doubt, it shows metal that has rusted, gold that is tarnished….a fire that is smoking, as if it is about to go out. The third card is what I call the card of 'New Birth'…rising from the ashes… this is the blank card that you chose. As you can see, Theoclea, images have now appeared on the blank card. It shows a magic wand in the right hand corner. A Phoenix, rises into the night sky. The sky shows the full Moon, and the Phoenix is flying on a path lit by many candles. The path leads up to the moon. What does this reading say to you, Theoclea?"

"Troyana, when I was initiated, a treasure box was given to me. It was 700 years old, and was put together by Orpheus. The Medallion and other things were in it. There was a parchment written in Orpheus' hand. I've read it many times. He wrote about the need for unifying opposites. It could be done by the Oracle who would be both a Priestess of Dionysus and Apollo. He wrote about the use of the Rose Medallion, the Token of Inanna. I've learned to use it. Then he wrote about a 'renewal', and he said that all of the powers of

Chapter Seven...The Sybil

the Oracle and the Temple would have to be used to bring that about."

"That's the only part of the parchment that I still wonder about. I've thought about it in many different ways, I've followed every path—allowed for the imagining of synchronicities. I'm still not sure, I feel something in the air, but it's not yet clear, even to me. I feel that it's some kind of a renewal. I keep thinking that renewal is necessary. I know one thing, Troyana, I keep hearing the words 'it's starting, it's starting, it's starting,' over and over in my mind."

Troyana picked up the deck turned it over, and then put it down once more.

"That was your favorite phrase, when we were children Theoclea, you used to say that all the time. 'It's starting, it's starting, it's starting...'.You always liked that phrase and that was the way that we always started our magical chants. You said that we had to say that to get the magic going."

"Theoclea, I know that you've told me that you're against this, but, I still don't know why you don't make more use of Vorios, and the other Magicians at the Temple. That man knows of the elemental life on the various planes. He can do wondrous things. Oh yes, he knows how to be a common illusionist, a sleight of hand magician, he knows all of the tricks. He has a collection of common stage magic, and entertains the children of the town—you know—rope and ring tricks; card tricks; mirrors; projections of all sorts— those things. He does that for his own amusement. He has told me that you have been doubtful about using his REAL skills."

"Theoclea, you have a Chief Magician who has wonderful skills. Vorios is well known in the larger world of REAL Magic. He comes to me for a reading every once in a while, and the cards rise from the deck without his even touching them! His specialty is Weather Magic and working with the Elementals. We've worked together on many projects. Vorios tells me that I have the ability to amplify his magic. He also finds that my ability to make symbolic pictures of the past or future appear on some of the blank cards can be of service to him. His Real Magic is first rate. Did you know that he can speak to the Dragon that produces the Dragon's breath that rises from under the Tripod Chair?"

"Yes", said Theoclea, "and I've asked him to stop doing that, but he claims that it is a necessity. He feels that it is his responsibility to do whatever is necessary to keep the image of the Delphic Oracle high in

Chapter Seven...The Sybil

the public consciousness. 'Imagine, Theoclea, if the dragon's breath stopped...where would we be then?' That's what he tells me! You know that my predecessors used all kinds of trickery. I don't want people to think that I'm like the others. I'm not a child anymore, even though I still see visions, and hear the whispers. I've been very serious about all of my duties, perhaps too serious in some ways. Sometimes I wish that things were the way they were when we were children," she sighed. "We were so serious about magic, and then we would all burst out laughing at the silliest things, didn't we Troyana?"

"Theoclea, did you know that Vorios and I once saved one of the coastal towns from complete destruction? Vorios had been doing his weather magic and saw that a tidal wave would be coming that would engulf an entire coastal town. He sent a message to me, and took me down there to see what we could do. We were on the beach and the air was stirring. Vorios said that we didn't have much time. We purified the area, he cast a circle, and then we called the Gods and Goddesses. All the while, the wind was whipping up. The air started to feel moist and we felt the first drops of rain. We didn't have much time to control things, so he built a fire on the beach, then we started chanting. We kept up the chant for some time, and then, I took out one of the blank cards, and…"

Troyana stopped in mid-sentence, and looked at the three cards that had been chosen in the reading. The three cards that Theoclea had picked were slowly rising up through the air. They continued to rise up from the table until they stopped at eye level between Theoclea and Troyana.

"Who's doing that Theoclea, is it me, or is it you?"

"I don't know," said Theoclea." You were saying that you and Vorios built a fire on the beach, and then you began chanting 'It's starting, it's starting!' You were on the beach, and then…"

"I didn't say that!" Troyana shouted! "That's not what I said at all!"

At that moment the cards fell.

They both looked seriously at the cards for a moment, and then burst out laughing! Troyana tossed the deck of remaining cards over at Theoclea.

Chapter Seven...The Sybil

"Ohhhhh........." Troyana, said. "Theoclea, you'll never change, you tricked me again!"

After their laughter died down they both looked at each other for about a minute.

"Theoclea," Troyana said, "perhaps we are not so different. My health and misfortune tie me to this chair that I sit in. Destiny has given you the Tripod Chair of the Oracle. We both listen for the whispers, and look for the signs."

Chapter Eight...
Pythagoras and Vorios

They sat on cushions in a large tent, where food and drink were being served.

"It's been a long time, old friend," Pythagoras said.

"Too long," replied Vorios. "Neither one of us have a reason to return here...we've gone our separate ways."

"When I got your message, I was concerned...I don't travel much anymore," Pythagoras said.

"I thought that if each of us traveled back to the old place, we might be able to draw from the conversations that we used to have. I miss them," Vorios said as he looked at Pythagoras. "I suppose that people think of us as Sages."

They both laughed. Vorios continued.

"You must be very proud of your student. Theoclea has done well. The book, the prophecies, she's much admired." Pythagoras smiled.

"Yes, I'm very proud of her. I've heard that she's going to visit the Festival before the Mysteries of Eleusis, and give a speech to the Pilgrims. She's done her utmost to raise the public opinion of the Oracle."

"I know," replied Vorios, "She's not like her predecessors. She doesn't rely on my gifts, or the work of the other magicians. Yet, there are times when my work might benefit her. Perhaps you taught her too much about the scientific method and sacred Geometry."

Pythagoras laughed. "Here we go again, my friend, our old discussion of Magic and Scientific methods."

"Vorios, you know that I've always believed that everything can be explained through mathematics, and geometrical symbolism. With the proper formulas, and insightful investigation, everything can be explained, even something as complex as the chain of events of what we call 'reality'."

"I note that you used the word 'insightful' in your remark," Vorios replied. "I believe, of course, that Magic takes into account the randomness, what we mistakenly call 'chance'. Magic relies on knowledge of Synchronicity, 'feeling' about probability, and

Chapter Eight...Pythagoras and Vorios

insightful powers that allow us to intervene in the flow of 'reality'. There are too many things, too many possibilities that occur each second for us to take all of it into account. Magic exists in the world of "Mythos" the world of dream, meditation, perhaps words and music, and other things that appeal to all of the senses and allow us to achieve altered states. Magical powers allow us to view the situation from the most important vantage points and sense the flow. The flow is like a stream that changes constantly according to the weather, the impediments, like rocks, and many other things. A knowledge of Nature, and being conversant with the elements is crucial. Magical tools, like sacred knives and other objects are sometimes used."

"Vorios, how I've missed our discussions!" Pythagoras said.

"So have I," Vorios replied.

"Vorios, I've known for some time that my concepts of Geometry cannot as yet measure the roughness of nature. A mountain is infinitely more complex than a cone, a coastline represents a chaotic random quality that is not in a curve."

"On one of my visits to Theoclea, well after she had become the Oracle, she gave me a piece of parchment that contained a drawing. She said that the image appeared to her in a vision. She felt that the image was something that I could decipher, that the image was meant for my eyes. Perhaps a mathematician of the future had something to do with it. The image had been copied from Theocleas' original drawing by one of the artists at Delphi. I wasn't able to understand it at the time. Lately, though I've looked again at that image have begun to feel that it may be possible in the future to have a Geometry that can take much more into account than I may be able to imagine."

"I think that you may be right, Pythagoras!"

"Here's an example, for you Vorios," Pythagoras said. "If you take an upside down black triangle and you place it against a right side up triangle, you get a six pointed star. If you duplicate this and add some randomness, reflective qualities, and chance, you come up with shapes and designs that look more and more like the complexity of nature. The drawing from Theoclea seemed to imply that."

"Very interesting Pythagoras. Here's a different situation for you to ponder," Vorios said. "You are walking down a street, you look ahead, and you 'think' that you see your brother and a woman dressed in yellow walking across the street. A donkey cart moves forward and blocks your view, then the cart moves on

Chapter Eight...Pythagoras and Vorios

and they are gone. Did your brother and a woman in yellow actually walk across an intersection of the street? You have a strong mental picture of the event. You believe strongly that that is what you saw. Yes, you saw it. It happened. But what if you were detained for a few seconds by an item in a vendor's stall? When you reach the intersection you don't see your brother and the woman. Did they actually cross the street, seconds before? Because that was not part of your reality, you can never be sure. There are so many possibilities here. Time is a factor. Reality exists in YOUR viewpoint, and you can't even be sure of that! Pythagoras, is it possible that you and I don't even exist, that we are characters in an author's imagination?"

"Well, Vorios, on that last point, you've really left me. You know that 'logos' has become the primary realm of my thinking, history; facts; figures; careful scientific investigation, and experiment. I must admit though, lately I've been open to the randomness and synchronicity that you talk about."

Vorios studied Pythagoras carefully.

"Perhaps we are both getting old, maybe it comes with old age. I too am more open to your ideas about careful investigation, about using numbers in more than just a spiritual way."

The conversation ceased for a few moments. Vorios withdrew a red ball from his pocket, he handed it to Pythagoras who inspected it. Pythagoras then gave it back to Vorios. Vorios put his hands behind his back, then put his fists in front of him.

"The ball is possibly in one of my hands. Where is it?" Pythagoras touched the right hand. Vorios opened his fist and the ball was not there.

"Is the ball in my left hand?" Vorios said.

"Not necessarily, Vorios, you said 'possibly'." Vorios opened his left hand and the ball was not there.

"Where is the ball?" Pythagoras shook his head—

"I have no idea where it is."

"Look in that bag that you brought with you," Vorios said.

Pythagoras looked at his bag, reached into it, and felt something. He looked and there was the red ball. He took it out and inspected it.

"Well," said Vorios. "What do you think?"

Pythagoras continued to inspect the ball. He smiled. "It's not the same ball!"

"What makes you think that?" Vorios said. Pythagoras thought for a moment.

"I suffered a wound to my hand on the way here. There is a gold-colored salve that I use, it's all over my

Chapter Eight...Pythagoras and Vorios

hand. Some of it rubbed off on the ball when you gave it to me. Not all of that could have been rubbed off in the brief moment when you held it behind you. The ball in my bag had no gold salve mark on it. You must have placed it there when I walked in," Pythagoras said in a satisfied way.

"Ah, yes, Pythagoras, you've go me there. The ball with gold salve mark is on the floor where I dropped it!" Vorios picked up the ball from the floor. Sure enough, it had gold salve on it."

"Vorios, come now, you can do better than that!" replied Pythagoras. Vorios reached into his bag and withdrew a small bowl with what appeared to be a black salve of some kind in it.

"This is the black salve that I use for my wounds." He took some of the salve out, and applied it to the red ball, mixing it carefully with the gold salve that was already on the ball.

Pythagoras studied the motions carefully, momentarily transfixed. The gold, black and red seemed to mix together in Vorios' motions. Gold, black and red were the colors of the Delphic Oracle! For about a minute, Vorios mixed the colors round and round the ball. He closed his eyes, then opened them widely, and tossed the ball in the air, where it hovered right in front of Pythagoras' eyes! A small cloud then appeared above the ball. Tiny raindrops fell from the cloud onto the ball; there was a whisper of a sharp clap of thunder; a small flash of lightning, and then the ball vanished!

"Ah," said Pythogoras, "Yes, I like it! I like it very much!" He leaned forward and said, "Okay, what's the secret, I'll tell no one, of course!"

"I think that there are some other things that we should discuss," said Vorios.

"Of course," replied Pythgoras. "You continue to amaze me Vorios. Is there no limit to the magic that you can produce?"

"Yes, my friend, there are limits."

"Like what?" said Pythagoras.

"Like spontaneous wounds that appear suddenly, and then heal in a matter of a few minutes. A gash, as if made by a knife or a sword. The person sees blood, feels pain, and then in a matter of minutes, the blood is gone, and there is no trace of the wound. Such an event is called a 'Stigmata'. No magician would even try to produce that, it is beyond the range of magic. A magician who would try to do such a thing would only wind up severely hurting himself. When a stigmata

Chapter Eight...Pythagoras and Vorios

occurs it shows us that there are other realms far beyond what we know."

"Stigmata' you say, Vorios. Do such things actually happen?"

"Yes, they do, Pythagoras, but it is extremely rare. I have never seen it, I've only read about it in books. The person who experiences this has touched a Spiritual Gate, and perhaps has had a glimpse of a Way or Path that no one has seen before. It stays in my mind as an example of all that we may never understand, or even try to control."

"Yes," said Pythagoras,"I'm sure that there are realms out there that we may never touch or see. Now, Vorios, about the secret of your trick. Rest assured, it will stay a secret with me!"

Vorios smiled and studied Pythagoras face for a moment.

"Old friend, let's talk about the idea of a renewal of the public's confidence in our Greek Pagan Institutions. Orpheus predicted that things would deteriorate, and then a renewal would occur. It doesn't seem to be happening in the way that he thought that it would. Of course 700 years have passed, yet, with Theoclea, I feel that we have an opportunity here ...

let's talk about it...then perhaps I'll let you in on the secret."

"Yes, okay," said Pythagoras.

"I must tell you though, Pythagoras, there was a bit of REAL magic involved in my trick!" Vorios said.

Pythagoras smiled. "I thought so!"

"By the way, Pythagoras, the red medallion that Theoclea sometimes wears. Have you ever seen another like it?"

"No, Vorios. It seems to be a one of a kind, she hasn't spoken to me about it."

"Pythagoras, don't you find it strange that another red clay medallion from the same place and time period has never appeared? One more thing Pythagoras, as a scientist, do you know how the crystal lights work? I've always assumed that it is some kind of magic of a kind that has been lost to us over time."

"To my knowledge, Vorios, no one has ever been able to figure out scientifically how they work. It seems to be impossible to break them. I heard a story some time ago that someone in the distant past was able to break one somehow into smaller pieces, and all of the pieces glowed and acted like smaller crystal lights! There is a story that thousands of years ago our forebears arrived in Greece from some distant land and

Chapter Eight...Pythagoras and Vorios

brought thousands and thousands of crystal lights with them. I believe that they are all still with us and all of them are still working!"

Vorios looked at Pythagoras, and slowly a broad smile started to appear on his face.

"Perhaps we shall know the truth of all of this some day," he said.

Chapter Nine...
The Dancer

Morain climbed the steps that led to the Garden of the Temple. The Roses were in bloom, and she had been told that Theoclea was speaking to the Chief Magician, Vorios in the garden. As she approached the garden gate, she overheard part of the conversation between them.

"The air can be made to stimulate the movement and the amount of moisture in the clouds. This can be done by communicating with Elemental beings that exist on a different plane from ours. The drought that we've been experiencing, for instance, can be ended quickly by this kind of communication. It can be done spontaneously, but it's better to make the preparations days before by first lighting a fire, and then…"

"Oh, Morain," Theoclea said, as Morain reached the top of the stairway and carefully opened the gate.

"Vorios has just been telling me about his visit with Pythagoras last week".

"Yes, Morain, it's wonderful to see you, I don't get to see much of you these days, Vorios said. Morain extended a hand to Vorios.

"I know, Vorios, we must arrange a special time to get together and chat. I'm happy to hear that your friendship with Pythagoras has continued."

"Pythagoras and I are old friends, Morain, even though our paths seem to have diverged," Vorios replied.

"We can still get into deep discussions. Well, I must go, I have a new student named Seron, who must have his lesson now. It's nice to have seen both of you again. Theoclea, will you think about what I have proposed?"

"Yes, Vorios I will. I'm pleased that you've continued your teaching," Theoclea replied. He then said goodbye, walked to the gate, and disappeared down the stairs.

"Morain, you may have overheard some of our conversation. We were discussing the possible use of magic to end the drought that we've been experiencing. You know that I don't like to use magic, but there

Chapter Nine...The Dancer

are times when it may be a necessity." Morain looked at Theoclea, and felt for a moment that Theoclea was more than uneasy about having made that last remark. There was a strange tension, something new about Theoclea's emotional state.

"There's nothing wrong with discussing the weather with your Chief Magician, Theoclea," Morain replied.

"I have good news for you! Panelle and I have been arranging things for the visit to Eleusis. We've been able to make arrangements to see the fire entertainment and the drumming event, and we'll be going to the market as well. We've also made plans for you to see the rituals that you've wanted to see."

"Wonderful, Morain, and, of course, I also want to see the dancing. I hear that Bella Festa will be performing, and I've always wanted to see Bella and her troupe. Morain, she dances with a battle ready scimitar! Don't tell Panelle about this, but I've heard that Bella is so beautiful that she's broken many hearts, including Pythagoras'. Her hand movements are supposed to be exquisite. I've imagined her dancing in my mind, but I really MUST SEE IT! I've already mentioned this to Panelle, Morain. It's something that I really want to see!"

"I'll talk to Panelle and we'll see about fitting it in," Morain replied. "Theoclea I'll have to leave you now, enjoy the garden, it's a beautiful day. Panelle is waiting for me to discuss the details further." Morain opened the gate and left Theoclea alone in the garden.

She descended the stairs, and finally came to the level that contained the meeting room that was used for guests. Panelle sat quietly waiting for her, her long gray hair resting on a book that she was reading.

"I just spoke to Theoclea," Morain said, "and she insists that, during the Festival, she wants to attend the performance of Bella and her Troupe, Bella-Festa."

Morain joined Panelle on a couch in the meeting room.

"Yes, Morain, she told me that, and I've made arrangements for us to meet Bella. Rumor has it that Bella's so beautiful that she's broken many hearts, including Pythagoras"

"Theoclea told me about that," Morain said—"It's common knowledge."

"Her dancing has been described as being incredibly subtle, very sensuous, very controlled," Panelle said. "Her style is the highest of all the dance styles. Theoclea wants to see it. We're going to meet in a few

Chapter Nine...The Dancer

days with Bella to discuss the details of Theoclea's visit to the dance performance in the Tent City."

"I'm not much when it comes to dancing," said Morain.

"I know what you mean," said Panelle." I like the outgoing exuberance of those dancers from the Ivory Coast, for example."

"Theoclea wants to see them too," Morain said.
"Really?" said Panelle, "well, that's more like it!"

A few days later, Morain and Panelle sat in an same chamber of the Temple reserved for meeting guests, and. after being informed that Bella had arrived, they made themselves ready for her visit. The moment that she entered, Bella displayed a commanding presence, sure of herself, yet at times momentarily intimidated by the austerity of the Temple , and the two famous figures that appeared before her. With a flourish, she immediately offered her hand to Morain.

"Morain what a pleasure, I've heard and read so much about you, I'm thrilled to meet you...ah, but you're an Empath, so you already know how I feel!" Morain smiled. She sensed an artistic honor about this woman, a no-nonsense approach.

"There are limits, Bella to what I can feel," Morain said. Bella then held Morain's hand in hers for a moment and smiled. After executing a complex turn of the hand, Bella faced Panelle.

"And you are Panelle, the Protector, of course." She extended the same hand toward Panelle, but twisted the hand in a way so that the thumb and first finger were offered first, the other fingers following behind and finally, the arm being outstretched, the palm was offered. Panelle hesitated for a moment, admiring the complexity and control of the gracious flowing movement. She said—

"Why ...yes, Bella, what a pleasure!" She placed her hand in Bella's. Morain and Panelle noticed that Bella wore an austere dancer's black top and pantaloons. They had heard that some dancers prefer to only wear colorful clothes during performances, and wore comfortable, black clothing at other times.

"I feel as if I already know both of you, from all of the stories of your magical protection and gifts of empathy, what an honor to finally meet you," Bella said. More greetings and some gifts were exchanged, and then Bella relaxed and sat down on a convenient cushion.

Chapter Nine...The Dancer

Panelle commented on Bella's graceful hand movements. Bella raised both hands, palms up, and said, "Ancient hand movements done in the right frame of mind can call up great energy. Surely you both know that in ritual, hand gestures are very important, they can change the feel, the flow of events. I have always wanted to discuss this with Theoclea." She brought her hands together in a prayer position, lowered them to just in front of her heart, then bowed slightly, and placed her hands on her lap.

"So, now let's create a plan for Theoclea's visit to one of my performances. Did you know that the Bella Festa troupe will be performing for five nights and one afternoon during the seven day long festival? There will be other dancers before us, of course, to warm up the crowd...and then we'll be the main attraction! Let's see for Theoclea's visit...perhaps the afternoon would be best! Then again, the last evening might be perfect. We'll reserve three seats in about the third row, and put up some special decorations in the colors of the Oracle, yes, the Gold, Black and Red of the keys, I can see it! And then..."

Morain and Panelle looked at each other, and Panelle spoke firmly.

"I'm afraid that that is out of the question. You must NOT KNOW that Theoclea, Morain and I are there. NO ONE must know that we are there. "

"What?" replied Bella...not know that you are there?"

"Yes, sighed Panelle, "we will have to put up protective Magical Wards around the tent days before your performance. There are certain proprieties that we must maintain. NO ONE is to know that we are present. We will dress like all of the other Pilgrims. Most importantly, Spells will have been put in place so that no one will want to inspect us in any way, we'll be completely uninteresting, and blend into the fabric of the event seamlessly, with nothing to arouse anyone's interest whatsoever.

"But, I don't understand!" replied Bella.

Morain spoke emphatically.

"Theoclea has to blend in with the flow of the performance, should she go into a trance or disturb the flow of events, the result would be unpredictable, and no one would be adequately prepared for that occurrence in such a large crowd. We've had to do this in the past when she wanted to leave the Temple and be in an unfamiliar place with unfamiliar people. I think though, that the idea of using the Red, Black

Chapter Nine...The Dancer

and Gold colors of the Keys in the decorations would please her. She says that she has imagined your dancing in her mind, but that there's no substitute for actually being there."

"Oh, and I was so looking forward to meeting Theoclea," Bella said.

"Theoclea has decided to have a party sometime after the Rites of Eleusis, when she's back at Delphi, and has rested from the visit. She'll be inviting many people, and has stressed that many of the entertainers and merchants that she meets at Eleusis will be invited," Panelle replied

"Well, that's a small consolation, I suppose," said Bella. "I can understand that you want secrecy. I will treat each show as if I felt that she was there! Yes, that's the way to do it. Each show shall have the same intensity, the same excitement!"

Morain looked at Panelle, and they both smiled. "It... doesn't always work out the way that you want it to, Bella," Panelle said. "That's why we have to be so very careful."

"I was planning something special for her, I was going to dance up to her, or maybe offer my sword to her...there were so many possibilities of things that I wanted to do! I was hoping to show her part of my collection of knives and swords. You may not know this, but I have a special magical rapport with them. I can speak to knives and swords. One must speak to them, know them, and listen to them in order to balance them, and have them do things for you."

"Perhaps you will be able to do that at another time", said Morain, with a shudder.

"Yes, perhaps," Bella said, a little dejectedly.

Panelle then blurted out—"I hope that you don't mind my asking this Bella, but, um...is it true that you had a long term relationship with Pythagoras?"

Morain looked aghast for a moment, and then said, in a low voice..."Yes, umm...anything that you say will be in the strictest of confidence, you know that in the Temple, we don't get any news of the outside world." Panelle kicked Morain's foot that rested behind a cushion.

Bella replied, "Come now ladies, I've heard that you have people everywhere that give you news of the outside world." She smiled, and said "It's okay. Yes, Pythagoras and I were lovers, it's true. As in all relationships, it ended badly, with things being said that shouldn't have been said—that's about it. He's gone on, and I've gone on. There's not a whole lot more that I can tell you. One has to treasure the good

Chapter Nine...The Dancer

memories. We have both agreed on that. That's what we'll always have. He has even come to see me dance on occasion. Some years ago I even took a music class with him."

"Well, it's getting late, and I should be off." Bella stood up. They all said their goodbyes, and Bella left the room. Morain and Panelle sat down once again.

"I don't believe that you did that!"said Morain.

"What?" Panelle said.

"You know," asked her about Pythagoras!"

"Well Morain, the truth is that we don't get enough gossip at the Temple, and I'm starved for it!"

"I know," said Morain, "it's all so serious."

"So," said Panelle, "Eleusis...we're going to have to treat each situation differently. When she goes to the market to see the merchants and their wares, we can't protect her in the same way. When we go with her to see the drummers, and the fire entertainment, we will presented yet another situation."

"We'll just do our best, you remember what has happened in the past," Morain replied.

"Yes, said Panelle, in a low voice, "That's what I'm worried about. I certainly DO remember what has happened in the past!"

Chapter Ten...
The Dance

The tent city contained over five hundred tents and was growing each day as more and more pilgrims arrived. Some had been traveling for many weeks, perhaps even longer to have the once in a lifetime experience that the Mysteries promised. Many of them had Theoclea's book with them. The scheduled appearance of Theoclea had swelled the numbers, and the tent city appeared to be larger than ever. The tents were multi-colored, and each tent had a personal symbol displayed on the front, depending on the Spiritual path that was being taken..

The pilgrims came from every city-state in Greece, as well as surrounding countries. The Priests and Priestesses of Delphi, and others who were part of the entourage had decided to camp behind the stage that had been erected on the plain of Eleusis, away from the tent city. In this way the Guardians could protect the visitors from Delphi. To Theoclea, the sight of all of the tents at night was magical. Each tent was lit by lanterns and candles of all sizes. There were lighted pathways, from one part of the encampment to the next. The drummers and fire entertainers had their own space, nearer to the stage. There was a large tent at the farthest edge of the tent city where the special entertainment was to occur.

Panelle had put up protective Wards at various points in the tent city weeks before they arrived In this way, Panelle, Morain and Theoclea could visit the tents with anonymity. They usually dressed as pilgrims, and had already witnessed rituals that Theoclea had insisted that they see.

The dance performance was being held in the large white tent. To the right of the tent, far in the distance one could see the lighted 'Gate of Eleusis', a name that had been chosen for the gate to the fairground. One could also see the strands of white crystal lights that formed a kind of 'Headdress of Lights' flowing away from the gate poles.

Chapter Ten...The Dance

There was a raised stage inside of the large white tent, and several dance troupes had already performed. There was one troupe devoted to 'authenticity', preferring the traditional music, costuming, and moves. There were troupes and solo performers that danced in black and white to the popular music of the day, and others who preferred to show the style of the region that they had come from. Women from the islands danced in yellow skirts made of a grassy-like fabric. They were wearing garlands of flowers. No one wore roses, knowing that roses were one of Bella's trademarks. Most of the dancers ended their performances with dances to up-beat rhythms. Each troupe had their own musicians, playing reed flutes, mizmar-like instruments, tablas, frame drums, and more.

All of the dancers knew the vocabulary of moves, hip bumps, shimmys, Egyptian and Turkish moves, and more, but the costuming and the approach of each troupe was unique. The jewelry was usually made of silver, and came in an almost infinite variety of designs, and shapes. Some performers attempted to dance to intricate polyrhythms, others chose simpler slow and fast beats. None attempted to do any sword work, knowing that the sword dance would be Bella's specialty.

Finally the moment came that everyone had been expecting and waiting for, the performance of the Bella-Festa troupe. There was a hush as an announcer appeared, and, after giving a list of their awards and achievements, with a flourish he brought them on!

Their entrance was spectacular. They were the only group of the evening to enter playing finger cymbals. The shimmering effect of the zills was reflected in the clothing that they wore. They wore silver coin bras, chokers, cholis of various colors, black pantaloons, full gold skirts, tassle belts, and jewelry from exotic places. Two members wore spiked wristbands, and all of the dancers had tattoos in various places. There were roses, and other flowers in their hair. They quickly formed a circle, after going clockwise around the stage. Three of the women entered the circle and created a blur of spinning, and shimmying movements, accompanied by the intricate hand floreos that were Bella's trademark. All the while the zills kept up the excitement. Then, the group divided in half, as if creating a curtain.

The musicians stopped. Only the reed flute player continued with a slow mournful song. The audience had heard it before. It was music that only Bella danced to. No other dancer would even attempt to

Chapter Ten...The Dance

dance to the song. It was Bella's song, slow, mournful, forlorn at moments, rising to hopefulness, and nobility at other times.

Bella entered from behind the back stage curtain. She wore the three colors of the Delphic Oracle—gold, black, and red. Her personal color, silver, was reflected in the jewelry that she wore. Her pantaloons were black, her skirt was gold. She wore her trademark hip scarf, with a white and gold symbol of a rose. The scarf was fringed in white. She wore a red rose in her hair. In all respects she matched the clothing of the others in her group, wearing a coin bra, choli, and tassle belt. Everyone knew that she did not have a tattoo, or spiked jewelry. She preferred a softness and fluidity to her look and movements.

The drummer joined the flute, playing a slow beladi rhythm. Bella raised her right arm, and started with a simple floreo. Snake arm movements followed. She proceeded to perform five or six more hand movements coordinated perfectly with the music. Intricate controlled body movements, slow taxeems, and arm undulations followed.

Then, the sword carrier appeared from behind the curtain and the musicians stopped. There was a hush in the crowd. Unseen by the others, the three hooded pilgrims in the middle of the fifth row leaned forward in rapt attention.

The sword that Bella used was not the usual dancer's stage sword. It was a real scimitar that had actually been used in battle. The sword was sharp, and everyone knew this. Not a sound was heard in the tent, the sword handler put the sword and cushion down on the floor in front of Bella, who sat before him. Bowing before her, he gave her the sword, took the cushion, and retired to the wings of the stage.

She looked at the sword and whispered something to it. Then, Bella raised the sword, and gently placed it on her head. She slowly moved up to her full height, the sword continuing to be in balance, as the drummer started playing a medium beat. Bella held the sword out to the audience on the right of the stage, moved to the left, and showed the sword again. She moved to the center, tantalizing all by balancing the sword, taking it off to show it to everyone, then placing it on, balancing it once again. She motioned to the drummer to play a slow quiet heartbeat. Bella once again whispered something to the sword, and placed it on her head. The sword was balanced, and she slowly moved to a sitting position.

Chapter Ten...The Dance

Bella knew that her concentration could not be broken. The balance was crucial, every move had to be carefully controlled. She slowly went over all of the moves in her mind. From the seated position, she moved forward to a kneeling position, the sword carefully balanced on her head. She proceeded to perform torso rotations, and slow turns, a berber walk, and finally, a layback. Slowly, her back and head were lowered, until it seemed that the point of the scimitar would touch the floor. With the utmost control, she moved to the upright position, all the while the sword stayed in balance. Finally she returned to the sitting position, on her knees, the sword still balanced.

The audience applauded. For a split second she looked at the three pilgrims in the fifth row. For an instant the magic slipped, and she KNEW. She KNEW! The balance of the sword faltered, it started to sway visibly. Some saw it, some did not.

Panelle sensed the faltering magic, an imbalance in the flow, and leaned forward. The scene was frozen in her mind, she was able to see it dimly lit from three vantage points, and was aware that the Wards and the Spells were weakening. Morain turned quickly, feeling disturbance in Theoclea's mind, perceiving Panelle, deep in thought. The sword continued to sway. It seemed as if the lights had dimmed. Panelle was able to see the flow of the magic in terms of black and white amorphous shapes that flowed into each other, like lights and washes that were in motion.

There were shapes in the mix that should not have been there. The new shapes receded, but there was a wash that remained. All of this occurred in a few seconds that were stretched out in Panelles mind. Then, just as suddenly, the lights came back, and the sword slowly steadied itself.

Bella felt that something had gone wrong, but, as the sword steadied, she could not remember what had distracted her. Her mind clouded for a second, and then she regained full concentration. Slowly she stood up moving from the sitting position to a standing position. The sword remained in balance. Panelle leaned back, still troubled, aware that the Wards and the Spells had returned somewhat.

Bella faced forward, hands out in a 'come hither' position, raised her arms above her head, and brought her hands together in the 'prayer hands' position. Her hands parted and, the arms plunged downward then out and around in a circle, meeting once again above her, left palm up, and the right hand directly over the left hand. Her middle fingers then joined

Chapter Ten...The Dance

making the "Gates of Eleusis" gesture. She swept into a quarter turn to the left, as her arms swirled in a circle, to the left, back, and then up. Her hands came down, her body stayed in the quarter turn but she faced forward. She turned her body forward, and turned her hands to the crowd so that all could see the 'Gates of Eleusis' gesture. She then parted her hands, and with a gesture of indescribable grace and complexity, her hands described the "Headdress of Lights" that flowed away from the gate poles. All the while the sword balanced itself.

The audience went wild, one by one they stood up, giving her and the troupe a standing ovation. She removed the sword, bowed, started to move off, and bowed again as the applause continued. The audience kept her on the stage for a full ten minutes or more. Someone rushed up with a garland of roses for her. She bowed once again and moved with the troupe off to the wings, knowing that there would be at least three or four encores. The audience started clapping for more.

She had a vague feeling that there was a thought that had caught her attention during the performance, but she could not remember it, she looked at the audience as she moved toward the back of the stage, but all was forgotten in the wake of their appreciation. She bowed again and waved goodbye and retired to the wings with her troupe members who surrounded her. As the clapping continued, one of the women in the troupe embraced her. Another of the members approached her with awe.

"What was that move, the last one, the delicate hand work when you were still balancing the sword? We've never seen that before! How did you do that and keep the sword balanced?"

Bella looked at her and faltered for a moment—then shook her head and said, "An inspiration of the moment, perhaps. One is perhaps…blessed at such an event. It's something that rarely happens…it's like… opening a new Gate that one has not been aware of before." Tears appeared in her eyes, but she simply wiped them off, and smiled. The clapping continued with shouts of 'more, more'.

The audience continued to applaud, and the whole troupe was obliged to return to the stage, where they performed three or four rousing encores. During the encores, Theoclea continued to look at the troupe and the dancing with wonder-as if she were a child again. Panelle, though, glanced at the stage, but her attention kept returning to Theoclea. From

Chapter Ten...The Dance

the moment that the magic had been restored and the hand gesture had been made, she was troubled. Her eyes rested on Theoclea. Something had happened. Some other magic had intervened. The flow of events had momentarily taken an unexpected turn. She glanced at Morain, who looked back at her with a concerned look.

Morain and Panelle sat uneasily through the encores. When all was over they all left unnoticed.

"Wasn't that wonderful?" Theoclea said, as they left.

Chapter Eleven...
The Elements enter

The drummers had set up their tents in an area of the tent city that was on the other side of the stage. It was far enough back from the stage so that the drumming would not interfere with the entourage from Delphi. In this way, they could play until the hours of the morning without unduly disturbing most of the pilgrims in the tent city who were camping far from the stage.

The best drummers and troupes were from the lands south of the Mediterranean, and of those troupes the Najir Ketsch were the best. They had all kinds of drums. There were drums with goatskin heads, and wood bodies of mahogany and other exotic woods. The drums came in all sizes and shapes. There were hand-carved hollow log drums, and talking drums that could be raised and lowered in pitch. Some of the musicians had turned clay pots into drums. They accompanied the drums with all manner of shakers, bells, rattles, and gourds.

The night before Theocleas' speech was to be given, Morain, Theoclea and Panelle decided to attend the performance of Najir-Ketsch. The performance was in an open air arena. There were seats and benches arranged in the round, and in the center there was a large fire pit. The firewood was being placed carefully in the pit when the three women from Delphi arrived. Their anonymity was maintained by the Wards and Spells that Panelle had put in place. The drummers were seated in one section of the arena, where they could be seen and heard by all. A simple wooden stage had been built for them. Two fire tenders came out and there was a ritual lighting of the fire. Theoclea Morain and Panelle were able to see all that was going on from their vantage point.

After the fire was lit, one drummer, the leader came forward and started by playing a heartbeat on the goatskin head. The other drummers joined in, one by one, each one adding another color to the texture of sound that was being created. The shakers,

Chapter Eleven...The Elements enter

bells, and rattles were the last to enter, adding more excitement to the dense, earthy sound.

With each entry of a new instrument the texture of rhythms became thicker and more exciting, each drummer listening and reacting to the subtle changes, the beat changing somewhat as each new intelligence and color joined the whole. The last player to enter had a large gourd-like rattle. The sound of this rattle dominated the texture and raised the excitement to a new level.

Suddenly, a dancer appeared dressed in a leopard skin, followed by another dancer on stilts. The stilt dancer was wearing a stylized lion mask of white paste with orange hair all around. The mask was made all the more frightening by the bone-white teeth that were set in the bottom of it. He danced with an attitude, a wild exuberant dance, while the dancer in the leopard costume seemed to goad him on, by doing all sorts of gymnastics.

A fire-eater appeared, dancing as well while juggling with fire wands. Each time he appeared to be eating the fire, the crowd responded with huge appreciation. Two more entertainers joined him while the stilt dancer and the Leopard left the arena. The two new additions to the program were spinning fiery balls in the air and each spin created a whooshing sound that entranced the audience. It was a sound seldom heard, and yet the signature whoosh of flame is something that is primal.

The air was stirred up by the spinning balls, when other entertainers appeared with hoops. There were flaming wands attached to them, and the stirring of the air increased noticeably. The skies, that had been clear, suddenly showed an onrush of clouds, like an army that suddenly moved in and took position, obscuring the moon.

The air was full of stirrings that first came from the East, then from the South, West, and North, creating a great whirlpool of air. The howling of the wind caused the drummers to stop. The fire entertainers likewise stopped their performance. The wind raged for about thirty seconds, and then all was quiet.

The fire dancers returned for the huge fire display that had been planned. Firecrackers were buried in the ground, and fireworks were ready to go. There was to be a dragon that would walk around the grounds, setting off firecrackers wherever he went. There were to be fire dancers who would stage a mock fire battle with two large flaming swords. A huge muscular man would come out with flaming chains and slap them

Chapter Eleven...The Elements enter

on the ground, setting off groundworks. Finally, there was to be a fireworks display with shells, and mortars; repeaters and fountains; roman candles and cakes; tubes; mines; fountains and cones; smoke and snakes; sparklers; spinners; jacks and wheels, and all manner of firecrackers

Morain was concerned when it appeared that some of the groundworks seemed to go off prematurely, about ten feet away from where they were sitting. She glanced at Panelle, who had closed her eyes and was deep in concentration. Suddenly everything stopped, and Morain was sitting in an absolutely quiet arena.

All motion around her had ceased. She detected some kind of an anomaly going on. The feeling of being frozen in a frame of black and white was one that she had experienced before. Something was dreadfully wrong. Morain looked at Theoclea, and Theoclea looked back, a look of grave concern on her face. Morain closed her eyes and saw a chain of events as if seen through Theoclea's mind, as their two minds momentarily became one. She saw that one of the groundworks was about to explode. The resulting fire would spread and set the other fireworks off, quickly resulting in injury to many of the spectators, including the visitors from Delphi.

Theoclea slowly joined her right hand to her left, and made the same motion that Bella had made in her performance, the hands clasped, the thumbs, little fingers and index fingers touching. She held her hands up. Then in a sweeping motion, she parted her hands, as if describing the white lights on the Gate. In an instant, the action resumed.

A sudden explosive outpouring of rain occurred. The rain came down in torrents, drenching the groundworks and aerial fireworks immediately and forcing an end to the program. Morain's face was grave and she looked at Theoclea. Theoclea looked back a Morain, and then at Panelle, whose face showed the strain of concentration and concern. Morain spoke first:

"Theoclea, what's going on?"

"Yes, Theoclea what is happening?"

Panelle said.

Theoclea looked at both of them, and Morain sensed that there was something that was being kept secret from her. She had a feeling that Theoclea would have preferred to be more open, but dared no to. Theoclea's face showed an almost maternal sorrow at the preceding events. Morain sensed a strange mix of anxiety and fear that she had not felt from Theoclea before.

Chapter Eleven...The Elements enter

Tears started to appear in Theoclea's eyes, and in a low voice, she said—

"It's starting...this may be difficult...but this path has to be taken...and I'm the one who has to take it. There may be those who do not want to see this happen...and they made their presence known here tonight, but the Gate has been opened...it's starting...there's no turning back. Please trust me...I *see* no other way."

Chapter Twelve...
Before the Speech

Morain and Panelle stood in front of a tent that had been put up for Theoclea. The tent was directly behind the rear of the stage. There was a covered path that went from the tent to the steps that led up to the rear curtain of the stage, and the lighted gate could be seen in the distance. Theoclea was in the tent preparing for the speech. The tent contained a bed, and a dresser, and other things. All had been prepared with her comfort in mind.

In front of the stage there were countless pilgrims. Some had camped out on the plain for two days or more, with more people streaming in every moment. All had to pass through the lighted 'Gate of Eleusis', and other gates that had been set up. The donation urns were placed all over the plain of Eleusis, and each urn had a Guardian to protect and empty the urn when it was full. There was a Guardian at the 'Gate of Eleusis', and Guardians at the other Gates.

On one side of the front of the stage, a contingent of Counselors had a special place. They had come to honor Morain. On the other side of the front of the stage there was a contingent of Guardians, or Protectors, there for a similar reason, to honor Panelle. There were Heralds, whose magic made their voices, and the voices of those on stage heard by everyone. Music played, a signal that events were under way, and people started to take their places. One of the Heralds was on stage and spoke to the crowd, trying to slowly bring order to the event.

"Take your places...there will be more music, drumming and a fire display, then we'll start." The drummers and fire entertainers took to the stage.

"Well, Morain, here we are, the final evening, and the speech. Thank the Goddess that we're leaving tomorrow afternoon. The Wards that I've put up in different parts of the tent city have worked well. They've protected everything in the city, as well as providing a dome of magic over the city," Panelle said. "This whole journey has been difficult. I hope that she

Chapter Twelve…Before the Speech

doesn't plan any more like this. I was here for a week before the event, cleaning up other people's magic. It's been exhausting."

"I know, Panelle, I'm tired too. I've taken her to all of the places that she wanted to see. She insisted the other day that we go to the market and see the goods for sale. Dear One is such a child. Sometimes, though, I know that she's able to keep her secrets, even though I've been with her almost constantly."

"When we were at the market, she stood in front of a vacant space, and said—*'Look Morain—candles and Goddess figures for sale.'*

"Dear One," I said, "there is nothing there, its a vacant space." She said, 'No Morain, look, the Goddesses are all sitting, and the candles are in front of them'.

"Theoclea," I said, "there's nothing there!"

Panelle looked thoughtfully at Morain and said—

"That's not unusual, is it? I mean, we all know that she sees things. She's been seeing things since her childhood."

"Yes," said Morain, "I didn't think that it was unusual. What was unusual is that we returned later to the market, and in the vacant space there was a merchant's display of Goddess figures and candles."

Panelle started to frown.

"Well, that's still not unusual—she's always seeing things that are going to happen, and then—and then they happen. Most of the time, it's something mundane." Morain stared at the ground and glanced briefly at Panelle.

"The unusual thing about that day is that she walked over to the stand and insisted on lighting the three candles in front of one of the Goddess figures. I protested—'Dear One, the candles, we haven't paid for them! The merchant's not here!' *'Oh,' she said, 'it's all right, Morain, I know him, he told me that it's all right to light the candles. He said that I could light the candles any time, even if he is not here!'*"

"No, Dear One, I can't light the candles for you. Why are you behaving like this? Where is this coming from?"

'Well, then I'll light them myself!' she said. She insisted that I give her the lighting stick. I told her that I couldn't give it to her. Then she shoved me away. I said 'Where is this coming from, you've never been like this before!'"

"WHAT?" said Panelle, "repeat that last part."

"She shoved me away, and I said 'where is this coming from?' Then I said something like 'you've never behaved like that toward me before.' I thought about

Chapter Twelve...Before the Speech

leaving her for a moment, to calm down, but then I grabbed her hand, and pulled her away from the display. She blinked her eyes several times, and looked strangely at me. First her face showed confusion, and then I thought that I saw a knowing grin on her face, as if she had a secret to share."

'I'm sorry, Morain', she said. 'You're right, I don't normally behave like that! It's not me.' Then she said, *'It's starting, Morain, it's starting'.* Her grin turned to a frown, and tears appeared in her eyes. I hugged her, sensing that she needed reassurance."

"WHAT?" Panelle place her right palm on her forehead, "AND YOU DIDN'T TELL ME ABOUT THIS?"

"No," said Morain, "I didn't think that it was important."

Panelle looked frantic. "Morain, whenever there is significant behavior out of the normal flow of events it could be... if you had told me about this right after it occurred, I could have prepared for...well... Whenever the flow of events changes abruptly, it's a sign that something is being tampered with! You should have told me immediately! Goddess be, the sky could fall on us for all I know!" Panelle closed her eyes and assumed an intense expression. She sensed something...

"The Wards have dimmed slightly—I don't like it!"

Suddenly, the tent curtain parted and Theoclea walked out, motioning Morain and Panelle to join her. She was wearing a gold tunic fringed in black, and the red headdress of the Oracle. The Red Key was on a thong around her neck. She walked ahead of them... and then told them to stay back. The plan was for her to go on stage unnoticed, and take a seat behind a gold black and red curtain. After she was seated and had meditated for a few minutes, they would be first to walk on stage, for a tribute to them had been planned by the Counselors and Protectors. After the tribute they were to walk together to the left of the stage and await Theocleas' entrance from behind the curtain. She would walk to the front of the stage and then motion them to join her—Morain would stand on one side, Panelle on the other side.

All was going well. Panelle and Morain walked on stage. Theoclea was meditating. There was to be a tribute to Panelle and Morain. All the while Theoclea meditated.

Morain walked to the center of the stage first, and addressed the crowd. There was thunderous applause. She called for silence. She was dressed in black. She

Chapter Twelve...Before the Speech

thanked the Heralds for their magic—a magic that allowed her voice to be heard by everyone in attendance. She faced the Counselors in the audience, who were in the special section to the left. She did this by bowing to them, and sending a wave of Empathy toward them. The gesture was reciprocated by them... They all bowed, and sent a controlled wave of Empathy back to her—controlled, so as not to overwhelm her. Then, Morain called for Panelle to join her.

Panelle was dressed in a golden tunic, her long gray hair parted, hanging down in front of her. Panelle spoke about the magic that had been set up in the tent city. She spoke of the difficulty of setting up the dome of protection and the Wards, and the Spells. She thanked the Guardians and Protectors for their assistance during the week-long festival. She bowed to them, for they were all seated in a special section to the right. They stood up and bowed back to her—they knew that she guarded a National Treasure.

Then, Morain and Panelle both thanked the other notables like Sephera, and Demetrios...the people who had been instrumental in organizing the event. They thanked the entertainers, and others. When they were finished, they both walked to the left of the stage to await Theoclea's entrance. As they stood waiting for Theoclea, Panelle's sense of uneasiness grew. The Wards were weakening, the protection that she had put in place was faltering. She sensed that whatever was happening was somehow only felt by her, and not by the Guardians and Protectors in the audience.

Finally the curtain parted and Theoclea appeared. There was once again thunderous applause from the crowd. A heartbeat was heard from the drummers. She looked confident, and walked slowly to the center of the stage. She looked to the right, and to the left, and smiled at the crowd. When she reached the center of the front of the stage, she saw that the altar that she requested had been placed there. She had a bag with her and placed it on the altar. Her smile slowly disappeared as she turned to the right once more and looked at the Gate of Eleusis. It was to the right of the section where the Guardians and Protectors were seated. There was a walkway at the far right that led from the stage to one of the gate poles. The walkway was part of Theoclea's design that Sephera had given to Demetrios. Theoclea knew what she had to do. She had been waiting for this moment for a long time. She walked slowly to the right of the stage.

"What is she doing?" Panelle whispered to Morain.

Chapter Twelve...Before the Speech

Morain gripped Panelle's arm, sending a wave of calm for the moment.

"Panelle, trust her, this is something that she must do. I sense that she's waited a long time for this—trust her."

Theoclea reached the walkway, and walked down slowly. The crowd was silent, for the Counselors had been alerted by Morain to send out a wave of understanding and patience to everyone. The walkway was lined with tiny candles that were also a part of Theoclea's design. As she walked, she thought of the other gates that she had touched, milestones in her life. She looked ahead and saw that there was a Guardian standing by the Gate. She looked at him, and he smiled a knowing smile. He stepped back a few paces, bowed to her, and moved out of her way, beyond the Gate. She finally reached the gate pole. Theoclea looked up at the crystal lights, and admired the way that they trailed down, forming the hair of the headdress. It was her tribute to Inanna. She bowed her head, and with her hand trembling, she slowly reached forward and touched the Gate. With her other hand, she touched the Red Key. A feeling of giving of herself filled her, and she took one step forward, touching the side of her head, and a shoulder to the Gate. Her trembling ceased, and she felt something…a quiet strength…flowing through her…she lingered for a few more moments, then stood back and bowed her head. Theoclea turned and started up the walkway. All eyes were on her as she reached the edge of the stage and returned to the center where the altar was placed. She bowed her head in thanks to the crowd, and nodded once more to the Gate. Then she took the bag off of the altar. In the bag was the Medallion of Inanna. She reached into the bag and took the Medallion out. She motioned to Morain and Panelle to join her.

Panelle held back, a look of panic on her face. She grabbed Morain and said—"She's going to wear the Rose Medallion, the Token of Inanna. I told her not to!"

"I told her that its' magic could interfere with the Wards and other protections! I can feel it, the Wards are going down, anything can happen! She's not protected, Morain, we can't let her do this!"

Morain looked at Panelle, tears forming in her eyes. "Panelle, I'm oath bound. I can't tell you everything that she says. I don't know what she's going to do or say, but we have to trust her, Panelle. Remember, Panelle, she's not only the Oracle, she's the greatest of all the Oracles, the one that was promised by

Chapter Twelve...Before the Speech

Orpheus. Come, we must join her, trust me, and trust her. This is the moment when both of us must stand by her on the stage."

"Okay, Panelle said, "but I don't like it!" They joined Theoclea on stage. The applause continued. Theoclea placed the Medallion around her neck. The Wards and other protections went down.

Chapter Thirteen...
The Speech

The applause continued. Theoclea bowed slightly to Morain, standing to the left of her, then turned and nodded gratefully at Panelle, who stood at her right. She continued to look at Panelle. Panelle looked back, a worried look on her face. Theoclea turned her head slightly and gave Panelle a slight smile and nodded. Panelle understood. Theoclea turned toward the audience, and raised both hands up—to quiet the crowd down.

All stopped, even the distant sounds, as Theoclea looked down, and took a deep breath. Then she looked up, and straight ahead. With a strong voice, that was amplified by the Herald's magic, she said,

"It's starting."

There was a silence after this, and a murmur of voices here and there could be heard from the crowd. "It's starting, It's starting". They echoed her words, the murmur continued, as if waves were breaking on a distant shore. Then the murmur died down.

"IT'S STARTING !" she said, louder than before, as if each word were to be pondered. The crowd responded even louder than before—more people realizing that Theoclea expected a response.

"It's starting, It's starting, IT'S STARTING!" could be heard as more and more people raised their voices in response. Their combined voices sounded like larger waves that were breaking against broken columns. Somewhere in the back of the crowd, the drummers started a slow heartbeat. Their beat followed the voices and all merged. Then everything died down, and there was silence once again.

With a voice that was scarcely a whisper, but heard by all through the Herald's magic, Theoclea whispered, as if sharing a secret.

"It's starting..."

Whispered murmurs of what she said were once again echoed heard here and there, and then died

Chapter Thirteen...The Speech

down. Theoclea then assumed her normal voice, assured, calming, soothing.

"The **Renewal** has started...and the key to its' success is YOU. She touched the Red Key and held it out for the crowd to see. Her voice was raised now.

"The Key to the success of The Renewal is YOU. YOU HAVE THE KEY!"

The crowd erupted in loud applause—they didn't expect to have the Oracle acknowledge *them* in such a direct manner, they all had heard that *she* was different.

In a trembling voice, full of emotion, she continued to hold up the red key and said, **"THIS IS THE KEY TO ALL ALTAR ROOMS OF THE PAST, PRESENT, AND FUTURE. IT IS MORE THAN THAT—MUCH MORE! IT IS THE KEY TO ALL OF THE LOCKS OF THE CHAINS THAT BIND YOU!"**

The crowd erupted with wild applause...Some shouted her name... when the noise died down, she spoke once again in a calm, assured voice, "Do you know where you are standing?"

"You are standing on the Plain of Eleusis, the place where Demeter and Persephone were finally reunited after the months of anguish—Demeter, searching for Persephone, Persephone searching for an answer to the plight that had taken her from her life on the surface. Hades had made her the Queen of the Underworld. This is the very place where the dark and the light were placed in balance. When that balance has been achieved, then wondrous changes can occur in our lives. Our very lives depend on change and renewal. The seasons of our lives change! Change is inevitable!" The crowd erupted with an outburst of wild applause. This was the Theoclea of the book, 'WHISPERS' that they had read or heard. Then, everything was quiet again.

With all of the emotion that she could summon up Theoclea recited the last part of a poem.

> "Twas on the plain Eleusis where they met,
> Mother and child ; and all tearful regret
> was wiped away between them, as they sang
> and held each other...
> and the high world rang!"

It was as if she had hit a gong! The applause continued as more and more people realized the significance of where they were.

"Those are the words of a poet of the future. A poet who will be discriminated against because of his

Chapter Thirteen...The Speech

beliefs!" she shouted. She motioned to the crowd to hold their applause by raising both hands, and held up the Rose Medallion, the Token of Inanna for all to see.

"Those words appeared on this medallion."

"You have heard of it. Some say it's blasphemy for Theoclea to wear the image of a foreign goddess, an ancient Goddess, a Goddess who is not part of our pantheon. The medallion contains magic. Yet, others say 'she can't be in her right mind, or she's the Oracle, she can do whatever she wants to do!' Theoclea, the Delphic Oracle….the eyes and ears of Greece. She can *see* the past and future, she can hear the past and future in the whispers. She can *see* the past and the future in signs and visions. That is how I *see* myself! I *see* You. Not just all of you in the crowd, but people in the future who look toward us. I am the eyes and ears of Greece. I *see* more, I hear more. It's both a blessing and a curse perhaps." She paused and gazed over at the Gate.

"I am *different*. Many of you have read, or have had read to you portions of my book. I am the Oracle who wants to make sure that all of the people in our great Greek state have a chance to *hear* what I hear, *see* what I see. People of the future will look toward us and wonder how our ideals survived. I am asked, "How did you come to write that book, *'WHISPERS'?*"

"I hear the whispers from the great ones of the past and future. They have contributed to the book so that *you* can hear the words that convey their thoughts. Some of it may be thoughts of my own, I don't always know."

"You may say 'She is different from the others'. All that I know, my friends, is that yes, I am different, different from all of you. It can be a curse or a blessing, to be different."

"It is my sacred duty to this land and its' people to sit on the Tripod Chair two days a month. I feel and smell the tendrils of smoke and go into a trance, so that I can hear the whispers and see the visions. But it's mostly the whispers. So, I will tell you of some of the most important whispers that I've heard, whispers that are important to *you* here today, or *you* in the future who look toward us in the far time of renewal. We too today are in a time of renewal. Doubt and disbelief in magic are here, even though there may be more magic in the air now than there will be in the future. To make the magic you must be *open.*" She sighed and wondered...would they remember her words? She continued.

Chapter Thirteen...The Speech

"You all know that I have chosen to be a Priestess of both Dionysus and Apollo. What you may not know is that I hunger for knowledge of other faiths. I read, or have read to me the words of the Monks of the East. People read to me of the ancient Sumerians. I am different in that I can go to these places in my mind as well, and hear more words."

"You honor me for being the first Delphic Oracle to be both a Priestess of Apollo and Dionysus. You must consider this—a follower of Apollo reaches for the highest good, the highest philosophy of humankind. A follower of Dionysus must look at the dark side, the wine, the midnight revels, and the madness. *Both* followers can slip and fall into the abyss. Transformation can come when one falls, and seeks guidance, or when one rises up to try to grasp the next gate."

"Each of you is free to do this. Remember to seek the guidance of others, the Counselors, or the Protectors, if you feel that you are falling. They are here to help you. I wrote the book to empower *you*— each one a Priest or Priestess in your own way. I am your eyes and ears. I can't comment on all of the sayings in my book, '*WHISPERS*'. I have certain ones that I feel are important in our renewal, and the renewal that is to come in the future. I'll comment on some of them."

Do you hear the voice saying 'Know Thyself?

"Those words adorn many gates. A gate is a path, or a way. Every day gates are open to you. Consider each one carefully before you move on."

Have an openess for all great things that come from the Human Heart, Beauty, Virtue, and other things.

"Value those who say and write of these things, cherish their bravery to be different."

You have felt both anger and love in your hearts... go the way of Love.

"Yet always remember that True Love means knowing when to let go- that's not easy, for one way or another love ends. Cherish the moments when love flourishes...cherish the memories of Love."

Laugh gaily as a child laughs

"When I feel myself becoming too serious, I revert to my childhood, a time when I laughed freely, played with others,

and saw the world in a different way. I can still tap this energy, and you must do it too."

Know and Pick the fruits of every Art.
"Honor the Artist in all ways. Do not be so quick to form opinions, give the artist your time and consideration"

Enjoy Nature in her Beauty
"Always remember that you are a part of nature. When you destroy nature, you destroy a part of yourself. You are a part of the process. Ground yourself. Feel yourself as a part of it."

Understand other's happiness and pain
"We can't all be Empaths with the gifts and training of my counselor, Morain, but we can try and be aware of empathy, try to understand how wounds can be healed."

Beware that your being may change into its' opposite!
"My Guardian and Protector Panelle is very aware of this. Changes of this sort can happen quickly or slowly. They often warn of changes in the flow of magic. They warn us of changes in the flow of events, of unforeseen synchronicities.

They can reveal a greater whole, or an abyss. Walk this path very carefully, you may lose yourself, or gain great wisdom."

What are you willing to sacrifice for immortality?

"Some say, 'Theoclea, why are the words of the others so important?' I will tell you. Many of the others have, or will sacrifice their freedom, so that we may have their thoughts.

Many have sacrificed so that you may benefit."

"I'd like to share with you some words that the Medallion said to me, during this week, while I thought about what I would say to you." She raised the medallion up for all to see.

"Shed your fears and shame, don't speak like one in a dream! There is a time that is coming when Gods and Goddesses of many faiths will have five hundred million ten and five servants. There will be a pathway made of thousands of candles that will reach from the Earth, the abode of Demeter, to the abode of Diana—the Moon!

The Token of Inanna, the Rose Medallion has given me these words to say to you. They will be written by a poet of the future, a man who will be exiled for his beliefs.

The Poet says more, and my words dance with his!"

Chapter Thirteen...The Speech

"Take note of my words, just as I speak them and teach them to the others. If you write about it, feel the renewal in the air! Delphi and Eleusis represented here as one. Our age is beautiful. Hunger has given the acorns their savor, and thirst has turned every brook into nectar. I say it again! The Token of Inanna, the Rose Medallion has given me these words to say to you. Our age will grow anew in the far future. I have a prophecy for you."

"*From us*—what we say and do—a renewal will occur in the future. The people of that time will be inspired by us. I have seen them, I have spoken to them! Our beliefs will not always be present. Tears will be shed, wars will be fought. Magic will be dispersed. The Dragon and the Gryphon will cease to be."

The crowd started shouting "No! No!"

"Can we, at this time, let that happen?" Theoclea asked.

More people entered "No No!"

"No, we shall not let that happen," Theoclea said. She was in tears now, and the crowd responded with spontaneous tears and shouts. There was a roar of thunder, and then a bolt of lightning crossed the sky. A light drizzle started. Theoclea started to fall—she reeled back—her eyes momentarily rolled. Morain and Panelle caught her. The drizzle continued quietly. They held Theoclea up and she regained consciousness. Morain and Panelle motioned to the crowd to be quiet. Theoclea seemed confused for a few seconds, and then stared at the face of Inanna on the Rose Medallion. Morain and Panelle continued to hold her up.

The crowd quieted down. Slowly, Theoclea turned the Medallion over to the blank side. In one hand she held the medallion, and the other hand touched the Red Key.

In a voice that was heard by all, through the Herald's magic, she said—

"The Medallion Speaks!"

There was a hush in the crowd when she said those last words. She looked up at the sky, and then at the crowd, and then as if sharing a secret, she said,

"The Medallion's words dance again with mine—it says—Look to the stars—your age will grow anew in the far future, and from you, something new will be formed. From the most sacred waters of *your* hearts,

Chapter Thirteen...The Speech

our ways will return. Remade in a way that trees are new, made... new again...when their leaves are new."

Theoclea visibly started to lose her balance—but she motioned to Morain and Panelle not to move. She summoned up all of her strength and continued.

"The letters are dimming, I can't make out the last part. Ah, yes. "Because of *you*...others will be able and ready...to ascend...to the moon...and...to the stars!"

She dropped her hands, looked upward and fainted. Morain and Panelle grabbed her and held her. Her eyes fluttered, and she could barely move. Her right hand was rising and pointing upward. Her hand shook, but she continued to point. Her eyes continued to flutter and roll.

Then someone in the crowd looked up and shouted,

"What's that? Look, up in the sky!"

"An omen", someone else said.

"What is it?" said a woman with a child, sitting in the front.

The twilight sky, a deepening dark blue with fiery patches of red, showed clouds that had streaks attached to them. The clouds seemed to be forming something. Someone shouted—

"Look, a Phoenix!" The words spread.

"A Phoenix, an Omen, a Miracle," someone said. For a while all eyes were on the sky, but gradually people's attention was brought back to the stage. A rumor had started—

"She's dead," someone said. The rumor spread quickly as the Phoenix continued to form. Morain and Panelle looked at each other and tried to revive Theoclea.

They lifted her up, and as they lifted her they both noted that there was blood on her right shoulder. Suddenly, Theoclea regained consciousness, looked at both of them and then at her shoulder. There was a gash. She saw the blood. Quickly she pulled the sleeve down so that no one else would see it.

Morain and Panelle lifted Theoclea up. Her eyes regained their clarity…She indicated to them that she needed some help. The crowd noise died down to a whisper, and then silence.

Theoclea looked up at the sky where the image appeared, and the image started to fade. She lifted an arm and gestured to it. While the Phoenix quickly continued to fade, the sky dimmed, and the stars started to appear. The Phoenix had faded to a wisp of a cloud

Chapter Thirteen...The Speech

when a shooting star blazed across the sky. Suddenly, Morain and Panelle felt Theoclea tremble. Her eyes regained their clarity...she indicated to them that she needed some help. The crowd noise died down to a whisper, and then silence.

Theoclea lifted her right arm out in a 'come hither' gesture, her palm up. She quickly brought her left hand forward, and placed it directly over her right hand so that the thumb and all fingers touched. She folded over the middle fingers, so that only the thumbs, forefingers and little fingers were touching. Quickly, she brought both hands to an upright position, the hands still clasped. The fingers and the thumbs were all pointed upward. The sign looked like the 'Gates of Eleusis'. She parted her hands, palms up, and mimicked the flowing strands of white crystal light that flowed away from the gate, forming the 'Headdress of lights'.

"You are on the Plain of Eleusis!" she shouted!

"Remember my words, remember what Theoclea has said. All will remember that she was the Pythia, The Pythian Priestess, The Dragon Priestess of the Earth, my name, Theoclea means 'The Glory of the Gods and Goddesses'. I am a priestess of both Apollo and Dionysus. Inanna watches over me, as well," she whispered. Everyone heard what she said thanks to the Heralds.

Theoclea held her shoulder. There was pain, a wound, but she dared not show it. Then, she looked up at the sky again. She glanced at the wound, and started crying. There was a double roll of thunder, one coming a second after the other. Within seconds of that, two jagged lightning flashes were seen, one following quickly after the other, one came from one direction, the other from another. They crossed directly under the wisp of a cloud that was left from the Phoenix.

"The sign of the Delphic Oracle," someone shouted.

"Theoclea's sign," another said.

The crowd shouted her name 'Theoclea', over and over. She had just enough energy to manage a weak smile and wave to them, then she motioned to Morain and Panelle, and they escorted her off the stage. The crowd's applause and appreciation continued, as they all stood up and bowed toward the stage.

Night had fallen, and the full moon started to appear. The drums started, the panpipes played, and somewhere in the distance the dragon roared.

She continued crying all the way back to her tent. The crying became more intense as they approached

Chapter Thirteen...The Speech

it. When they reached the tent, she motioned for them to stop. She seemed to be trying to regain control of herself. She looked at Morain, and whispered,

"Even I, Morain, who all my life have..." There was more that she wanted to say, and Morain sensed that. Theoclea started to enter the tent, and told Morain and Panelle to wait outside. Morain said—

"Theoclea I thought that I saw a gash on your arm. You know that I'm a healer as well. Let me look at it."

Theoclea looked quickly at her arm, to make sure that the sleeve was down.

She quickly motioned to Morain that it was something that she would take care of. Tears appeared in Theoclea's eyes once again. She whispered to Morain through her tears, "It's...It's alright. I...must have scraped my shoulder...on...the...Gate."

Theoclea entered the tent. Morain closed the tent flap and stood outside. Theoclea continued to cry, and then the crying stopped momentarily. She put the Red Key on an ornate plate decorated with images of Demeter and Persephone, and put the Rose Medallion away in a drawer. She looked for some bandages in another drawer. The pain had subsided. She lifted her sleeve to look at the wound.

It was gone.

There was no trace of it.

"Ooohhh..." she sobbed, and the crying returned. She continued this way for some time, then she gazed at the Red Key. Suddenly, she noticed something...beside the Red Key, on the plate, there was a seed of grain.

It was a moment that she would never forget—an event that would be with her for the rest of her life.

She would think about it every day.

From that moment on, it would shape her destiny.

She would tell no one about it, until she was alone with Pythagoras in the last moments of her life.

When the tears subsided, it was as if waves on the distant shore were receding. Then she whispered as she looked at where the wound had been and cried softly:

"Even I...all of my life...I see...I hear...but this!" The crying continued for a time, and then slowly, she fell asleep on the bed. In a dream she saw the amorphous lights once again, and part of a gate, then the lights slowly went out—the gate and the dream faded away.

Epilogue

Theoclea awoke the following morning. Slowly, the events of the evening before came back to her. She raised her sleeve and looked at the place where the wound had been. She started to cry again. Quickly she found a top with long sleeves, and put it on. She would wear long sleeves for a while and reveal what had happened to the wound to no one.

One of the newest Priestesses- in-waiting of Delphi opened the tent flap, and said, "Theoclea, I have breakfast for you! Why are you crying, Dear One, your speech last night was wonderful! Everyone is talking about it! It was charged with magic, the words were so inspiring. I'm so happy that I know you, Theoclea. We're all so proud, oh Theoclea, everyone is in tears when they think about your speech last night. Oh, but

I forgot to ask you if you're all right. We were so worried, and..."

Theoclea stopped crying and managed a smile.

"Oh, yes, I'm okay, but where is Morain?"

"Oh, yes, Morain had to go into the tent city for something. She said for you to eat your breakfast, and that she would be right back. I was to make sure that you ate something." Theoclea was hungry, and she reached for a pastry. The new Priestess stayed with her.

"Did you really think that the speech was good?" she asked.

"Why yes, Theoclea, everyone is saying that!"

"My dear, you are one of the new Priestesses at the temple, what is your name?"

"I am called Psychera...after one of the newest of the Goddesses," the girl replied.

"Ah, yes, I see," said Theoclea.

"Psychera, did you know that the face on the Rose Medallion shows one of the oldest of the Goddesses, Inanna?"

"No, Theoclea, I didn't know that," the girl said.

"Inanna's symbol was the Rose, my dear."

"Psychera, have you ever seen the Rose Medallion, and the Red Key up real close?" Theoclea said, as if sharing a secret. "I'll show you how they work together."

Theoclea showed Psychera the Red Key, and took note once again of the seed on the plate. She took out the Rose Medallion from a drawer, and explained its' use, and how they were used together. Then she placed the Medallion and the Key around her neck. She picked up the seed from the plate.

"Psychera, I saw the Mysteries of Eleusis very clearly in a vision a year ago. It was as if I was really there the vision was so vivid. I cannot tell you about anything that I saw or heard, for The Mysteries must remain secret, on penalty of death—even for me. I can tell you something about this seed, though. There are two gifts that the Goddess Demeter gave to humankind. The first is the seed...the grain—agriculture. From a simple seed, our civilization started. The seed in itself appears to be dead.

Indeed, without being buried in the ground, without water or sunlight, the seed will appear to us as dead. To commemorate this death we bury it in the ground. With the right conditions, the seed experiences a reincarnation of sorts, it is reborn and becomes a plant or a tree that graces us with all of its' treasures."

Psychera pondered this and said, "I understand, Theoclea. What is the other gift that Demeter gave us?" she asked.

"The Mysteries!" Theoclea replied.

Several minutes went by, and then a voice from outside the tent said, "Theoclea, it's Morain, are you up?"

"Yes, said Theoclea, come in Morain... I was just chatting with our newest Priestess." Morain entered and nodded to both of them. She studied Theoclea's face for a few moments and then said, "Things are better today, dear one. I can tell."

"Why did you have to go to the tent city, Morain?" Theoclea said.

"Well, your speech was so compelling, that I wanted to give you a gift." She handed Theoclea a gold colored bag. Theoclea opened it and inside of it was a candle holder with two Goddess statues, and three candles of red, black, and gold.

"How thoughtful of you, Morain, and very fitting, as well. The Goddesses are Demeter and Persephone. Where did you get this candle holder?" she asked.

"I bought these from the merchant," Morain said.

"He told me to tell you that you can light the candles at his stand any time, whether he's there or not!"

Book Two- Atlantis

Chapter One...
More Whispers

Theoclea looked out the window of her bedchamber. She saw geese that appeared to be flying across the moon, which was barely in the waxing crescent phase. She turned, sat down at her writing desk, and dipped her pen in the ink bottle. Her cat was nestled against her and sleeping.

'More Whispers', she wrote in big letters on the title page of a notebook. She looked satisfied with this, and turned the page. She began writing again.

Prologue

Many of you have read my first book, 'Whispers'. I am the Delphic Oracle, The Pythia, The Dragon Priestess of the Earth, and my name is Theoclea. I live in the Temple of Delphi. I am the first Oracle to have chosen to be both a Priestess of Apollo and Dionysus. I have the ability to see into the future as well as into the past. My powers have been growing, and each year I can see more. I had my first vision when I was a child, playing with friends. For two days a month, I sit on the Tripod Chair, in the subterranean chamber at the Temple of Delphi. The Dragon's breath comes up through cracks in the floor, I inhale the Dragon's Magic, and it helps me to go into a trance. I am asked questions, and the answers come to me through the God Apollo. Perhaps there are other Gods and Goddesses involved in the process as well.

I know that I am different. I have visions. The important thing here is that I consider *words* to be part of my magical gifts. I seem to know what to say, and do in many situations. I am grateful for the guidance and gifts that the Gods, the Goddesses and the Earth have given to me. I am grateful for my Protector, Panelle, and my Counselor Morain. They help me when I faint or have other troubles. They're there for me. There may be some of you who attended my speech to the pilgrims the night before the Mysteries of Eleusis began some time ago. If you were there, you know that I quoted from my first book 'Whispers'. I commented on the sayings and the bits of wisdom that I wanted to convey, and I used the Rose Medallion to see the words of a poet of the future.

To use the Medallion, one must first look at the face side. The medallion is made of reddish clay and is about three inches wide. The face side has the image of a woman, the Goddess Inanna, one of the first Goddesses— a Sumerian Goddess, whose symbol was the Rose. After looking at the face side, I look at the blank side, and touch the Red Key. I don't always touch the key, but it seems to help. The Red Key opens the doors to all of the altar rooms of all the religions of the past, present, and future. It also unlocks all of the locks of the chains that bind you. After looking at the face side of the Medallion, I look at the blank side. Then, a story, a poem, lyrics to a song, a saying, might appear on the blank side.

There was Magic that occurred during the speech, particularly at the end. I cannot comment on it. It was a surprise to me. A Phoenix symbol appeared, and other things happened. It was all a surprise, and also a shock to me- you must believe that. I think of it every day.

The story of that speech, and the planning of my trip to Eleusis, with my Guardian, Panelle, and my

Counselor, Morain, has been documented elsewhere. All of the events leading up to the speech, the places I visited, the entertainment, the market, all of this has been described by others.

Of the story of my childhood, my friends, Anka and Troyana, much has been written. There are many stories about one of my teachers, Pythagoras, Vorios, the chief magician at the Temple, and others who share the life of the Temple with us. Looking back on it all, especially the speech, the events seemed to favor the Apollonian side of my quest. I don't feel that there was all that much of the dark nature, the dark of humanity in the speech at Eleusis. It was a speech of renewal, I had been planning it for a long time, and it was meant to be uplifting—a reaching for the higher gates.

This book will relate my ideas about the dark side of human nature. Dionysus for me represents those qualities of the dark side—the drinking of the wine, the midnight revels, the madness—things that when taken further down to the lower gates, without control or moderation, can lead to all kinds of problems. I may or may not succeed here in offering my views through poetry, song lyrics, story, dreams, and sayings. In the end, the balance is what matters, the balance of the dark and the light, the Sacred Masculine and Sacred Feminine—The Union of Opposites. Our reverence and connection with the Earth, the Four Directions, and Spirit must balance whatever is dark within us. Somehow, I feel that seeing and knowing must be a part of this.

Chapter Two...
The KeyRose Reading

Theoclea rose from the desk and looked out the window once again. The birds were gone and a cloud obscured the moon. She took the KeyRose box off of its shelf and sat down once again at the writing desk. She touched the leather Red Key attached to the brass plate.

She opened the box and proceeded to set things up for a reading. Theoclea smiled as she handled the thirty images on fine paper. A nearby crystal lantern illuminated the black cloth and the pieces. One by one she placed them on the right side of the cloth, as usual, making sure that all of the images could be seen. She always left the blank pieces in the box.

Theoclea looked down at all of the familiar pieces on the right side of the cloth. The Ancient Mother; the Drum; Music; the Dance; Balance; The Rose; The Guardian; The Bulls-eye; The Fingerprint; The Pentacle-Man; The Column; The Storm Cloud; The Lightning flash; The Knife; the Red Key; The Rose Medallion; Magic in the Air, and others.

Many of the pieces reflected her own contributions—The KeyRose allowed her to add images to the blank pieces, making this set her own distinct set. Theoclea had been given the KeyRose box and the Rose Medallion, when she became the Pythia, Pythian Priestess, the Dragon Priestess of the Earth—the Delphic Oracle.

She held up her right hand and slowly placed it over the images. One of the pieces seemed to be singing to her. It was the Pentacle-Man, a man with outstretched arms and legs within a circle. She placed it in the center of the cloth. She gazed at the other pieces. Usually, there was another piece that wanted to sing and play with the first piece. Yes, there was—The Rose. She placed it below 'The Pentacle-Man' in the center. Another piece was usually needed. Nothing came to her, so she let her hand do the picking. Her hand picked two familiar pieces that often came up in

Chapter Two...The KeyRose Reading

her readings. The Fingerprint, and the Guardian of The Gate. Where most people had an aversion to the second piece, seeing a soldier, she always imagined him as a Guardian of some kind. She continued to gaze at the pieces that had been chosen.

Her hand continued to travel over the pieces, the Lightning Flash and the Storm Cloud felt warm to the touch, so she added them to the central images. She picked up another piece called The Knife.

She looked at all of the pieces that she had placed in the center of the cloth. Usually five or six pieces called to her in a reading. Something was still missing, yet she didn't feel the need to add an image on a blank piece. The images were all there. Not every reading was accurate, she started to feel as if this reading was not complete...as if something else was about to happen that would reveal more to her.

She looked at all of the images on the right and the 'Ancient Mother' called to her. As she looked at the Ancient Mother and placed her in the center, she recalled the poem about the piece that had appeared to her on the Rose Medallion. She whispered the poem.

ANCIENT MOTHER

Ancient Mother,
what do you see,
moon-lit mirth,
infinity?
The past, the future,
the shore at night,
all are part of your
luminous sight.

The verdant plain,
the lake of gloom,
the perfumed garden,
where roses bloom?
The risen sun,
the sunbeams' motes
the foam-born singer
with the sweet-scented notes?

Ancient mother, I hear your song,
a song of hope, for all day long
it calls to me
when I'm alone...
the heart-gladdened-notes,
from the incense-throne.

Chapter Two...The KeyRose Reading

**They speak of Eleusis
what a joyful scene
when Demeter the mother
met Proserpine.**

**You sing of that joy,
You sing of that place,
You sing of a time
when the human race
shall seize the thunder
and forget the shame
and sing joyful songs
that honor your name.**

**Ancient Mother we hear your song
calling all of us together
in a joyful throng.
Our voices will rise in a
candle-lit swoon,
and the sound will be heard
by the Stars and the Moon.**

She placed the Ancient mother with the other pieces in the center. Of all of the pieces she loved this one the most and it was on the cover of her 'Whispers' book. Next, she had to pick the piece that she would never choose, and, as usual, she picked 'The Rigid Structure'. She placed the piece on the left side of the cloth.

Theoclea closed her eyes so that she could see the remaining pieces in her mind. They floated about, as if carried by a wisp of air from the East wind. She opened her eyes and gazed at the remaining pieces on the right side of the cloth.

She turned them all over so that she couldn't see the image sides the Theoclea looked over at the gold-colored flat basket with a dark star in it, and four roses placed between certain points of the star- The Pentacle and the Rose. Placing her hand on the Pentacle and the Rose, she felt the power of the symbols of Apollo and Dionysus joined together to form a pentacle. The four roses at four of the inside points represented the powers of Goddesses creating balance.

Theocleas' personal Pentacle and Rose was always highly charged. The Dragon whose breath seeped up into the chamber under the Tripod Chair had finally told her a secret. The Pentacle and Rose had to be charged once in a while in order to keep working, and the charging was done in a secret ritual.

Chapter Two...The KeyRose Reading

Theoclea placed her hand in the center of the star in the usual way. Then she took her hand and placed it over the remaining pieces on the right that had all been turned over. Today, one piece felt warm to her touch. She picked it up, and turned it over. It had the image of the Red Key.

She put the pieces and the cloth back in the Black Lacquer box, and put the box on the shelf. Theoclea touched the crystal lantern, it dimmed and went out. She lay down on her bed, and sleep quickly enveloped her, while her cat was nestled against her. The cat suddenly stood up, arched its' back, and looked about as if someone or something else was in the room. After a minute of walking around, satisfied that no one else was there, the cat jumped back on the bed, and fell asleep against Theoclea.

Chapter Three...

The Vision

Theoclea was sitting on the ground, the KeyRose pieces were on a black cloth in front of her and she looked at them, taking her time. She had added pieces over the years—a sun piece for Apollo, red, black and gold keys, a lightning flash, a cauldron of fire, a dragon, grapes that represented Dionysus, and other pieces. She was taking her time... perhaps contemplating a question. The Red Key was on its' thong around her neck and she touched it. She felt the warmth of the key as its aura glowed and slowly spread out, surrounding her in its glowing radiance.

She felt confident of the outcome, for she had done this before. She knew that there were grave risks involved, and that it was her destiny to do this. She felt a certain longing, perhaps to get the answer quickly... she had done this before...each time it was somewhat different...there was always a doubt whether it would happen again, she heard a whisper, she felt the Key.

"Theoclea, the Delphic Oracle," someone said.

"...like a child..." the same voice again. Then she heard a maniacal laugh and saw a hand holding a knife. The knife was bloody, as if it had just been used. It was serrated and sharp. The handle was blank on one side. The knife was turned over to reveal a sign, a gold crescent moon with a black arrow going through it. There was a red drop of blood under the moon, and under that there was a stylized letter 'D'.

The hand had a firm grip on the knife. The man's right arm had a tattoo on it, it was the same sign as on the knife- a gold crescent moon with a black arrow running through it, and a red drop of blood below the moon. The image faded, but the laughter remained, then the laughter died down to murmured unintelligible whispers. A rock appeared, a rock that had been lifted and set in the ground so that both sides could be seen. One side had not seen the light of day for thousands of years, perhaps even longer. A Red Key

Chapter Three...The Vision

was hanging on its' thong on the rock. The whispers remained.

From the whispers, she felt a faint stirring of the air about her. A wisp of air from the East wind blew a few of the KeyRose pieces off the cloth. The East wind with its' logic, reason, and air of certainty stirred up a small whirlpool of air, a small whirling dervish of air started to grow in front of her, and one by one the KeyRose pieces were caught up in it—blurring into each other ...the whirling grew—it surrounded her... getting slowly larger and larger.

A warm red aura was emitted from her Key, she felt it, and it grew and protected her. She was in the midst of a growing storm. Gusts of wind increased sharply in speed and force. She was in the center, as a storm cloud gathered. The wind was now approaching from the South.

Indeed, the South Wind entered with its' passionate fire, an explosion of fire, the fire of a giant volcano spewing its' lava hundreds of feet in the air. It was an eruption that was heard by people in places half way around the earth, said to have been the loudest sound ever heard on the Earth. It was heard by people living on islands thousands of miles away. The Red Key glowed—it embraced her—the wind heated up.

She was in the center of an event of horrific proportions. Lightning flashed everywhere. She could see the sea slowly receding, revealing a sea floor that had not seen the full light of day in thousands of years, and even then it had been encrusted with a thick coating of ice.

In the center of the storm there was a lull. Theoclea was in the center, in a glowing red protective aura. The sounds of the volcano, gave way to the crackle of the shifting magnetism in the air.

There was a sudden movement of the earth that she stood on. The sea was receding quickly and could finally be seen to be miles and miles away…all died down to a dull roar.

Then at the moment when the sound reached a whispered hiss, a wave aproached, a wave of a magnitude that had never been seen on the earth. A wave of horrific size, a mile high, and it was moving toward the land.

The whirling got faster. The West Wind entered with its water and she felt droplets, the air was moist with water, but not healing water—all was flying, whirling about her. The wave rose higher and higher as it approached the land. The hiss of steam could be heard as the volcano instantly turned the water in the

Chapter Three...The Vision

air to steam. The wave continued to rise, approaching the shore faster and faster. She couldn't see the top of the wave. Suddenly it came crashing down!

All was chaos as the North Wind entered, with its rocks and soil, the very earth was shaking around her. The land was sinking into the sea in a huge landslide. The rocks were flying, there were flying sacred crystals of a multitude of shapes and colors—the power station was destroyed in a matter of seconds!

So many colors, crystals of different shapes...the crystal energy destroyed forever. There was a smell of pumice in the air...the smell that comes when lava hits the sea, cools and floats on it. The air was full of ash that choked her. There were screams that were drowned out by the cacophony of the chaos. The Red Key glowed, and she knew what she had to do. She had done this before, and she knew that there was a risk, but it was her destiny.

She walked forward and entered the heart of the chaos—the Red Key glowed....the aura protected her. There was a risk, others had faced it. One of her sister Oracles died doing this. It was Theoclea's destiny...things were flying outward and inward as she walked through the storm.

Whispers abounded, downward, upward, inward, outward—all was a mass…a blur…a whirling…pieces of columns flying upward, parts of roofs falling downward. A colossal statue of a man holding a shield with the gold crescent moon and the black arrow through it flew by, and smashed into what appeared to be a huge sign showing children of many colors holding hands with a rising sun between two pillars in the middle.

Bodies of people drowned by the water, or burned by the fire were whirled upward…inward…outward… whirling crystals…a multitude of colors and shapes. The pieces flew around her, a mass of crystals, water, air, heat.

The knife appeared again with the arm and the tattoo of the gold crescent moon and the black arrow. The laughter started again—"like a child," a face appeared, a man with a bald head, and an earring in one ear. Once again "like a child," the voice said. Tears streamed down Theoclea's face, mingling with the water, and the tears of the many millions of people who died that day.

Theoclea cried out—Your death…your death … YOUR DEATH!" An image appeared of knives of various sizes whirling and dancing with rocks and stones and crystals of all shapes, colors and sizes.

Chapter Three...The Vision

Once again, Theoclea shouted as loud as she could—"YOUR DEATH...THAT KNIFE!" An image appeared and disappeared so quickly that she could scarcely make out what it was. Finally, there was bright light...the Red Key glowed...the KeyRose pieces still whirled around her and the whirling of the air started to die down. She grabbed at the pieces and she placed them in her pocket, were there more? Yes—another, and another, and another. She walked forward, she was outside of the storm, her aura subsided, but the key continued to glow.

She reached into her pocket, and took the pieces out. She looked at them, the blank sides faced her. They were made of solid gold. Before she could look at the image sides, the image of the bald-headed man with the earring and the tattoo appeared again and the maniacal laughter started again, getting louder and louder like the vision of the giant tsunami... then all crashed, and Theoclea awoke with a start, sweat pouring down her forehead, her pillow soaked with sweat and tears. Psychera her Priestess-in-waiting rushed into the room "Theoclea, are you all right? I heard you shouting!"

Chapter Four...
Pythagoras arrives

Morain, Theoclea's counselor walked down the flight of outside stairs carved into the mountain. Finally she arrived at the bottom of the stairway and opened the gate, where she saw Theoclea wandering about the lower rose garden.

"Theoclea, you sent for me. I have good news, Pythagoras has arrived!"

"That is good news, Morain. Please go and tell him where I am, I have things that I must talk to him about. Also, please remind Vorios that I wish to speak to him, later this afternoon, perhaps in about an hour in the south arbor."

Morain left the garden, and about five minutes later Pythagoras stood at the bottom of the stairs. It had been thirteen years since Theoclea's initiation as the Delphic Oracle. Pythagoras presided as the High Priest at the portal of initiation. Three days afterward, he left Delphi, and for thirteen years he had been away. During that time he helped to start a school in a neighboring country, and had traveled widely. He opened the gate and walked into the garden.

"Theoclea!" he shouted.

Their eyes met and he walked slowly toward her. She smiled. When he finally stood in front of her they spent a few seconds affectionately looking into each other's eyes. Slowly his face moved toward hers, he kissed her, and they embraced. "How many years has it been?" he said.

"Thirteen," she replied. She gazed at his face and then stared at the Black Key on a thong around his neck. A frown appeared on her face.

"You used to have the Gold Key," she said.

"Yes," he sighed. "Life has taken away the Gold Key, and given me the Black Key, and a wound. The wound has healed over time, and I've been given spiritual guidance. One must go on, and reach for higher levels."

"Yes," she smiled, "one must go on." He looked around the garden, and then looked back at her.

Chapter Four...Pythagoras arrives

"You've done so much, the book 'Whispers' has been widely read in Greece, and elsewhere, I'm proud to tell people that I was one of your teachers!"

She smiled, and said. "Some of your wisdom is in there, in the book, Pythagoras."

He gazed nto the distance, then looked into her eyes, and said, "I've been away too long, I know. I heard about your speech at Eleusis, Theoclea. People are still talking about it—an inspiring speech, where magic took place—a sign of the Phoenix in the sky—and then your sign of the Delphic Oracle appeared. It has been recorded in the sacred books as a most incredible event, a miracle some say."

"Pythagoras, even I don't understand all of the events that surrounded the speech, there was more that happened that day." She absent-mindedly touched her right shoulder. "Perhaps someday I will able to tell you more."

"How are the children?" Pythagoras said.

Theoclea looked at Pythagoras' smile, and her face brightened.

"When were you told?"

"About a year ago, Vorios told me. He said that you told him that it was okay for me to know. So, how are they, what are they like?"

"They are lovely, Pythagoras, a true blessing to both of us. When I think of my initiation ceremony, thirteen years ago—you were the High Priest. I knew that we had a choice as to how to celebrate the Great Rite. I knew that we would be left alone toward the end of the initiation, that we would be led to a chamber, that we had a choice—to do it symbolically, or to actually perform the Great Rite. Until we walked into the chamber I still didn't know. We had been ritually cleansed and purified all day in many ways, and then, when you looked at me and held me in your arms I knew, the choice was made. During the next nine months, when you were away, it became apparent that a child was to come from our union despite all of the precautions. All of the Priestesses and Priests were very excited about that. The conception of a child from the Great Rite at the initiation of the Oracle was an event that had not occurred at the Temple of Delphi for hundreds of years. The big surprise to all of us was that twins, a boy and a girl were born."

"My travels to other countries, my founding of a school at Crotona, these things have kept me away." Pythagoras said.

"I know, Pythagoras, and for their own protection, they don't know who their parents are. I must tell

Chapter Four...Pythagoras arrives

you this, they are truly a blessing, not just to us, but to everyone that they meet. I must go now—I have a meeting to attend. You'll see, Pythagoras, the children will be part of the children's chorus, and have parts to play in the first ritual, 'Orpheus returns to the Underworld', the ritual that we wrote together when I was your student. Pythagoras, you have something to look forward to."

She kissed him on the cheek, smiled and walked over to the gate, turned around, and looked back at him.

"The children are lovely, and talented, Pythagoras, you will see what I mean. I must go. Rest here awhile, this garden was one of your favorite places." She left him alone in the garden, and memories of the year that he spent teaching her and the others came back to him. It was so many years ago, and here he was back at the Temple, for a performance of the ritual. It had been performed every year since then. He walked around, admired the roses, and remembered.

Chapter Five...
Vorios and Theoclea

They were in the South Arbor of the Temple of Delphi where some of the trees still held fruit, but it was getting past their season. The air had a chill to it, and the leaves were already falling, as a quiet rain wet the leaves. In the center of the arbor there was a clearing where outdoor rituals were held. A fire pit was lit in the center of the clearing. There was an altar in front of the pit, and on it there was a sun disk, and there were other symbols of Apollo. There was also a large crystal on the altar. Vorios picked up the crystal, looked at it with interest, and then put it down.

"Vorios, I asked you to come here because I had a dream—a nightmare. In the dream, I seemed to be going through the process of divination that I experience when I'm in the chamber with the Tripod Chair. I was doing some kind of divination with the KeyRose set. The elements suddenly started to enter and became restless. I heard a man's voice laughing and saying things to me.   Suddenly the stirring of the elements increased and I witnessed a horrific catastrophe. A wave of incredible size hit a shore, and a landslide started. There was the sound of a volcano...I can't possibly tell you how loud the sound was. There were buildings, and the largest one was hit and there was an explosion of a multitude of crystals. There was a chaotic whirling of crystals, and statues flew through the air, bursting into signs on buildings. People's bodies, bits and pieces...it was a nightmare. In the midst I heard a voice. I saw a bald-headed man's face. I screamed something back and I saw his arm with the tattoo of the gold crescent moon with the black arrow piercing it, a drop of red blood below the moon. He had a knife that had red blood on it, and I saw knives and stones whirling as if in a dance. I had a vision, but it appeared and disappeared so quickly that I could barely make out what it was. Vorios, you're my Chief Magician. I've already told of the dream to Morain my counselor, and Panelle, my guardian, but they don't seem to know what to make of it. They told me to talk to you. I thought it best to tell you about it now, before the guests arrive and we start the ten-day festival of the 'Two Rituals of Balance'.

Vorios had a deeply thoughtful, worried expression on his face. He turned and picked up the crystal from the altar, looked at it intensely again, and then put it down.

"Theoclea, the symbol of the gold crescent moon with the black arrow going through, with a drop of blood below it is the ancient symbol of a people that were supposedly wiped out hundreds and hundreds of years ago. What I'm going to tell you is conjecture based on legends. Your vision of a catastrophe in the dream may have been a vision of the destruction of a continent called Atlantis that existed over 9000 years ago. Legend has it that almost the entire continent vanished beneath the sea in a couple of days. There could be many explanations for that. There are stories that there were two factions of people that lived side by side in an uneasy peace on that place, The 'Children of the Law of One', and 'The Sons of Belial'. One story tells us that sometimes one faction would get the upper hand, and sometimes the other faction would be victorious. There might have been others involved as well. There is a theory that after the continent was destroyed there was a diaspora, and many of the Atlanteans left the island. There were predictions of a catastrophe, and perhaps twice before the island, or continent, had been destroyed."

Vorios paused, as if wondering how much more he could reveal to her. Then, he continued—"There is conjecture that the citizens of Atlantis may have mapped the world, and were a great seafaring nation. I believe that remnants of that civilization are all over the known world. This much I know to be true—one group of people settled on the island of Thera, off of the coast of Greece. Many hundreds of years ago the soldiers of Thera attacked Athens. They were beaten back and defeated. The battle was ferocious, but our magic was stronger, and because of that we won. The Greek army then invaded Thera and killed every last man and woman on the island—the children were left in the care of others, and never told of their ancestors. That was done because the settlers on Thera claimed to be descendants of the Sons of Belial—people from Atlantis that represented the most arrogant aggressive, war-like people that have ever lived on the face of the Earth, according to legend. They represented the ultimate Evil, and they had to be wiped out. That is why I said that they were finally destroyed hundreds

Chapter Five...Vorios and Theoclea

and hundreds of years ago. We then settled the island with our own people."

Theoclea gazed into the distance, and thought about what was said.

"Vorios, but what of this man that I have described in the vision, the man who speaks to me, the man who laughs, the man with the tattoo and the bloody knife?"

"The tattoo would indicate to me that he is one of the 'Sons of Belial' Theoclea," Vorios replied.

"Vorios, you speak of conjecture, theory, supposition, legends, stories, and beliefs...I want to know the facts."

Vorios just stood there in silence, not knowing what to say. He knew more, but Atlantis was not a subject that he was comfortable talking about.

Chapter Six...
The Planning

Panelle and Morain sat on the cushions in one of the meditation rooms, their eyes were closed, and they were in their own worlds of thought. After a few minutes, Morain, Theoclea's Counselor opened her eyes and picked up a writing tablet and a stylus. She wrote something down. She was dressed, as usual, in a black robe fringed with a gold Greek key design. Panelle, Theoclea's Guardian and Protector opened her eyes after a few more moments. She wore her temple clothes—a gold colored robe fringed with the same Greek "key" design in red.

"Okay, Panelle, let's get down to business on the planning of this event."

"Yes," Panelle agreed.

"I've got my notes here somewhere...here they are," she said reaching under a cushion. "First Day—Opening remarks, then, it's feasting and rehearsing, with workshops relating to the first of the two rituals—'Orpheus returns to the Underworld'."

Morain chimed in—"Second Day, more of the same. Pythagoras and Theoclea will give a workshop at 1:00 on the 'Dark night of the soul,' and Troyana's workshop, will be 'The Hanging Man', at 3:00."

"On the third day in the morning and afternoon people will meditate and congregate for private rituals, and in the evening, the first ritual will take place," said Panelle.

Morain took some notes on that, and then said, "On the fourth day there will be rehearsals for the second ritual, 'Artemis and the Handless Maidens'. On the fifth day there will be more rehearsing, ritual workshops, and preparation...and after a feast in the evening, The Priests and Priestesses Choir will sing. Then Bella and her troupe will dance for us and the Children's Choir will sing."

Panelle burst in—on the sixth day, the second ritual, 'Artemis and the Handless Maidens' will be performed in the late afternoon. On the seventh day,

Chapter Six...The Planning

everyone will start to say their goodbyes and during the day some will leave. On the eighth, ninth and tenth days things will wind down as some stay and some leave. The vendors will probably stay on until the tenth day, and then pack up and leave. A perfect plan for a ten day long event! You do know that Pythagoras will be playing 'Orpheus' this year."

"Yes, I know," Morain said."

Panelle thought for a moment and then replied. "The surprise will be that the 'singer' in the ritual will be his daughter, Alcena. Someone has to make him aware of that. His son, Abderus, the other twin will be one of the 'Shades' guarding the gate to the realm of Hades. Perhaps Vorios should tell him about this."

"Yes, that's most appropriate," replied Morain. "In the first ritual, Anka, Troyana, and Bella, the dancer, will be the three Goddesses. Anka will be Artemis, Bella has chosen to be Gaia, and Troyana hasn't decided yet. Theoclea will be Hecate, and Vorios will be Hades. By the way, Anka has chosen to be Artemis in the second ritual as well," Morain said.

"Well, that's a surprise, Artemis was Anka's least favorite role when she was a child, growing up with Troyana and Theoclea. I think that we're overlooking something obvious here," said Panelle.

"What's that?"

"Well, people are bound to talk about Pythagoras... after all, what kind of a father leaves his children and doesn't see them for thirteen years? I tell you it's scandalous—there's a lot of gossip going around. I hear things."

"Well keep all of that to yourself," Morain replied. "Remember our Oath...we are not allowed to discuss what goes on in the Temple, especially the most sacred matters—none of this can be discussed, even amongst ourselves—nothing is to be allowed to leak out to the outside world without Theoclea's permission, and even there..."

"Yes, yes, I know all about our Oath...and what about Pythagoras and Bella, together again...you do know that they had a long term relationship, don't you?" Panelle replied, exasperated.

"Keep it to yourself, she told us that they were on somewhat friendly terms and that's good enough for me! Besides, Pythagoras was specifically invited this year. It's possible that he didn't know of the children's existence until some time ago. Perhaps Vorios told him. They're still close friends, you know," Morain replied.

Chapter Six...The Planning

"Well, I still think that it's scandalous behavior on his part, and a choice piece of gossip."

"Keep it to yourself," Morain said emphatically, "remember THE OATH!

Panelle paused, choosing her words carefully—"What do you think that Vorios, a Magician, and Pythagoras, a Scientist and Mathematician talk about when they get together? I hear that they meet once or twice a year in one of their old secret meeting places."

"I'm sure that we would not understand much of what they say to each other. I once overheard part of one of their conversations and I didn't understand one word," Morain replied.

Chapter Seven...
The Stone and the Merchant

In the days before the start of the ritual week there were all kinds of displays set up in the Great Hall. There had been other events leading up to the event including the raising of a great stone outside of the Temple, weighing almost 15,000 lbs. Over one hundred people had participated in the event. It involved the intricate pulling of three ropes, with more than thirty people on a rope, pulling, braking, and angling. The stone was sometimes pulled on log rollers, and sometimes on a sled that would eventually lead it to its' destination—to be one of fourteen other stones that created a semi-circle near the Temple of Delphi. The task also involved the feeding and housing of the people. There was also the preparation of the space for receiving the stone, the mixing of the mortar, and the purchase of the remaining fifteen stones that were to be used in the next ten years to complete The Stone Circle.

There were many people involved in this event. Almost all of the members of the Najir Ketsch Drum and Dance Troupe pitched in. Members of the Bella-Festa Dance Troupe helped as well, and Bella was expected to arrive in a few days. There was Reena, the music teacher, conductor of the Children's' Choir, and teacher of drama and writing at the Temple orphan's school, a woman who was a singer, a well-known soprano, an actress, a composer, who helped even though she was limping from an injury. There was a panpipe player who participated, and entertained the crowd when they were resting. There was also, the Artist in Residence at the Temple—Chrissa, whose laughter and smile lifted everyone's spirits when the going got tough. Morain and Panelle pulled on the ropes as well.

Theoclea was deemed to be too delicate for this—they didn't want to risk losing a National Treasure. Yet, in the next few weeks, she was to prove to everyone that she was stronger and more resilient than they thought.

Chapter Seven...The Stone and the Merchant

On the days before the opening of ritual week, the Great Hall was filled with merchants, artists, displays, jewelry, clothing, altar tools, and altar objects of every kind. Silver, gold, precious and semi-precious stones were seen everywhere. Theoclea's friends from her childhood were there, Anka had brought stone displays, and Troyana did card readings. There were large placards with symbols from the thirty pieces of the KeyRose decorating the hall. There was music. The Najir-Ketsch drum and dance company gave a concert, and Demetrios was there from Eleusis with his musicians. Sephera was also there from Eleusis. Bella, the dancer had not yet arrived, but she sent word that she would be there for the rituals. Vorios was waiting for the arrival of Pythagoras. Panelle had put up special Wards and Spells to protect the Temple, and Morain, Theoclea's Counselor worried about the effect of all of this on Theoclea, the Oracle. Her concern proved to be basically sound, but once again, our Oracle, Theoclea, proved to be someone to be dealt with, and anything but powerless!

The Artist in Residence, Chrissa, the head of the Orphan's School Music and Art Department, set up easels with large placards showing some of the symbols on the KeyRose pieces—The Ancient Mother, the Large Spiral, and other pieces. Interspersed here and there, were Chrissa's large drawings of cards from Troyana's deck. Chrissa had the magical ability to do intricate drawings of what appeared as images in other people's minds.

She was able to see and draw the images in Theoclea's mind, for Theoclea presented them to her in a special way. The images that came to Troyana's blank cards were likewise drawn by Chrissa to any scale. She could also see and draw the images on the Rose Medallion, when Theoclea presented them to her.

The Merchant was also there, the one from the market at Eleusis. He had his goddess statues and candles. The curious thing was that everyone seemed to know him, He wore a large floppy hat, and it was he who directed the Stone Raising. He had been around for the raising of all fifteen stones, and eventually was given the job of directing the operation. Everyone knew him—it should not have come as a surprise that his presence was felt. Everyone had seen him, for he was a fixture at all of the events. He played a keyed instrument, and was always present at the bonfires. It was simple, everyone knew him, including Morain, Panelle, and Theoclea. No one, of course,

Chapter Seven...The Stone and the Merchant

could remember the first time that they met him. His Goddess figures and candles sold briskly.

As for Chrissa, the Artist in Residence, Panelle and Morain had their opinions.

"She's one of the few employees of the Temple who lives at the Temple, but has a secular life as well. It's that 'bohemian' aspect of her life that makes me suspicious and cautious about her. Why did Theoclea choose her above all of the other artists who applied for the job? I know that there were others who had magical gifts as well." Panelle said.

"It's simple," Morain replied, "I can meld minds with Theoclea, I can send calming, understanding emotions to her, together we can solve problems, involving the outcome of the immediate future. But I can't draw."

"I can't draw the images that appear on the Rose Medallion. I can't draw, and neither can you Panelle! Neither of us can receive images of the blank 'sybil' cards from Troyana. Chrissa can do all of that and more! She also writes poetry, she's the head of the Music and Art program, a vital part of the curriculum of the orphan's school. Everything that is taught at the orphan's school revolves around Music and Art. She works well with Reena, the music and drama teacher who conducts the Children's Choir. Now that woman can sing, she composes music as well, and she's an actress. She has magical gifts as well, although I'm not sure of what they are! She lives outside of the temple in the town and has a rather 'bohemian' life as well! Let's face it, Panelle, we need people from outside of the community of Priests and Priestesses who can sing, dance, write poetry, play musical instruments, perform plays, and teach these things to the children at the school. Just look at us, Panelle, we can't sing, we can't dance, we don't write poetry, and neither of us can play a musical instrument, not even a drum! We know our positions, and know how to apply our magic, and we do it well, and that's that!"

"Well, you don't have to be so depressing about it. We are indispensable, aren't we?"

"Yes, yes, we are," said Morain. "Look, you always wear gold, with the Greek key design around the sleeves and hood of your robe. You also occasionally wear a medallion with your glyph on it. As a result of that everyone in Greece knows who you are, and knows what all of that stands for. I wear black, with the Gold Key design around the sleeves and hood of the robe, and most of the time I wear a medallion with my glyph on it. In all of Greece, I am the only one to dress like

Chapter Seven...The Stone and the Merchant

that! Theoclea always wears gold, red, and black, and now she almost always wears the Red Key and the Rose Medallion—need I say more? Now this artist, Chrissa, she's happy, she sits with her glass of wine, and a box of chocolates, and just draws and paints away. She wears all of the colors, depending on her mood of the day! Jewelry, rings, pendants, necklaces, and more! She wears whatever she wants to wear. The same is true of Reena, the singer...she wears what she wants to wear, usually fabulous fashionable clothes. I don't know what she eats and drinks, but she's happy too! I almost envy the two of them—having the freedom to wear all of the colors. When is the last time that we had a true Healer permanently at the Temple—someone who dresses all in white, Panelle?"

"Well, Morain, it's been a long time. It's just that ...we've all been in good health...and we can always go into the town to see a healer. You don't have to make all of it sound so depressing. Well, I think that I'll take a look at what the merchants have—when I get depressed I have the urge to buy something."

"Fine," said Morain. "Just leave me here to do your job of looking at the crowd as well as my own, checking in on Theoclea's emotional life and well-being." Panelle smiled a weak smile, and walked off.

"I'll relieve you later," she said.

Theoclea stood in front of the Merchant's stall. She nodded her head at him and he smiled back, a toothy smile, he didn't have all of his teeth. She lit the candles of red, black and gold in front of the largest of the Goddess figures.

"It's been a year since I last spoke to you Alwin," she said, in a low voice, looking around to see that no one heard her. "You look well, I didn't actually get to see you at Eleusis," she said.

"Yes Theoclea, and you look well, too, I was there for your speech, at Eleusis, it was strong, uplifting, and magical, a speech that will always be remembered by all who heard and saw you."

She nodded in appreciation. Then, she turned around again, to make sure that no one could hear her.

"Alwin, when will I meet again, with you, and the… others?" she said.

"Soon, Theoclea, soon—you'll know when and where. It's been about five years since we all met, and one of the Sisters is not well. We have also lost Brynn, one of the Brothers."

"A pity," Theoclea said, "I only met him that one time, but I liked him." Alwin lowered his head, sadly.

Chapter Seven...The Stone and the Merchant

He brought out a very large fabric bag, and reached into it.

Carefully he brought out a shiny new Red Key. He kept the fabric bag on top of the Key, so that Theoclea could only see a portion of it. For a split second he raised the bag and lowered it so that she could see all of it. They both looked around, to make sure that no one saw the bag, or the Key.

"You're one of the few who have reached higher, and have received the Red Key," he said. "There are not many others who have reached a Spiritual position high enough to be able to give the Red Key to other people. Usually, only those who have had the Black Key and the wound can be considered for the Red Key, and the wound has to have been healed. They also must have reached for and attained higher spiritual levels and guidance. Most of all, they must *answer the question, and the question changes with each new situation.*"

He pointed at the bag.

"I just made these, a month ago, and they have been properly consecrated, and hand-tuned. It's time for me to give you another Red Key, my dear, so that you can pass it on to someone else. Perhaps you may need more than one this year." He put two keys in another bag quickly, and handed the bag to her.

"Thank you, Alwin," she said. He leaned forward and whispered something to her.

"You'll know when the meeting is to be held… and where… soon, Theoclea. We have to find another Brother to take Brynn's place. Perhaps you can think of someone to nominate, maybe someone who will receive one of these Red Keys."

Theoclea thought about this for a moment, and then smiled at Alwin. "I think that I may know someone who would fit in very nicely," she replied.

Chapter Eight...
Pythagoras and Vorios

Vorios sat at a desk in his chamber at the Temple of Delphi. On the desk was a clay medallion, the same size and color of the Rose Medallion, but on the face side there was an image of a bearded man. His hair seemed to be made of leaves, and leaves surrounded the bearded face. Vorios stared at the image intently, then turned the medallion over, and stared at the blank side. A frown appeared on Vorios' face. Suddenly, there was a knock on the door. Vorios put the medallion away, then approached the door.

"Who is it?" Vorios said

"Pythagoras!"

Vorios opened the door and the two men looked at each other, and smiled. They embraced each other as old friends. Vorios spoke first. "Pythagoras, you got my message about seeing me as soon as you arrived at Delphi."

"Yes, you said that it was urgent."

"First, Pythagoras, let's sit down, and chat. You must be very proud of your student, Theoclea. They say that she delivered one of the most inspiring speeches ever to be heard at Eleusis. The speech was charged with magic, I hear."

"Yes, Vorios I am proud. She always felt that she was destined to make that speech. It was part of the first vision of the future that she had as a child. Her magical powers are her secret, I can't really say what she is capable of in that area. How much of that magic was yours, Vorios?"

Vorios raised an eyebrow at the question and looked straight at Pythagoras. "You of all people should know not to ask a question like that. I'm oath bound, of course to not reveal any of the secrets of the magic that is used at Delphi. Especially any magic that might involve the Oracle. Even my most advanced students like Seron are never taught all of the key processes".

"My mistake, Vorios, I should have known better. Now, what's the important matter that you wanted to discuss?"

Chapter Eight...Pythagoras and Vorios

"It concerns Theoclea. She had a dream, she even asked me to discuss it with you as soon as possible. In the dream she seemed to be seeing the destruction of Atlantis, or the island of Thera, or both. She described the vision in detail, she even spoke of the destruction of a crystal power station."

"A power station? Do you mean that she actually saw it being destroyed? There have been legends, stories..."

"Yes, and there's more...she saw a man with a tattoo on his arm...he was holding a bloody knife. The tattoo was the gold Crescent Moon with the Black Arrow in it!"

"The Sign of the Sons of Belial! Incredible! I had a feeling that her powers were increasing. She told me that she can see further and further into the past, with increasing accuracy. The same has been true of the future!"

"Yes, Pythagoras, she told me the same thing."

"Pythagoras, my field is magic. I know something of the crystal magic that may have been used, but it has never been duplicated. I'm somewhat vague about Thera and Atlantis. You're the scientist, the historian, an expert in Sacred Geometry. You spent eleven years in Egypt.

Theoclea (The Delphic Oracle) and Pythagoras in Eleusus and Atlantis

I suspect that perhaps you know much more about Atlantis. What's going on here, Pythagoras?" Pythagoras stared at the floor, then closed his eyes, and took a deep breath. How much of it could he reveal?

"I learned about Atlantis during my years in Egypt. The Priests in Egypt told me that there were ancient books of Atlantis buried somewhere near a huge statue with the paws of a lion and the head of a man, The Sphinx. There were bits and pieces of knowledge that were revealed to me, until I had a fair picture of what might have happened. Vorios, you know the stories, the legends—Atlantis was a great seafaring nation. They had mapped the world and had outposts all over the world. That's conjecture. The fact that the world is a sphere is a belief held by some. The island of Thera, off the coast of Greece, may have been already a thriving outpost of Atlantis, well over 9000 years ago, when Athens was first being developed. Legend says that all of the Atlantean cities were modeled on the capital city of the continent of Atlantis. Even when large portions of the world were covered with ice over 10,000, 15000, years ago, the continent of Atlantis was supposedly always in a temperate to tropical zone, located far, far beyond

Chapter Eight...Pythagoras and Vorios

the Pillars of Hercules." Pythagoras paused, Atlantis wasn't a subject that was discussed amongst his usual circle of friends. He sighed, and continued.

"There are theories that the continent of Atlantis was in another place where the magnetism and activity of the Earth was powerful, but unstable. The locations of Thera, or the Pillars and the capital city may have been like connections in a vast magnetic field. The legend says that when Atlantis was destroyed, the volcano on Thera erupted, and Thera was almost destroyed. Fortunately Thera has built itself again, several times as a matter of fact. There have been periodic eruptions, though, on Thera, during the past 9000 years. The legends say that the locations of all of the Atlantean outposts were carefully planned, and not always because they were the most likely ports for a seafaring power. Each outpost city had triangular buildings called Pyramids. There were many other similarities. There is a theory that the Atlanteans could harness the magnetism and other energies of the Earth with giant crystals. The only drawback to that may have been that the main continent and many of the outpost cities were located in parts of the world that showed the greatest instability... volcanoes, earthquakes, tsunamis and the like. I suspect that you've already heard much of this, Vorios. That's about all that I learned from the Egyptians. I believe that the books on Atlantis still exist, but they're buried somewhere in Egypt, perhaps near that huge statue with a man's face, and the body of a lion, or beneath it, perhaps." Pythagoras knew more, but there was only so much that he was willing to say.

"A pity, said Vorios, much could be learned from those books, I'm sure. Pythagoras, I've set up the board for a game of Gemaia, hoping that you would join me." They both sat down at opposite ends of a table with a board that contained black and white square.

There were 12 semi-precious gemstones in front of one side of the board, and the same number of stones, type and quality, were set on the opposite side. Both men took the game seriously, and silence was observed. The first moves were quickly made on both sides, and then both men settled in for the midgame. Neither one of them spoke, but the time elapsed between moves became longer and longer as each man tried to imagine the possibilities that stretched forward in time.

Vorios made a move and then looked up at Pythagoras.

Chapter Eight...Pythagoras and Vorios

"I understand that you and Theoclea will be giving a workshop on 'The Dark Night of the Soul'."

Pythagoras idly played with a crystal lantern that sat on a black square on the third row of the board. The lantern was lit. He touched it and paused, as if rethinking the logic of the move. He stared at the board, and his hand went back to his chin. He looked up at Vorios and said—

"Yes, and that same afternoon, on the second day, at 3:00 Troyana will give a workshop on one of her cards 'The Hanged Man'."

They maintained silence for a few minutes and studied the board.

"The children, Vorios, how are they doing?"

"Well, Pythagoras, they've been raised with the orphans, like any other children of the Temple. They have no knowledge of who their parents are. We've done this for their protection."

"I've been away for thirteen years, Vorios. You told me about them last year. Why didn't you tell me sooner?"

"The Oath of Secrecy, Pythagoras...let's just say that...someone did not think that there was any reason for you to know."

"Have they shown any unusual abilities, gifts, anything that I should be aware of?" Pythagoras said.

"No magical abilities, neither the boy nor the girl have visions, nor do they seem to have an interest in mathematics or science. They have shown extraordinary abilities in other areas."

"And what would that be?" Pythagoras replied.

"The girl, Alcena, can sing like an angel," Vorios said, smiling. "She composes her own music, and has occasionally sung some of your music, Pythagoras. Her voice is very pure, and she has an unusual grasp of nuance. It's the kind of nuance and ornament that we used to hear from wandering singers from the countries and islands north and west of Greece. She can sing unaccompanied, and can convey the most delicate of emotions with her voice alone."

Pythagoras stared at Vorios and then down at the board. He decided to move the lit crystal to an adjacent square. "And what of her brother, the boy?" Pythagoras said, satisfied with his move.

"Abderus writes…he writes verses, stories, poetry, prose, and recites for the other children. Occasionally we ask him to write and recite something for the Temple, for a special occasion."

"Are the verses any good?" asked Pythagoras.

Chapter Eight...Pythagoras and Vorios

"They're much more than good. They're way beyond his years in wisdom. They resound with a strange clarity of purpose, yet there are layers upon layers of meaning. He knows how to use symbols, metaphor. He seems to love the sounds of the words and the effect can be rather striking. You will hear both of them, they will perform in a concert during ritual week, you'll hear him recite, and then hear her sing. The girl is also going to be the singer in 'Orpheus returns to the underworld', and the boy will be one of the 'shades' that guard the gate to the land of Hades—The Underworld. The Priests and Priestesses have a name for the twins. They only speak the name in private, the twins have never heard it.

"What's the name?" Pythagoras asked.

Vorios looked at the board and placed his hand on a shard of selenite and moved it to another square with satisfaction. He looked up at Pythagoras and said, "They are called 'The Star Children'."

Suddenly, Pythagoras' crystal lantern piece dimmed and went out. He looked at it and said, "Vorios, did you see that?"

"What?" said Vorios, who had been staring out the window.

"Look at the crystal lantern piece!"

"Did you turn it off? Pythagoras?"

"No," Pythagoras replied, touching the piece in the right place. It didn't go on.

"Something's wrong," Vorios said. I'll have to check all of the Temple magic in the next few days."

Suddenly the lantern went on again. "That should never happen," said Vorios.

"Vorios, what do you know of the technology of the crystal lanterns?"

"Nothing, I've assumed that you, a scientist, a mathematician of all people must know the workings of these lamps!"

"No one knows the secret of the crystal lanterns, it's some kind of lost knowledge," Pythagoras said. "Perhaps a lost magic art that we cannot duplicate."

"A pity," replied Vorios. He gazed up at Pythagoras, and said—"Theoclea wants the truth about Atlantis. She told me that conjecture, legends, stories, and the like are not enough. She will settle for nothing less than the truth, Pythagoras, in the end she'll have to know."

Pythagoras sighed, gazed at the board, and then looked up at Vorios. "In certain circles, discussions of Atlantis are frowned upon, as if the subject was unfit for scientific examination. Science and Mathematics

Chapter Eight...Pythagoras and Vorios

have become, for some, orthodox and dogmatic. I'm not that way, but I'm careful about what I say."

"I know that, Pythagoras, there are many magicians who would never speak of it either, fearing that they may be thought to be ignorant of the magical arts...and certain dogmatic beliefs that magicians hold to be true. Pythagoras, you of all people know that Theoclea is different. There has, to my knowledge, never been anyone like her. There are, perhaps, only a few people that I've known who have worn the Red Key. She won't settle for legends and stories. If anyone ever had the ability to get to the central point of the stories and legends—to *see* and *know* Atlantis, perhaps even better than the Atlanteans themselves—Theoclea is the one!"

Pythagoras sighed, and they went on with the game.

Chapter Nine...
The Workshop

In the next few days people arrived and were greeted. Finally, opening day of the annual Week of Rituals of Balance began. All went well with the feasting and the greetings on the first day. On the second day the pre-ritual workshop of Pythagoras and Theoclea proved to be especially rewarding. Pythagoras started.

"I am Pythagoras. Thirteen years ago I taught at the Temple of Delphi, for a year and a day, and one of my students was the remarkable woman who stands before you to my right. During my tenure here as a teacher, one of her assignments was to collaborate with me on a new ritual, eventually to be called 'Orpheus Returns to the Underworld'. After her initiation, about three days later, my mission at the

Temple was over, and I left Delphi. A year after she was initiated as the Oracle, the ritual was performed at the Temple of Delphi for the first time. The ritual has been an annual event every year after that. And so, I am now back after being away for thirteen years, traveling, founding a new school in Crotona, and walking my life's path. I am grateful for having been invited back this year to play the role of Orpheus." He gazed around at the faces in the audience, some were familiar, and many were unfamiliar to him.

"The ritual is a Mystery Ritual, similar to the 'Rites of Eleusis'. Before the ritual everyone swears an oath of secrecy—not to reveal the important aspects of the ritual to anyone. There are certain things that you can do. You can sing part of a song, or chant, if you remember it. You can quote a line or two of the poetry, if you remember it, and if you come upon similar poetry that is not in the ritual, you certainly may quote that." He turned to Theoclea. "If you agree with this oath say AYE!" All of the participants said 'AYE'! "Then we shall move on!" He gazed at Theoclea for a few moments.

"I need not tell you of the remarkable gifts and achievements of this woman who stands before you. Her Prophecies have averted foolish wars in which many thousands would have died. She has predicted earthquakes and other calamities, so that we were prepared for them. With the help of the Rose Medallion; the Red Key; the KeyRose box, and other divination tools, we have given her questions large and small, and have received guidance. We have all been able to share in her wisdom by reading the little book that she has written, called 'Whispers'. I give you Theoclea, The Delphic Oracle. Her name Theoclea means 'The Glory of the Gods and Goddesses'."

She wore the colors, red, gold, and black, of the Delphic Oracle. She also wore the Red Key, and the Rose Medallion. On a table in front of her was the black lacquer KeyRose box with the leather red key on a brass plaque on the top of the box. She nodded and smiled at Pythagoras and then, took her time looking at all of the audience members. Finally, she spoke.

"I am Theoclea, the Pythian Priestess, the 'Dragon Priestess of the Earth'- The Oracle of this Glorious Temple, The Temple of Delphi. I am the first Oracle to choose to be a Priestess of both Apollo and Dionysus. As a Priestess of Apollo, I know the heights that humankind has reached for. I have touched the higher gates, and I have seen the Guardian. As a Priestess of Dionysus, I have seen and touched the lower gates as well. For two days a month, I sit on the

Theoclea (The Delphic Oracle) and Pythagoras in Eleusus and Atlantis

Tripod Chair, in a subterranean chamber below the Temple. I inhale the dragon's breath that comes up from the crossing of two cracks in the Earth that meet under the chair. That spot is called 'The Hearth at the Navel of the Earth'. The dragon's breath helps me to go into a trance. I answer questions put to me by the pilgrims who visit the Temple. It is said that the God Apollo supplies the answers to me, but I think that there are both Gods and Goddesses involved in this. I wear the Red Key and the Rose Medallion, with the face of the Goddess Inanna on one side. Those of you who have read my book,'Whispers', are aware of my thoughts on these matters. Pythagoras has told you of the Oath of Secrecy. I have only one more thing to add to this. Sometimes during a ritual, there is a moment of personal revelation. We've all seen it and experienced it. If anyone feels that a moment of personal revelation is at hand, please allow it to happen. The Rose Medallion may be helpful to us today. It is also called 'The Token of Inanna'. There is a woman's image on the face side. One must stare at the face side for a minute or two. The face is the face of the Goddess Inanna...one of the oldest of the goddesses. Her symbol was The Rose. I also hold the Red Key, when I use the medallion."

Chapter Nine...The Workshop

The Red Key was on a thong around her neck and she showed the key to everyone. "The Red Key opens the doors to all of the altar rooms of all of the religions of the past, present and future. It unlocks all of the chains that bind you." She stared at the face of Innanna, then turned the Medallion over. "After a few minutes, I turn the Medallion over and poetry, a story, and other words appear on the medallion . The Rose Medallion shows the writings of the poets and thinkers of the past and the future. Each year when I use it I can go further back in time and further forward. They all whisper their poetry and writings to me. They speak of many things, and that is precisely what Pythagoras and I will do now in this, the pre-ritual workshop." She reached toward the table and held up the KeyRose box.

"The KeyRose box contains thirty images usually on gold-colored paper. The thirty images are used in divination, and there is a book that explains their use." On the easel that we have set up, there are two pieces...the Ancient mother and the Large Spiral."

Theoclea and Pythagoras continued, by using writings and song lyrics that they, and others, had created. When the workshop was over, everyone quickly left, because they all wanted to hear Troyana's workshop at 3:00 on 'The Hanged Man'. Vorios started to walk toward the door, when he saw Seron, one of his students walking ahead of him.

"Seron, slow down!" Seron turned and stopped. Vorios caught up with him, and put his hand on the boy's shoulder.

"What an experience that was, Pythagoras and Theoclea together in one workshop! The ritual is going to be magnificent."

"Yes, great workshop, I agree Vorios, everyone seemed to find it most interesting," Seron said.

"Well, Seron, we're very fortunate that they both shared their feelings and wisdom about the upcoming ritual. I had no idea that the two of them together could be so charming. Parts of that workshop were actually very amusing, in spite of the title 'The Dark Night of the Soul'. Now come along, Seron, we don't want to miss Troyana's workshop on 'The Hanged man'."

"Vorios, I'll have to miss it. I have writing to do, for tomorrow's class with you."

"Nonsense, my boy, you're excused! Troyana's workshops are amazing, now come along I'm sure that we shall both find the workshop enlightening."

"But Vorios, Psychera and I…"

Chapter Nine...The Workshop

"Yes, Seron, I know all about your romance with Psychera, Theoclea's Priestess-in-waiting, well, she'll have to wait. Troyana's workshop is more important right now. Have I ever told you how Troyana and I worked together to create the magic that saved a coastal town from certain destruction? Come along, boy." Seron showed a certain reluctance on his face, but then agreed to go.

Chapter Ten...
The Hanged Man

They reached the Great Hall where Troyana's workshop was to be held. Chairs were set up, and Vorios had reserved some chairs up front. People were quickly filing into the Hall. Vorios and Seron sat down in front. The seat next to Seron seemed to be empty, but slowly the face and upper torso of a woman appeared. The rest of her was invisible! Vorios saw her and introduced Seron to Anka. She was wearing the magical henna that the inhabitants of Hydros wore when they left the island. All of the people of Hydros walked about in the nude when they were on the island. Off of the island they could follow certain proprieties. They could make themselves entirely visible or partly or completely invisible...it was their choice. They always had the magical henna with them, and a bow and arrows, as well as other objects that could also be treated and made invisible by the henna.

Everyone's attention was suddenly brought back to the front of the room where a large easel was being set up, and something was on the easel, covered by a large sheet. The Temple bells chimed three times, and Troyana came out of a side room of the Great Hall. The crowd noise died down, as she rolled the chair that she sat in across over to the easel. The chair was on wheels, and had been made for her by Vorios, many years before. She smiled at Vorios, and took her place beside the easel.

"Many of you know that Theoclea, Anka and I grew up together." She nodded to Anka, who was seated next to Seron. Anka was studying Seron, and he turned to her with a look of annoyance. Anka smiled with her pearly white somewhat sharp-looking teeth turned toward Troyana, and nodded to her.

"Anka, Theoclea and I played together. Anka's gift was that she could see the future with divination using stones. Theoclea had visions of the past and future. Anka and I were there when Theoclea had her first vision. That vision of a tree falling saved our lives. My gift was the use of cards for divination. I designed a

Chapter Ten...The Hanged Man

deck of cards. How many of you have seen the card deck that I use?" she asked.

Many hands went up, for merchants had been selling the basic deck for years, calling it The Sybil's Deck, for Troyana was known as 'The Sybil'. Troyana took some time to discuss some of the important cards in the deck. She was building up to something, and knew the right moment to reveal it.

"What you may not know is that occasionally a new card will appear on one of the blank cards that I always carry with my deck. I don't always decide to keep the new card, it depends on whether I'm reading for myself, or for a friend, or other circumstances. Recently a new card appeared. It has also appeared in dreams that I have had. I must thank Chrissa the Artist in Residence at the Temple for making a large representation of the card so that we all can see it." She turned and dramatically pulled off the sheet that was covering the easel. There was an audible gasp as the audience members viewed the card.

The card showed a man hanging upside down by one foot. There was a gibbet-like structure formed by two uprights and a crosspiece. The uprights appeared to be rough-hewn and the crosspiece was smooth. The man's hands were tied behind him, and one foot was tied with a rope to the crosspiece.

"Does anyone want to comment on this image?" Troyana asked. Several hands went up and she pointed to a man in the third row.

The man stood up and said, "There appears to be new growth on the upright poles. Perhaps this indicates new life."

"Anyone else?" Troyana said. A student in the back of the room was recognized.

"Perhaps this indicates a turning point, a turning of values upside down, a conversion experience required before further progress."

"Interesting," Troyana said.

Another person, one of the Priestesses said, "Perhaps the fact that his hands are tied means that we cannot grasp the situation, that we're out of touch that we need to know more."

"Very good," said Troyana.

Another participant, one of the Priests of the Temple was recognized. "His legs are crossed to form the number four, indicating that the man has a sense of who he is, his knees are bent showing flexibility."

Chapter Ten...The Hanged Man

Another hand went up. "There's a sense here that nothing can be done, perhaps patient inaction is needed."

While this was going on, Anka periodically turned to Seron and studied him. Her face, arms, and upper torso were tattooed heavily. Each time that Seron sensed that she was appraising him, he glanced at her, smiled weakly, and pretended to be engrossed in the workshop. A hand went up, and the next person said— "He must be 'sitting on the fence', waiting for someone else to take action." Another of the Priestesses in the room raised her hand and was recognized.

"We win by surrendering. We control by letting go. He has made the ultimate surrender, he has sacrificed himself!" Other hands went up—

"Seeing from a new angle," one person said. That one caused some laughter among the participants. Vorios' face showed concern. He studied the card thoroughly, looking for any missed details. He didn't laugh. Troyana continued.

"What each of you said was noble, wise and very positive in most cases, but look deeper. Does anyone see the tattoo on his right shoulder? It is a gold crescent moon with a black arrow going through it. There is a drop of blood beneath the moon." There was a complete silence in the room. "Does anyone know the significance of this?"

No one raised their hand. Finally, Vorios raised his.

"Vorios," Troyana said and pointed to him.

"It is the sign of the "Sons of Belial."

"Yes," said Troyana. The man is a traitor. This is a card of SHAME. I showed it to Pythagoras, and he said that images like this one are painted on the walls in countries like Egypt and other places. The faces in the paintings are very realistically rendered, so that there is no doubt in anyone's mind who the person is! When a crime is committed an image of the person is painted in this position on a wall, not to be removed until the person's death, or some kind of retribution is made. To interpret an image, one must first see if the image has a well-known interpretation. That should be considered first—then all other judgments weighed against it. This is the image of a traitor, an image of betrayal!"

Morain was in the audience and she started to feel a steady rise in Troyana's emotions.

"The card is saying that not only shame, but eventually death comes to the traitor, the instigator of a betrayal! She lowered her voice, and then said. "Do not be fooled by 'easy' interpretations. Remember this. If you are going to use the cards as divination tools, especially when you read for others, you should know the history of the images on the deck. Not just the interpretations that are fashionable for the time that we live in. It is significant to me that this image not only appeared on one of my blank cards, but appeared in a dream as well! The man wears the tattoo of the 'Sons of Belial'—making the appearance of the card a possible Omen of Betrayal. It is because of a betrayal that I lost the use of my legs! It was because of a traitor's actions that I sit in this chair before you! Do not overlook the obvious when you read the cards. Always look for the original meaning of an image! You may have seen the images on Theoclea's KeyRose divination tool. You do not need to seek a master to interpret the KeyRose images! In the case of this new card that I have presented to you, I hope that you can see as I do, that the original meaning, the shame and betrayal of a traitor, the damage that can be inflicted by such a person, can have many consequences."

She took the thong off from around her neck, and said, "You all see that I still have the Black Key, not because of the wounds that I received to my legs, they will never heal. It is the wound to the mind, the wound to the soul that must be allowed to heal before one can reach a higher Gate." She paused for a moment and sighed.

"I thank you for being an attentive audience and hope that your stay this week will be informative and enlightening." Applause started, and everyone rose to give her a standing ovation. She smiled at the crowd and acknowledged the applause.

As the applause started to die down, Anka continued to appraise Seron. He wore a black robe with long sleeves. He turned to her and showed her that weak smile once again. He said something like "what was it like when you were all growing up?" She looked at him, and then at the card on the easel. Then she turned her head and looked back at him again.

"We learned about…Magic!" she said. "We learned to see more than what was there in front of us!" She smiled back to reveal her pearly teeth. Seron noticed once again that some of them appeared to be very sharp. Finally, she just vanished.

Troyana started to wheel her chair over to Vorios and Seron. "A fine workshop, Troyana," Seron said as Troyana came up to them. "Well, Troyana you two have much to talk about, and I have a dinner

Chapter Ten...The Hanged Man

engagement with Psychera, please excuse me." With that Seron said his goodbyes to both of them.

Troyana looked at Vorios, and said, "Well, Vorios, what do you think?" He looked at her and kissed her hand. "Vorios, I had to...It was something that I haven't talked about with anyone for years! I had to get it out. There was no sense in holding it in. When the card appeared, all kinds of memories came back—all of the disturbing thoughts.I still haven't let go of them. She reached both hands out to Vorios, and he held her hands and stared at her. Tears started to appear in her eyes and suddenly she let it all out. She placed her head in his hands as she was crying.

"It's okay, Troyana, let it all out. The people who were responsible were dealt with years ago, tried and executed. "You have had to live with the memories. You're a brave and powerful woman. You shared your wisdom and opinions with us. We all should be eternally grateful for that." He looked back at the card with a troubled look. It was the face on the card that bothered him. It was blurred, as if the artist had made some mistakes, or the paint had been smeared.

Chapter Eleven...
The Meeting

Theoclea, Anka, Troyana, and Bella sat in one of the smaller ritual rooms that led to Theoclea's bedchamber. Incense was burning in a censer. There was a circle painted in white on the floor. On the four walls were candle holders, each one had a white candle inside and there were globes of different colors that fit over the candles. There was Red for the south, Blue for the East, Green for the West, and Yellow for the North. In the colored glass a symbol was etched for the Elements associated with the directions.

Anka sat in the West. She had always been associated with Water, for she lived on the island of Hydros. Sometimes, when they were children, she sat in the

North, the place of Earth, for she was the one who used stones in divination.

In the morning, they briefly met with Bella. When they met, Bella was in awe of each of them, Troyana and Anka were well known for their feats of divination with stones and cards. All of the stories of how Theoclea, Troyana and Anka grew up together and played at magic were well known to every child in Greece. It was part of the curriculum in the schools. When they parted, and each went their way as adults, the stories about the three of them ceased, and Theoclea became the one whose achievements and writings were known.

Theoclea, Troyana and Anka were equally in awe of Bella, for, of course, everyone knew of Bella, the Dancer, and her Troupe, Bella-Festa. She showed them a small part of her knife collection. Theoclea told Bella that stories of her performances were well known. She briefly mentioned that they were all aware of Bella's long-term relationship with Pythagoras. Anka said "I'm curious about your childhood. I haven't been able to find any writing about it. "Yes", said Troyana," what was your childhood like?"

"I was born on the Island of Kerkyra. When I was about four years old, my family moved to Thera. My

Chapter Eleven...The Meeting

father was a gem cutter, and very skilled at the cutting of gems and minerals. We lived happily on Thera until I was about fourteen. My father and brother were taken captive by an evil man, who was the head of a band of brigands and thieves. He told me that if I did not do what he wanted me to do, he would kill my father. I did what he forced me to do. I was only with him for a month, or so and then I found out that he had killed my father in front of my brother, and tortured my brother for information that my brother didn't have. That night, I stole a knife from the kitchen. There was a man who was guarding my tent. It was pitch dark, and I jumped out and swiftly covered the guard's mouth and slit his throat. No one heard a thing!" Theoclea, Anka and Troyana all looked at each other with wide eyes, then back at Bella.

"My father had taught me how to do this. I made my way back to my father's house, and found my mother, dead in the kitchen. I knew that my father had buried an emergency cache of gemstones in the back yard. With the gemstones and the help of my knives, I made it off of the island and landed in Athens. I met a band of wandering entertainers and joined them as a dancer. One day, as we were performing on the streets of Athens, a very beautiful woman approached me and told me that she liked my dancing, and that she knew of a fine dance teacher. She told me that she had been a dancer once herself. She turned out to be one of the wealthiest women in Athens. She had no children and adopted me, and treated me as her own child. Her husband was a fine man, rest his soul. From that time on life has been good for me. So, what do you think of my childhood?"

Theoclea, Troyana and Anka were speechless. Finally, Troyana spoke, "A difficult childhood…like mine with my accident, the betrayal, and my illnesses."

"I can certainly understand," said Anka. My childhood was not quite as gruesome and difficult. I was always treated like someone who was…different. Troyana and I were always concerned about Theoclea and her fits, the times when she went into a trance and passed out. Things like that."

Bella told them that she had agreed to have lunch with Pythagoras, and would have to leave them. Theoclea nodded to her, and said, "One more thing, Bella, do you have a personal sign, a personal glyph of some kind that represents you?"

"Yes, Theoclea, as a matter of fact, I do"

The four agreed to meet again, and after some formalities, Bella excused herself. Theoclea, Troyana

Chapter Eleven...The Meeting

and Anka closed their eyes when Bella left. They meditated for a few minutes. Then they looked at each other, and all of them smiled.

"She's the One," Theoclea said, "the fourth one, the one who's been missing all of these years." They all agreed. "I'll invite her back again this afternoon, and we'll tell her about the bonding ritual.

"Have we decided on what we are going to do at the bonding ritual?" Troyana said.

"Yes," said Anka, "We have to decide. This is a good time, what'll it be a spell, a chant, the stones, the cards?"

They were silent for about a minute. Then, Theoclea spoke: "I'll send word to her about meeting this afternoon. We must all have our knives and personal glyphs with us, more than that I don't know yet. When did we ever decide before what we were going to do? We'll decide this afternoon. We never knew what we were going to do when we were kids! Why should it be any different now?" They all laughed.

"I'll just tell her to meet us here again this afternoon," Theoclea said.

"She's in for it!" Troyana replied.

"Yes, said Anka, "I hope that she survives the bonding, shall I bring some stones, just in case we need them?" Anka asked? I've been walking around the temple, even in places about a half mile to a mile away from the Temple, and I have begun to know the stones. I'll keep doing this, I have a feeling that this time, I must know all of the stones that are anywhere near to the Temple. If there are stones that I don't see, the other ones that I have seen will spread a rapport with me, that's how it works!"

"Of course, Anka, we always used the stones at out bonding rituals!

They all laughed. "It's just like before, when we were kids," said Theoclea—

> "Let's make the sign
> and do the chant:
> an adventure—
> the three become four!"
> they all
> made
> the sign of the Gate of
> Eleusis, and chanted
> 'It's starting, it's starting, It's
> starting' three times.' Then
> they laughed again.

Chapter Twelve...
The Bonding

In the afternoon, Bella joined them once again. She sat in the North, which was the place that they had chosen for her. They all meditated for about five minutes. There was a cauldron in the middle of the circle that they sat in, and it was lit. One by one they opened their eyes, then Theoclea spoke-

"It's been a long time since we did the bonding ritual. We all know the proprieties of ritual, the purification, the casting of the circle, the calling of directions, the calling of the Gods and Goddesses, purification of the members, and the rest of the proprieties. We have to decide on the WORK OF THE CIRCLE. I think that we should each draw our personal glyph on a piece of paper, then, we can stick our knives through the paper, and place the knives and paper on the ground. We can then each pass the knives around to each other, as each of us gets a knife, we can say a prayer, silently, or out loud. Then when each of us gets back our knife and glyph, we can chant."

"The three become four
with the rising sun.
Our lives are bonded
Let this WORK be done."

Troyana and Anka nodded their heads in agreement. It was only Bella, who had a troubled, confused look on her face. Anka chimed in. "One more thing, I have a magic rope." She held up her hands and nothing seemed to be in them. "The rope has been treated with the magical Henna, we can feel it, but we cannot see it. I propose that part of the working be that before we do the chant, Theoclea will bind each of our hands together and then bind her own and attach the rope to my hands, then we can chant." Bella smiled slightly, and pondered this. She reached over to Anka and felt the invisible rope.

"I'd like to add something. We can all warm our hands over the cauldron, and throw in some flash salts and incense at the beginning to make sure that our

Chapter Twelve...The Bonding

hands are properly purified." Troyana said. The others agreed, with the exception of Bella, who continued to look troubled.

"How long has it been since the three of you did a bonding ritual?" They all looked at each other.

Troyana said, "Twenty five years?"

"I thought so," said Bella! "What is this a craft class...with fake magic of flash salts in the cauldron? What is a bonding without BLOOD? What is a bonding without SACRIFICE?"

The three others stared at her.

"Here's what I propose. We have a first knife—the Burning Knife, that we put in the burning cauldron before we begin, and we put a rag and a pair of tongs in front of the cauldron on the rocks. Now about the chant..."

'The three become four
with the rising sun
Our lives are bonded
Let this WORK be done.'

"The sun's not rising now, its afternoon, and 'The three become four', has been overly done! I propose that we change it slightly."

With the blood of each sister

Our signs become one
Our lives are bonded
Let this work be done!

"Now, before we tie our hands together, with the invisible rope, we have to do something else. We'll use a second knife, The Blood Knife, and a third knife, the Sacred Knife. We will pass these knives from one to another. I'll be the first, since I'm the new one. I'll use the second knife call it the Blood Knife, to make a quick cross cut in the middle of my left palm. When enough blood has come out, I'll use the Blood Knife again."

She held up another knife.

"THIS, a third knife, will be our Sacred knife. With my blood on the Blood Knife, I'll make my glyph on the Sacred Knife that we are using, then, I'll pass the Blood Knife and the Sacred Knife on to Anka, and she'll do the same thing, draw the blood, and with the blood knife and inscribe her glyph over mine. In this way our blood will be mingled on the Blood Knife and our left palms...and also the glyphs and our blood will be joined on the Sacred knife." She gazed at the other three to see if they understood, then she continued.

"Theoclea, I think that you should be next, and then Troyana should be last, because her magic is

Chapter Twelve...The Bonding

that she can amplify other people's magic. Then, we should...mmm... Troyana...you can sprinkle some of this..." She took out a pouch and showed that it had some silvery dust in it... "Sprinkle some of this on the Sacred Knife and this dust will seal the blood. We'll then put the Sacred Knife on this cushion that I have brought."

She brought out a cushion from behind her. "Okay, then I'll bind our hands together with the invisible rope, I can feel it. When we are all bound tightly, I'll bind myself, then we can do the chant—

With **the blood of each sister**
Our signs become one
Our lives are bonded
Let this work be done!'

"We'll do the chant as long as we want to, getting louder and faster each time, until we feel that it has reached its' peak! When our hands are all bound tightly together and the chanting is over, I know how to untie any knot, so that I can get one hand free. I'll take the Blood knife , and cut the invisible rope off of my other hand, and then I'll carefully cut a small piece of my skin off of my arm and throw it into the fire, Then, I'll say something like this—

"I sacrifice a part of me by

tying it to this tree...
no that's wrong...it's from
another ritual. I'll say—

'I sacrifice a part of me.
There was a time
when there were three,
through blood and sacrifice
the three are now four,
the spell's been cast
we are NOT as before!'

"Then I will go around, and do the same to each of you. After I cut the skin off your arm, I'll give it to you and you can toss it into the cauldron. Then you can say the sacrifice chant—

I sacrifice a part of me.
there was a time
when there were three,
through blood and sacrifice
the three are now four
the spell's been cast
we are NOT as before!

"We'll go over it again a few times before we start. Then, I'll take the tongs and take the first knife out of the burning fire...THE BURNING KNIFE. It's going to be good and hot. I'll take the rag and hold the knife,

Chapter Twelve...The Bonding

and BRAND MYSELF on my left arm. Then I'll do the SAME to each of YOU! The other three gasped, and all three of them said together—

"Oh my God!" They had horrified looks on their faces. They were speechless for the moment.

"We will then be bonded, but we must test the bond before we can end the ritual," Bella said.

"Test the bond?" said Anka.

"Yes, of course," said Bella, "we must test the bond to see if it worked!"

They were all silent for a minute. Troyana spoke first.

"Does there have to be so much ...blood?"

"Of course," said Bella, "It's a bonding ritual!"

The other three then slowly thoughtfully agreed.

Anka said, "Do we need the part about taking the skin off?"

"Of course," said Bella, it's...a tradition! It's done that way all over!"

Theoclea was the last of the three to speak. She spoke almost in a whisper. "The branding part, can we just leave that part out?"

"Okay," said Bella, "I only put that part in to see what you would say when I said that, it was my little joke. We won't need that first knife, the tongs and the rag, but let's put plenty of incense in the cauldron at the beginning, and keep it going!" The others let out a sigh of relief.

"LET'S DO IT!" Theoclea said. I like all of Bella's suggestions. We'll call it 'Bella's Bonding Ritual!'" All agreed on that. "Now, said Theoclea, "for the testing part...I have an idea. Anka, did you bring the stones, are there little ones, larger ones and big ones?"

"Of course!" Anka replied.

They then agreed on the testing, and prepared for the ritual. They went through with the ritual as planned...and finally got to the testing part. Before the testing part, they had performed all of the proprieties of the ending of the ritual. They thanked the Gods and Goddesses, and dismissed the Directions. They performed ...all of the proprieties except one... they didn't open the circle. The circle remained. They all sat and meditated for a few minutes. More incense was thrown in the cauldron. Anka's stones were placed near the cauldron. Then, Bella stared at the Sacred Knife on the cushion. After a while Bella then nodded to Troyana.

Troyana closed her eyes, deep in concentration. Anka had completely covered herself with the magical

Chapter Twelve...The Bonding

henna, and was invisible. Theoclea closed her eyes. In a few moments she saw the scene, in black and white. Then, she saw the knife slowly rise from the cushion, and very slowly move through the air...it finally rested on one spot, and Theoclea saw that Anka was holding it, even though she was invisible. Theoclea saw all of the rest of it, she saw that the test would be successful and run its' course. There were amorphous lights in the background. It was all in black and white. She also saw more, much more...

Suddenly the light and color came back. Everyone's eyes were open as the knife slowly floated to one spot and then seemed to settle, as if held in Anka's invisible hands. Bella was staring at the knife, and it started to rise and spin faster and faster, then slowed down, and started to circle about six feet off of the ground. Slowly starting in the East, it started to open the circle, eventually moving to the South, then the West, then the North, and then back to the East. It hovered in the air. Anka appeared instantly, sitting in her usual spot, meditating.

Everyone was suddenly surprised when each one of the stones started to rise, when they were about six feet off of the ground they hovered together forming a small cloud of stones directly over the Cauldron. Anka nodded to Troyana and smiled.

Theoclea recited:
>'The Circle fades, look toward the North,
>
>>the Time is late and we
>>
>>>must go forth.
>
>What was a circle is no more,
>
>>but are we as we were before?'

She heard the others whisper "No!"

"No!" she shouted. She gazed into the distance and continued—

>"For we have been in the worlds between
>
>>and a mighty mystery we have seen.
>
>>So my fiends let's say our goodbyes
>
>>>and look forward to when,
>
>>in another circle, at another time,
>
>>>WE SHALL MEET AGAIN."

Anka sat in her spot, everyone suddenly realized that she was holding the Sacred Knife. All of the stones in the cloud fell into the cauldron, and all four repeated the last phrase.

>>WE SHALL MEET AGAIN
>>
>>WE SHALL MEET AGAIN
>>
>>WE SHALL MEET AGAIN!

Chapter Twelve...The Bonding

Theoclea said, "The circle is open but unbroken, merry meet and merry part and merry meet again!" They all shouted and laughed held hands and embraced each other. "It's just like when we were kids, and now there's a fourth," Troyana said. They all cried and hugged Bella.

"Theoclea smiled, and said, "It worked perfectly, and I saw all of it beforehand in a vision!"

"No!" Bella said, "really? You saw it all before it actually happened?"

"Yes," Theoclea replied. She looked down, and tried to hide her look of concern. She sighed.

"Don't forget, I can see the past, present and future, sometimes it's a blessing, and sometimes not. I don't always see everything, some parts are vague. But I see enough." She managed a weak smile, and then embraced Bella. They all embraced her, then left the ritual room and agreed to continue the testing of the bond. Theoclea went straight to Vorios' quarters and knocked on his door.

"Yes, who is it?" he said.

"It's Theoclea, Vorios, and I must ask you to do something for me!"

"Yes, Theoclea, come right in." Seron, one of Vorios' students opened the door.

"Theoclea, you know my student, Seron, he has just been given his lesson and was about to leave." Seron bowed his head, and said, "Theoclea." A wisp of a remembrance passed through Theoclea's mind, but it quickly dispersed in a fog of forgetfulness. Theoclea smiled slightly and said—

"Seron, are you having dinner again with Psychera tonight?" Seron blushed, and stammered…

"Why yes, I am!"

"Well, enjoy your dinner together," Theoclea said. Seron left, and Theoclea closed the door.

Vorios rose from his desk, and walked over to her.

"Vorios, have you consecrated and charged the new stone that was raised last week?"

"No, not yet, Theoclea, We usually wait two weeks or more to allow the mortar to set completely."

"Vorios, please do this for me. The stone must be consecrated and completely charged immediately!"

"We have had some power anomalies lately, Theoclea, but I will do as you have asked. I'll get to it right away. The Artist Chrissa can inscribe the proper symbols, and Reena can do the chanting and singing. The other magicians will help me with the energy and power part."

Chapter Twelve...The Bonding

"Fine, Vorios, thank you, it's very important that this be done quickly!" She left Vorios' quarters. He immediately set upon doing the task that was given to him.

Chapter Thirteen...
The First Ritual

That night, 'Orpheus Returns to the Underworld' was performed. The singer, Alcena, the child of Theoclea and Pythagoras sang 'The Orpheus song'. Everyone could see the tears building up in Pythagoras' eyes as she sang—after she sang, one of the men walked over and held him—he indicated that he was okay.

Later in the ritual, the boy, one of the shades that guarded the gate to the realm of Hades was portrayed by Abderus, the son of Theoclea and Pythagoras.

His role was to challenge Orpheus at the Gate,

"Why it's Orpheus. Have you come back to try again?" He laughed maniacally, then stopped and said, "who is that with you?" He looked shocked. "Why it's...THE OLD GODS...and voyagers!" Sheepishly, he said, "You may pass." Pythagoras nodded to him with a big smile. The ritual went on, as planned.

The fourth day was a day of rest, and rehearsals were started for the second ritual—Artemis and the Handless Maiden. There was more of the same on the fifth day—more preparations made for the ritual, which was to be held outdoors, and there were all sorts of outdoor preparations to be made. At night, there was a feast, and a concert afterward. The first group to perform on the program was the choir of Priests and Priestesses. They were led by Reena, the Music Teacher.

They sang songs, like–
"Calliope's Lament"
"Hymn to Polyhymnia"
"Second Pythian Ode"
"Seikilos' Song"
"Hymn to the Moon"
and "Kore Evohe"

They ended with a song from the Opera "Persephone," that had been composed by Reena. It was sung by Reena, with the accompaniment played

Chapter Thirteen...The First Ritual

by the Merchant, on his keyed instrument—the title of the song was 'Why is he so evil?'

"I liked that last piece a lot," Panelle whispered to Morain, who glanced back at Panelle with a dubious look.

Next on the program was the Bella Festa dance Troupe. At the request of Theoclea, they performed basically the same program that they had performed at Eleusis. Their entrance was spectacular. They entered playing finger cymbals. They wore their usual costumes of silver coin bras, chokers, and cholis of various colors, black pantaloons, full gold skirts, tassle belts, and jewelry from exotic places.

As in their performance at Eleusis, they quickly formed a circle, after going clockwise around the stage. Then, as before, the group divided in half, as if creating a curtain. The musicians stopped, and only the reed flute player continued with a song. It was music that only Bella danced to. Bella appeared from behind a curtain and walked to the center of the stage. She smiled and revealed that she had a secret.

"Tonight is the first time that I will be trying something new. The circumstances here tonight, may allow me to do this, you may never see this done again anywhere else so please be patient." She smiled at Theoclea, Troyana, and Anka, who were seated in the audience to the right, then the reed flute player started again

Bella wore the same costume that she had worn at Eleusis—three colors of the Delphic Oracle—gold, black and red. Her personal color, silver, was reflected in the jewelry that she wore. As before, her pantaloons were black, her skirt was gold. She wore her trademark hip scarf, with a white and gold symbol of a rose. The scarf was fringed in white. As always, she wore a red rose in her hair.

A drummer came out from the wings and joined the flute, playing a slow beladi rhythm. Bella continued with her usual repertoire of floreos, and snake arm movements. Slow taxeems, and arm undulations followed. Then, the sword carrier appeared from behind the curtain and the musicians stopped. So far the performance was exactly like the performance at Eleusis. There was a hush in the crowd. Theoclea, Anka and Troyana leaned forward in rapt attention. They knew that the sword that Bella used was not the usual dancer's stage sword. It was sharp, and everyone knew that. Not a sound was heard in the room—the sword handler had the scimitar on a cushion. As always, he put the sword and the cushion down on the floor in front

Chapter Thirteen...The First Ritual

of Bella, who sat before him. Bowing before her, she reached out her hands and he gave her the scimitar, took the cushion, and put the cushion down about six feet from Bella.

Suddenly, the performance changed. It was not to be a repetition of the Eleusis performance. The sword handler took out a serrated knife, with crystals all over the hilt of it. He held it up and showed it to the crowd—it was obviously sharp. He placed the knife on the index finger of his right hand, and made a small cut. The audience gasped, as a drop of blood appeared. He placed the knife on the cushion, took out a piece of fabric, wiped his finger, and retired to the wings of the stage.

Bella looked at the sword and whispered something to it. Then she looked at the knife on the cushion several feet away. She closed her eyes and whispered something else. She raised the sword, and gently placed it on her head. She continued with her usual performance, tantalizing the audience by showing the sword, balancing it, lowering herself backward toward the ground while balancing the sword—Bella did all of the usual moves, then returned to the sitting position, the sword still balanced on her head. She looked at the knife on the cushion six feet away. She whispered something. Then she looked at Troyana, who closed her eyes as if deep in thought. Troyana opened her eyes and looked at the knife on the cushion.

The knife started to rise from the cushion. There was an audible gasp from the audience. Troyana kept concentrating on the knife, occasionally glancing over at Bella. When the knife was about six feet off of the ground it started to move toward Bella. Soon it was directly overhead. It rotated, and was pointing directly down at the scimitar. Slowly it lowered itself, and finally the tip of the knife touched the scimitar. Both knives were perfectly balanced. The audience started to applaud, but stopped when Bella placed a finger to her lips. The applause stopped.

The knife started to float up again, rotated and moved back to the spot that was six feet above the cushion, where it slowly descended, and finally rested on the cushion. Bella turned to Troyana, and still balancing the scimitar, she held out her hands and made the "Gates of Eleusis sign to Troyana, and Theoclea. The audience went wild with applause. Anka reappeared sitting next to them, and Bella smiled at her. She gently took the sword off of her head and showed it to everyone. The sword carrier then came out, placed the

Chapter Thirteen...The First Ritual

knife under his sash, took the scimitar off of the cushion and left. All the while the audience kept applauding. The 'Gate of Eleusis' sign was repeated by all four of the bonded women, then Bella smiled at the audience and walked over to Troyana, leaned down and embraced her. They all embraced each other, then Bella sat down in the vacant seat beside Theoclea.

The next, and final group to perform was the Children's choir, once again, under the direction of Reena, the Music Teacher

The Choir sang these songs:
"First Pythian Mode"
'Hymn to the Sun"
"Hymn to Themus"
"Tecmessa's Lament"

One of the boys stepped forward. He had prepared a reading for the audience. He announced himself.

"I am Abderus, and I have written a verse for this occasion. I wrote the verse today after meditating on the 'Orpheus Returns to the Underworld Ritual'. After my reading, my sister Alcena will sing for you a song that she has written, also for this occasion."

He looked down at the floor, as if taking the time to assume a different character, then, after taking a deep breath he started:

"My poem is called—

The Dark Night of the Soul

I stood in a clearing,
it was the midnight of my fortieth year.
The forest was dark, and reflected the state that my soul was in.
All my life I had followed a path,
the path of a man who's soul sought life's pleasures.
It was a path of solitude, for I had never married,
never had children, never had given myself to anyone
in the way that men pledge themselves to another.
I wandered about the clearing, as if in a dream, thinking of all that had befallen me in the previous year.
The end of a love–
the loss of my dear Lady of Peace for whom I had almost pledged myself—only to lose her to a prolonged illness.
My heart yearned for her, I felt incomplete, my friend and confidant gone.

Chapter Thirteen...The First Ritual

Music had always been an important element in my life.
I was a musician of great renown...once...and yet even music did not move me as it once had.
My soul was out of balance—as if the Sacred Feminine and the Sacred Masculine were ghosts, lost in a fog. The Gods and the Goddesses had forsaken me and had allowed me to stray from the path.

A fleeting thought of ending it all
passed through my mind,
when all of a sudden I saw
an object on the path that was lit
by the full moon.
Walking toward it, I saw that it was
a rose that had fallen from a nearby rose bush.
As I gazed at it in the moonlight, it seemed to speak
to me—I listened, and it said,
'Of all the paths that one must tread
(before one departs for the land of the dead)
there is one on which you must pay the toll
and walk right through
the Dark Night of the soul—
and if by chance you might meet someone
who gives you the rose when the night is done,

there is something here that you must say—
'With this rose in my heart I'll greet the new day'.
I pondered these words, and then saw that another
was walking toward me.
Her soul was in darkness, but she could see
the hurt in my eyes,
the pain in my heart
the Wound was still bleeding
I had taken life's dart.
She picked up The Rose and gave it to me,
saying,
'I give you The Rose to set your heart free'.

And so my dear listener,
for that's who you are
I give you the Rose
You have come from afar.
Your mind is troubled
Your heart is not free
The gift of this rose
I pass on to thee.

He had finished…

Pythagoras turned to Theoclea, who was sitting across from him in the hall. His eyes were filled with tears. She also had a handkerchief in her hands. They exchanged warm smiles, and he walked over to her, and stood by her. The boy acknowledged the applause that was forthcoming...he held up his hands to quiet the crowd, and then said, "My sister, Alcena will now sing for you," and he walked back and joined the chorus.

A girl walked forward from the chorus. There was a look of wonderment on her face, a slight smile, her lips parted slightly as she inhaled a long breath, and then her mouth closed. She slowly opened it and said, "I have written a song for this event. My song is called **"The Pentacle and the Rose."**

Theoclea stole a glance at Pythagoras and nodded to him. He sighed and returned a smile back to Theoclea. His eyes went back to the child. With a poise that spoke of a maturity beyond her years, she stood at the edge of the performance area. Her hands were clasped together in the manner that was traditional when singing unaccompanied.

She closed her eyes and drew her hands apart in the palms up position. Everyone sensed that the gesture was one of being respectful for the gift that had been given her. She opened her eyes and gazed upward, offering her song to the Gods and Goddesses. She opened her mouth very slowly, so slowly that the audience held their breath in anticipation. Theoclea, Anka and Troyana followed every movement. In the audience Bella was especially transfixed by the child's hand movements and concentration. The girl then formed a perfect "O" with her mouth, drew in a deep breath, and sang:

> **There's a Rose that grows in moonlight,**
> **its petals wait for dew.**
> **On fern-braided trails,**
> **In luminous veils,**
> **its silver-sweet scent waits for you.**
> **It grows in lands of darkness,**
> **below in wondrous gloom,**
> **on opaline threads in lush amber beds**
> **it spreads its strange perfume.**
>
> **Up above it blooms near night-shade,**
> **in diamond motes of moon-beams,**
> **where on the ground a Pentacle lies,**
> **its' Poet-soul listens and dreams.**
>
> **The Pentacle's a symbol**
> **of air, water, fire and earth.**

Chapter Thirteen...The First Ritual

**as everyone knows
it points to the Spirit
with the Rose
it shows its worth.**

**If you come upon the roses,
and have the Pentacle too,
watch out for the thorns
and join them together-
The Pentacle and the Rose.**

There was a hush for a few seconds, and one by one the audience stood up and applauded the girl. They had simply never heard the symbol used in a song, and it touched all of them. Theoclea was visibly crying, and Pythagoras walked over to the girl, gave her a hug, and walked her over to Theoclea. He walked over to the boy, Abderus, and thanked him for his offering.

The concert was over, and congratulations were given all around, with everyone especially interested in the costumes and jewelry of Bella and her troupe. Abderus and Alcena hugged each other. The children had no idea that Pythagoras and Theoclea were their parents.

Slowly everyone departed for their bedchambers, looking forward to the following day when 'Artemis and the Handless Maidens' was to be performed. Like the 'Orpheus' ritual, the second ritual was also for men and women. It was a ritual in which men were confronted with a "primal" part of their nature, while women were to learn that their bonding with a strong Goddess like Artemis would teach them many things.

Both Men and Women learned that the balance between the Sacred Feminine and the Sacred Masculine created power within them that could defeat those that had lost control, and had fallen to lower gates, and into the Abyss.

The second ritual was not performed that year, due to the unfortunate events that unfolded the next morning.

Chapter Fourteen...
The Sixth Day

A scream was heard that echoed through the hall and the chambers that housed the High Priests and High Priestesses, and their attendants. Vorios was roused with a knock on the door from Panelle.

"Vorios, come quickly! I'll rouse Pythagoras. Something's wrong!" Vorios put on a robe, and then looked around the room. He sensed something. The Magic was down. Panelle's Wards and Spells were down as well. He opened the door to see Morain running down the hall.

"Quickly...it's Theoclea's chamber- follow me!"

Vorios followed, and glanced back to see Pythagoras running to catch up. They rounded the corner of the hallway that led to Theoclea's bedchamber. The

Priestess-in-waiting who stood the night watch in front of Theoclea's chamber, Psychera, lay on the floor, her throat was cut, and she was dead, lying in a pool of blood. Both wrists were cut as well. Morain pushed the door to Thoeoclea's bedchamber open, and rushed in. She gasped.

"Theoclea's gone! Someone has taken her!"

Panelle said, "All of the protection—the Wards and Spells, the Magic...everything is gone." An alarm was sounded and the Guardians and Counselors were instructed to search the entire Temple. They were asked to look for Seron, for Seron and Psyhera had been very close.

Morain and Panelle both closed their eyes. Normally, they may have been able to stop time in their minds, run the whole thing backwards, as if in black and white, meld their minds with Theoclea wherever she was, see what had happened, and be able to come to her aid. Nothing, nothing came to them, nothing at all, despite their powers. When they opened their eyes, they both peered through the hallway window. It was dark and rainy outside, and even the crystal lanterns seemed to have dimmed somewhat. There was lightning, thunder, and a sulphur-smell like smoking pumice was in the air.

"What is hidden from you I will now proclaim to you—

I saw someone in a vision...I saw you in a vision!"

"You did not waiver from the sight of me? If so, then your mind is a treasure, a priceless treasure!"

"How do you think that one who sees a vision sees it—through the soul, or through the spirit?"

"One does not see through the soul or through the spirit.

It is the mind that is between the two—that is what sees the vision!"

(from a fragment of Theocleas' writings)

Chapter Fifteen...
Theoclea Bound

Her hands. The first thing that Theoclea felt was that her hands were bound behind her back. She blinked her eyes, saw vague cloudy shapes in front of her, and realized that she had been drugged in some way. As the fog in her mind cleared she began to see that there was a man sitting in front of her. She heard his voice.

"Theoclea, we've never met, I'm a stranger to you, and my name is Davros." She looked to the right and vaguely saw another man, a big man, standing with his arms folded. He stood near an altar. She looked all around the room as her vision started to clear, then closed her eyes, trying to remember something.

The room was small for an altar room. Crystal lanterns on the walls illuminated the altar that was in the center of the room. Everything that had been on the altar was removed, and there were now papers, a wine glass, and two bottles of wine. One of the bottles was empty.

The man who had spoken sat staring at his empty glass. There was also a knife on the altar—it was serrated. The teeth on the knife were of different sizes and razor sharp.

"Theoclea!" the seated man said, "Open your eyes, can you hear me? I'm a stranger to you, we have never met. I'm Davros!" His head was shaved, and he had an earring in one ear. He wore a long sleeved black robe, that had wine or blood stains on it. "Theoclea, can you hear me?" the seated man said once again. The tall man stood, his arms folded, his head also shaved, a scimitar tied to the sash around his waist. He was bare-chested and had tattoos all over his chest. He wore white pants, had an earring in one ear, and was very muscular. The seated man poured himself a glass of wine, took a big mouthful, swallowed it and placed the bottle and the glass back on the altar.

"Theoclea, the Delphic Oracle, they said that she looked like a child, what do you think, Avram?" He

Chapter Fifteen...Theoclea Bound

glanced at the big man and smiled, and the big man returned the smile, his arms continued to be folded.

"She looks like a handless maiden, not an Oracle," Avram said, looking at her hands.

"Theoclea, do you know where you are?" 'Davros said. Theoclea's eyes were still closed. Davros looked over at his knife on the altar and quickly covered the hilt with a cloth. She opened her eyes, and as she gazed around the room, slowly she regained her vision enough to know where she was. Finally, she looked directly into his eyes, glanced around the room once again, and her vision cleared. She spoke—

"What have you done with the Priestess of this Temple? You are in the Temple of Gaia...do you realize what you have done?" She looked at the muscular man, appraising him carefully. He continued to smile, arms folded.

"Well, let's say that the Priestess is being detained, she is in... good hands," Davros laughed. "Nothing will happen to her as long as you cooperate with us. We wanted to capture you, and our plan was to take over this smaller temple on the road to Delphi. Our goal is much greater than a small insignificant temple such as this. We have you, and will have the Temple of Delphi and its riches within the week. We want the gold. We want the treasures, everything of value. We have over a thousand men, and you have only a few hundred guarding the Temple. We have neutralized the protective magic that Vorios put in place, and one of his students Seron, is one of our men! He has given us a lot of information, Theoclea. We're in no rush. We will have a siege situation here and you're part of the plan." Theoclea studied him took in a deep breath and spoke firmly.

"Do you know where you are? You say that your name is Davros, and that you are a stranger to me, **DO YOU KNOW WHERE YOU ARE, DAVROS?"** She glared at him and raised her voice—her eyes not straying from his. **"You are in the altar room of Gaia! You are using the altar as a table. Put back the altar objects, bring back the Priestess, then leave with your men!"**

Davros laughed. "My God, they told me that you were like a child!" He continued to laugh, and looked at Avram…who laughed with him.

"You are my prisoner 'Dear One'. That's what they call you, am I right—'Dear One'? I know all about you, Theoclea, shall I share some of your secrets with Avram, secrets about your son and daughter? We're going to capture your Temple and its' riches, and we have you as the bargaining point."

Chapter Fifteen...Theoclea Bound

"Nothing will happen to me," Theoclea said. "Now leave with your men or suffer the consequences!"

Davros laughed hysterically. He looked at the tall man, and said,

"Avram, this is too much, can you believe this? I must tell the others about her." He reached up and grabbed the glass from the table and poured some more wine. "Oh how crass of me, I haven't offered you a drop of wine!"

Theoclea turned her head in disgust, then looked at him again.

"Take that unconsecrated wine off of the altar, put everything back as it was, and leave, or suffer the consequences!"

"Do you believe this, Avram? 'Suffer the consequences'! Theoclea, there is nothing that you can do to us. We've neutralized Vorios' magic, as well as the protection spells and wards of Panelle, your protector....it's all been neutralized this morning, thanks to Seron's information. We can even turn off all of the Crystal lanterns as well! Yes, we have the power to do that! They'll give up the Temple, rather than see you harmed, you are their most priceless treasure!"

"You cannot harm me," Theoclea replied. Davros nodded to Avram and asked him to bring in something. Avram left the room. Davros looked at Theoclea again.

"You are both a Priestess of Apollo and Dionysus, am I right?" She said nothing. He continued to speak.

"Compared to me, and those that I serve, Dionysus is a God of Light! We've reached into the true darkness, seen the lower gates, touched them, and have welcomed the Abyss. You have no idea of what we can do." He took the knife off of the altar, making sure that the cloth still covered the hilt.

"I can cut off one of your fingers each day until… the people at the Temple will quickly capitulate." Theoclea said nothing, and stared at the knife. She looked at her right shoulder, then back at him.

"The blood…during the speech…was that you?"

"What do you mean?" he said.

"Was…any of that magic during my speech…did any of it…come from you?"

"Yes, a few tricks in the sky, just to…test some things. There was no blood…what are you talking about?"

Theoclea glanced at her right shoulder again and said—

"Hold the knife out to me, I want a closer look at it. You say that you are a stranger to me, and that we

Chapter Fifteen...Theoclea Bound

have never met, am I right? Have you consecrated this knife in any way?" she said. She stared at the cloth covering the hilt.

"Ha, I've killed many with this knife, that's how I consecrated it," he replied. He took the knife off of the altar and showed it to her, carefully concealing the hilt.

"How dare you place it on the Altar of Gaia!" she shouted! He looked curiously at her.

"They said that you were odd." He shook his head. He continued to hold out the knife, and she studied it, only the serrated edges were shown. The cloth covered the hilt. She nodded to him and smiled a disconcerting smile. He put the knife back on the altar. The muscular man came back into the room with a cage. "Theoclea, you have no idea of what we can do," Davros said.

The cage was set on the altar. Inside of it was a ferret. The muscular man took the ferret out and placed it on his shoulder.

"Theoclea, show me your right hand, hold it out to me."

"There is nothing that you can do to me," Theoclea said once more. "Your only chance would be to do what you cannot do—I see that."

She held out her hand. Davros said, "I will show you what we can do."

"We?" Theoclea said.

"Yes, he said, "I am a member of the Sons of Belial."

"I know," said Theoclea. Davros stared at her.

He motioned to the muscular man, who quickly took the ferret, and held it down on the table. In one stroke, Davros took the knife and drove it into the ferret's heart. It shrieked, and then died almost instantly, its' blood oozing out all over the altar. He quickly took the knife out and placed it with the bloody cloth still covering the hilt on another part of the altar.

Theoclea was shocked.

"You would do that? Sacrifice a living animal in such….a brutal way—on the altar of Gaia?" She stared at the dead ferret. "You would sacrifice an unprepared animal on the Altar of Gaia? Orpheus put an end to the blood sacrifice seven hundred years ago! There has been no blood sacrifice for seven hundred years! It is FORBIDDEN!"

She looked at the tall man. He no longer smiled, a look of worry appeared on his face and he looked away from Theoclea.

"Yes, Theoclea, and I will do that to you piece by piece until the Temple of Delphi and its' riches will

Chapter Fifteen...Theoclea Bound

be given to us." He waved the knife at her. The bloody cloth still covered the hilt.

She took a deep breath and tried to compose herself. She closed her eyes for a few seconds, then opened them, stared directly at him, and said once again—

"You cannot do anything to me." He looked at her uneasily for a few seconds. She continued.

"It doesn't matter whether you have neutralized Vorios' magic—you can do nothing to me!" He continued to look at her uneasily for a few more seconds.

"You have seen what I can do!" he said.

"I know what you can do," said Theoclea, **"You are not a stranger to me, I know about you, I have SEEN you in my visions."** The muscular man, who had been looking straight ahead, his arms folded, turned his head toward Davros, a look of concern, a slight hint of confusion in his eyes.

Theoclea continued. **"You will be dead within the next three days, maybe sooner. I have seen your death!"** Many of your men will die with you! I HAVE SEEN YOUR DEATH!" she shouted. The muscular man, Avram, showed puzzlement, a growing hint of fear in his eyes, both arms started to slip from the folded position. Davros felt a hint of fear, but he contained it well. He nodded, almost smiled at the muscular man. Theoclea continued to stare at him. **"It's YOU, the one in my visions. You have a tattoo on your right arm, the sign of the gold crescent moon with the black arrow through it, the red drop of blood below it! Roll up your sleeve!"**

Davros' smile disappeared, he turned to Avram and said, coolly—"You see, I have told you that they have spies everywhere!"

"Roll up your sleeve!" Theoclea repeated. Davros rolled up his sleeve and showed the tattoo.

"This means nothing, he said, your spies are everywhere!" He stared at the tattoo, looked up at Avram, then gazed directly into Thoeclea's eyes.

"If you have seen my death, Theoclea, what is to be the instrument of my death?" he said, the smile returning to his face.

Theoclea closed her eyes for a few seconds, then opened them. She remained silent looking back and forth at both of them. "If you have seen my death, Theoclea, in what manner will I die?" he said, glaring at her. Slowly she closed her eyes once again, and then opened them. Theoclea smiled at him.

"Are you asking me this question as the Oracle? You know that if that is so, I must answer you truthfully,

Chapter Fifteen...Theoclea Bound

is that what you want?" She raised her voice. **"Is that what you really want?"**

Davros leaned back and poured himself more wine. He looked at Avram. "They have spies everywhere their Temple is the richest Temple in the world." He turned to Theoclea, and said "Yes! Answer my question!" Theoclea looked from him to the knife.

"I have seen that knife in a vision. You will die by that knife. On the hilt one side is blank, on the other side there is the gold crescent moon with the black arrow through it. Beneath that is the red drop of blood, and under that the first letter of your name a "D" is engraved into the hilt! Take the bloody cloth off of the knife and show me the hilt!"

He took the cloth off of the knife, and the blank side of the hilt faced him. He turned the knife over, and what she said, of course, was true. Avram looked at the knife in alarm. Both hands were now hanging at his side. There was no smile on his face. It had been replaced by a look of confusion. He was no longer looking at Theoclea as a child. She almost spat out the next statement.

"That knife, that unconsecrated knife that you have used to take a life on the altar of Gaia—that knife will be the instrument of your death!" I have no

more to say to you, Davros, the Stranger." She closed her eyes.

Davros sat and looked at her for almost a minute. He placed the knife back on the altar, and looked at Avram. He saw confusion in the man's eyes, a hint of fear that he had not seen in this man before. Davros whispered, "They have spies everywhere, they could have..." He stopped in mid- sentence. "Anyone could have...many people have seen this knife, and..."

He stopped, stared at the knife, then gazed at Theoclea for several moments. He looked back at the knife, then up at Avram and said, "Take her back to the chamber, and keep her hands tied. When you get back, tie her feet as well, take the Red Key from around her neck and lock it to the chain that hangs from the wall. Make sure that the chain is strong, there are many chains that hang from that wall." He picked up his knife from the altar. "There is a box back in my quarters, take it and place the knife in it, then put a lock on the box, and chain it to the wall as well. Now get her out of here! I want Theoclea's chamber guarded day and night! Get this mess out here as well." He pointed at the ferret.

Chapter Fifteen...Theoclea Bound

Theoclea was escorted out by Avram, her eyes were closed. They walked down a narrow hallway, then made a turn into a somewhat wider hallway, and made their way through the maze of the building. They stopped at Davros' quarters, and Avram went inside and found the box for the knife, and a couple of locks as well. Theoclea sighed, and opened her eyes. They finally walked into the hallway that led to the chamber that she was being confined in. A potted plant was incongruously placed against the wall in the hallway. Theoclea stopped and looked at Avram.

"Avram, what did you do before you were a soldier?" she asked. He was startled for a few moments.

"I ...I was a farmer, Theo...Oracle...what should I call you?"

"Theoclea is fine," she said.

"Avram, why do you follow this man, Davros? He is obviously dangerously out of his mind...out of control. He has touched the lower Gates and fallen into the Abyss. He is unbalanced, there is not a shred of the Sacred Feminine in that man," she said.

Avram shrugged. "I am a soldier, I follow the orders of my superiors! That is what I must do! I know little of what you call the Sacred Feminine, the Gates, and the Abyss. It means nothing to me, I am a soldier! I do my duty!"

"Avram, do you have a wife at home, do you have children?"

"Yes…Oracle…Theoclea…I have a wife and a son and daughter," he replied. She closed her eyes, for about half a minute, then opened them, and smiled slightly at him.

"Avram I see a great future for you as the leader of your people. You will lead them in peace, and your line will continue to lead through your son and daughter! This will happen only if you decide not to listen to him in the end!" He stared at her. He looked at the floor for about a minute, and while he did that Theoclea looked at the potted plant. One of the leaves was moving up and down, up and down. She nodded slightly and smiled. She looked at Avram.

"It will all start tomorrow. It has already started. When it starts, you must decide—do not listen to him in the end."

Avram said nothing. He escorted her into the room. She lay down on a cot. He did as he was told. He took the Red Key, and chained it to the wall with a lock on the chain. He bound her hands and feet. He took the knife that he had under the sash, placed it

Chapter Fifteen...Theoclea Bound

in the box, and chained the box to the wall with the other lock that he had. He walked toward the door, stood in front of the door and turned to her.

"I am a soldier, I must do what I am ordered to do."

"No," Theoclea replied, "you are a free soul, do not listen to him in the end—you will know when the time has come!" He looked back at her.

"You said that many of my men would die, what is to be the ...how will they die?"

"Are you asking this question of me as the Oracle?" she replied. He waited a few seconds, and said "Yes". She closed her eyes for about thirty seconds, opened them, and answered his question.

"They shall be stoned to death," she replied. He shook his head slowly back and forth.

"Now I know that you...that isn't possible!"

"You asked for the truth Avram, and I've told it to you."

"But that's absurd!" he replied. "Yet...If so...I've heard that...you...stones...your friend, Anka..." She couldn't tell, but there may have been a lone tear in one of his eyes.

"Go Avram, don't listen to him in the end, you will see."

"I judged you wrong, Theoclea, you are not a 'handless maiden', and I can see that." He left, shut the door and nodded to the man who had been chosen to guard the door for the night watch. He went to get someone to clean up the blood from the altar room. Then he went back to the altar room. Davros was still there, staring at the floor.

"Two more things," Davros said. "Has that note been sent to Vorios?"

"Yes" Avram replied. Davros thought carefully for a few moments, then continued—

"Tell the men to get ready for the attack. It will have to be sooner than I expected. Oh, and get Seron to relieve the guard at Theocleas' door. He knows all of tricks of these Temple people. I want Seron on the night watch."

When morning came, Avram walked back to the hallway. Seron lay in front of the door, in a pool of blood. He was dead. There was a hole in his chest, as if an arrow had pierced his heart, and then had been removed. The door was open, and Theoclea was gone. The Red Key was gone, and the box with the knife was gone as well. The potted plant in the hallway had been moved a few feet.

Chapter Sixteen...
Theoclea Returns

Morain rushed down the hallway the next morning, awakening everyone as she passed by their doors. Finally, she reached the door to Panelle's chamber. As she pounded on the door she shouted out the good news.

"She's back, Theoclea's back. Anka saved her!"

They both rushed together down the halls and corridors, until they finally were admitted into Theoclea's bedchamber. Theoclea was sitting in a chair, talking to Anka, who was entirely visible, sitting in another chair opposite her. Hugs and sighs of relief were expressed, then Theoclea asked Morain and Panelle to pull up two chairs and join them.

"I was held in the temple of Gaia..." She then related her conversation with Davros, leaving nothing out...but his name...she called him 'The Stranger'... other than that, she gave them every detail. She talked about the conversation with Avram, how she saw the leaf of the plant moving and knew that Anka was there. Anka related that Seron came to guard the room. She had suspected that Seron was a traitor. Her bow and arrows were invisible and she shot him in the heart.

"My hands and feet were bound, The Red Key was chained to a wall, but Anka knew how to turn it around and unlock the lock on the chain," Theoclea said. "You know that the Red Key unlocks all of the locks of the chains that bind you." Anka related the rest.

"There was a box that contained The Stranger's knife that was chained to the wall as well. I used the Red Key to unlock the chain and open the box. I put the magic henna on the knife and took it. I also used the magical henna and painted Theoclea with it. Then we basically walked out of there and came back here! I have his knife with me!"

"Now there's no time to lose," said Theoclea. 'The Stranger' and his men are planning to attack today, I feel sure of that. They have a thousand men, heavily armed, and we have a few hundred at the

Chapter Sixteen...Theoclea Returns

most. I have a plan...first we must..." The others listened intently. They each were informed as to what they should do and expect. Theoclea told them what to tell the others. "I don't want anyone to panic no matter what seems to be happening...no one is to do anything that's not in the plan, although I have left room for...synchronous events."

She told Anka to get Troyana and Bella, and in about half an hour they were all together. Troyana and Bella embraced Theoclea and Anka, and they all simply sat down and meditated for a few minutes. Theoclea told everyone to react to things as they happen, "Remember, we are bonded together—we can accomplish anything. She purposefully did not mention Davros by name—she referred to him as 'The Stranger'.

"The attack is probably going to happen today. I want everyone in the Temple to gather in the Main Hall this afternoon at two o'clock. Everyone, the merchants, teachers, orphans, everyone must meet in the great Hall at two o'clock!" She turned to Anka.

"Anka, will you get Pythagoras and Vorios, and tell them to come here? I have to advise them as well." Anka nodded and they all left. In a few minutes, Pythagoras and Vorios appeared.

"Someone named Davros sent me a note. Telling me that the magical power will be neutralized today, and that he also has the power to shut off the Crystal lights! He says that he'll neutralize Panelle's Wards and Spells as well," Vorios said.

"I know," said Theoclea, and she quickly told them what had happened. She instructed them on what to do, and told both of them to refer to Davros as 'The Stranger'. The door suddenly opened, and Panelle rushed in.

"All of the magic, The Wards and Spells, everything is down! We're completely unprotected!"

"Not really," said Theoclea, "we have great power, my friends and we shall use it! Does everyone know what to do?"

Everyone understood.

Chapter Seventeen...
The Attack

The Temple Bells chimed twice. Everyone was in the Great Hall. Theoclea stood on one side of the room. Troyana sat about six feet away from her. Pythagoras and Vorios stood between them. Bella was nowhere to be seen. Way across the room, Anka could be seen—she was standing next to a huge window. She looked out of the window, and at the far right she could see the half circle of standing stones. The stone on the end, nearest to her was the new stone that had just been raised. The stones then went clockwise to the left, a quarter circle, and continued another quarter circle to the right. In and among the circle of standing stones were the few hundred men who guarded the Temple. They had bows and arrows, and knives.

She moved her gaze to the left and in the distance she saw what appeared to be at least a thousand men. They were rolling great machines into place—catapults, machines that tossed heavy stones. Next to the machines, men were piling up the heavy stones that they had brought with them. Each man was heavily armed. Anka felt Davros' knife in her pocket, smiled, and disappeared.

In the center of the room stood the children's choir, all around and behind them were the others, the vendors, merchants, Bella's Troupe, the Najir-Ketsch Dancers, Demetrios and his musicians, and the one hundred people who had raised the stone. Reena and Chrissa were there, and many others who had not left the Temple since their arrival. At the door, more people were coming in, for everyone knew that it was time to meet.

Two figures in black monks' robes entered and blended into the crowd. Slowly they made their way to the side of the Children's Choir.

It all happened in what seemed like a few seconds. One of the Monks seized Alcena, threw back his hood, and held a knife to her throat, the other Monk, a big man, threw back his hood, and folded his arms.

Chapter Seventeen...The Attack

"Theoclea," the first man shouted, as he held Alcena tightly. "Theoclea, we meet again!" There was a hush, and absolute quiet descended. The crystal lights dimmed and went out. "I told you that I could shut off all of the lights!" Davros laughed and shouted.

It was afternoon, and everyone could still see each other, with a grayish light coming through all of the many windows. Morain had been instructed to send out waves of calm, if anyone was threatened. She sent calm and patience to Alcena, as Davros held the knife to Alcena's throat.

Davros turned to Avram and said, "Grab the boy!"

Avram looked at him, and said, "The girl is enough, there's no reason to frighten another child. I have two children of my own." Avram continued to stand with his arms folded. He glanced for a few seconds at Theoclea, who was sitting next to Troyana, about thirty feet away, facing them, then back at Davros.

Davros glared at him, and said, "I'll deal with you later!" He turned his attention back to Theoclea.

"Shall I tell everyone your secrets, Theoclea?" Davros shouted.

"You will not be telling anyone any secrets, Davros!"

As she said this she turned and looked at the large stairway, to the left and further back in the hall.

"Look at me Theoclea," Davros shouted. "I have the girl, look at the men out there, they're ready to attack. Give up the Temple—you've lost the battle already!"

Theoclea continued to look at the stairway, then she glanced at the window, where a knife slowly appeared as if held by invisible hands. She looked at Troyana who was deep in concentration. She gazed intently at Alcena, and turned her gaze back at the stairway.

"Look at me Theoclea, or I'll cut the girl's throat!"

Alcena closed her eyes.

She felt calm coming from Morain, but she was frightened. Suddenly in her mind, everything stopped, everything froze and was in black and white, as if an image had gotten stuck in an ancient projector of some kind. Some motion returned. She saw the stairway, then the knife near the window, and then she heard Theoclea's voice whisper to her. "You will know when to bite his hand, kick him in the groin, hold his knife hand with your right hand, turn, and push him away with your left hand and body, then step back a few paces. and run toward me!" In a split second she SAW and KNEW what was going to happen!

Chapter Seventeen...The Attack

The light suddenly came back.

Alcena looked at the stairway.

"LOOK AT ME, Theoclea, or I'll CUT THE GIRL"S THROAT!" Davros said.

Theoclea continued to look at the stairway, and shouted, **YOU WON'T BE CUTTING ANYONE"S THROAT, DAVROS!**

Suddenly, Bella appeared at the top of the stairway, and ran down the stairs, saying "I'm sorry that I'm late. I fell asleep, and the lights were out... and when I...She stared ahead, and quickly looked at Theoclea, then saw Davros.

"DAVROS, she said. What are you doing HERE?" WHY ARE YOU...she stopped.

"THE DANCER, WHY WHAT A SURPRISE, WHAT A PITY, YOU WERE INVITED, AND I LOST MY INVITATION!" He laughed!

Bella looked quickly at the window and saw the knife.

"DAVROS,"she screamed!

In one second she quickly saw Troyana in concentration, and then saw Theoclea nod quickly to her.

"I AVENGE THE KILLING OF MY FATHER, I AVENGE THE TORTURE OF MY BROTHER!"

She stared at the knife…It took about five seconds for the knife to head quickly to the left of the window, turn at the corner, position itself behind his back and plunge into his back.

Alcena, bit his arm, his knife fell, she turned and pushed him away, and then ran toward Theoclea.

"I AVENGE THE KILLING OF MY MOTHER!" shouted Bella. Bella ran down the stairs…and ran toward Davros, her knife out. When she stood over him she plunged her knife into his chest.

"I AVENGE…MY FATHER… MY BROTHER… MY MOTHER!" She plunged her knife into him again and again. Finally, she stopped, dropped her knife and just stood there on her knees crying. "I avenge…" she whispered. Morain put her hand on Bella's shoulder and raised her up. She embraced her and slowly led her away. Bella turned to Morain and whispered once more "I avenge, my father my…" Then she just cried in Morain's arms. Her troupe members ran over to her, and Morain handed her over to them. She stood back and looked around to see if anyone else needed her, then walked over to Alcena, embraced her and whispered something to her. Alcena was crying and whispered back. Morain motioned to Panelle to join them.

Chapter Seventeen...The Attack

Theoclea turned and looked at Avram, who was staring at the floor, he had not moved at all, during all that had happened. His arms remained folded. She walked over and stood in front of him. One by one everyone turned to look at Avram and Theoclea. There was a hush, you could have heard a pin drop.

"Avram," she said, "I told you…" There were tears in his eyes. Theoclea paused, then she continued. "I told you not to follow him in the end…and you knew what to do!" He turned, and looked at her.

"I'm so…I'm so ashamed of myself. I…am… a farmer…how…I don't know…how I…"

He fell to his knees, and shook his head, crying. "I have a son and a daughter, I couldn't…"

Theoclea looked around, and saw Anka standing near the window, Theoclea nodded to her, turned and saw Troyana and Vorios, in deep concentration.

"Avram, stand up. I want you to look out the window." Slowly he stood up.

Still shaking his head, he said—

"I couldn't…I have a son…my daughter, I couldn't…" he looked around at Davros' lifeless body. "I'm glad that he's dead. I should have killed him myself." Theoclea guided him over to the large window that faced the circle of standing stones.

"Avram, look out the window," Theoclea said. Slowly, he turned and stared out the window. "Every stone within a half mile of the Temple is rising, small stones, medium sized stones, large ones, all are rising...a cloud of stones!" Theoclea said.

Anka, Troyana, and Vorios continued to concentrate. Avram saw this. The stones kept rising, and far out where his men were the stones that they had brought with them to hurl at the Temple were rising as well.

"Do you see the stone that we raised last week, Avram, watch it," Theoclea said.

The fifteen thousand pound stone showed lightning flashes coming from the top of it, more and more of them, each lightning flash found a stone, and charged it. The raised stone became a volcano of lightning. Thousands of flashes erupted, each one charging a stone. More powerful flashes came out, each one finding a stone that had risen beside the huge stone throwing machines that were in the distance with Davros' army. The eruption of lightning grew and grew, as more and more stones were charged. A gray wintry day was being transformed, the flow from the stone continued to get brighter and brighter.

Chapter Seventeen...The Attack

"Avram," Theoclea said. "Tell your men to return home. Each stone will follow one man. If at any time, you, or any of your men try to kill or harm anyone, in any way, the stone that rests in their yard, or on their farmland will kill them. The charged stone will follow you, and your men wherever you go, even if you go out to sea. Your stone will find you. It will always know where you are."

"As proof of this, the stones that are near the stone throwing machines will destroy the catapults in a few minutes. Avram, go and tell your men all of this. I predicted something about you Avram, and my prediction will come true if you take your men and leave. You will lead your people in peace and you and your children, and your children's children will be great leaders. Now go Avram, Tell them what I have told you, and tell them to move away from the stone throwing machines."

Avram looked at Theoclea, and said, "Thank you, Theoclea. If I can ever be of ...service...to you..."

"Yes, Avram...there may be a time. We may need a man like you...now go. If any of your men stay, it will be death for them." Avram nodded to her and left quickly. Everyone crowded around the window. They saw Avram rush over to his men, and saw them all quickly leave. Then they saw the great stone cloud follow the men as they all ran into the distance.

When Avram and his men were gone, the stones that they brought with them came crashing down on the stone hurling machines, smashing them to bits, then the stones rose again, and receded into the distance joining the cloud of stones, to follow the men until their dying days. The flow from the great stone stopped and suddenly all of the Crystal lights came on.

Panelle was the first to realize that the wards and spells were back, followed byVorios who realized that the magic of the Temple was on again. People moved away from the window, and they started to speak to each other, to make sure that friends were all right. Morain continued to send out a wave of calmness to everyone.

She walked over to Theoclea, and whispered in her ear. "Theoclea, come with me, there's something that you should hear. Alcena has something to tell you." Suddenly a thought appeared in Theoclea's mind. *'At some point, the children would have to be told...'* They both walked over and stood in front of Alcena. Alcena looked at Theoclea, and her eyes filled with tears. She spoke haltingly choosing her words carefully.

Chapter Seventeen...The Attack

"When he was holding me, with the knife to my throat, I was frightened. Suddenly in my mind, everything stopped...everything froze and... was in black and white. I saw the stairway, then the knife near the window, and then I heard your voice whispering to me. You said to me, *"You will know when to bite his hand, kick him in the groin, hold his knife hand with your right hand, turn, and push him away with your left hand and body, then step back a few paces, then run toward me!"*"

Alcena sighed, gazed into Theoclea's eyes, and said—

"I *saw* and *knew* what was going to happen!"

Alcena started to cry again. Theoclea and Morain embraced her. "Oh, dear child," said Theoclea, "that's exactly what I was thinking!"

"It's okay," Morain said. "You can tell us."

Alcena continued to cry, and then said, **"I think... that I saw...the...the ...FUTURE!"**

Chapter Eighteen...
Another dream

In the next few days, one by one the guests left, and by the third day the vendors had all packed up as well. Pythagoras remained, the Orphan's school had specifically asked him if he could stay on for a few months, and share his wisdom with the students. He readily agreed to this. The temple then settled back slowly into the usual routines. Within the next week, Theoclea had to do her two days in the subterranean chamber, sitting on the Tripod chair, going into a trance, and answering questions from pilgrims.

When the days were over, she started writing again, using the KeyRose Box, the Pentacle and the Rose, the Rose Medallion and the Red Key. One night, after she had written a few pages, she curled up in bed, with her cat beside her, and they both fell fast asleep. That night another dream appeared.

Theoclea was surrounded by a cloudy white mist. The mist was coalescing slowly into shapes, taking far longer than usual. The vision of the scene that she was viewing slowly became sharper and sharper. Finally, she saw that she was standing on sand. She was there. She looked behind her and saw that there was a vast sea, stretching out into the distance. She turned around, and there was a hill with steps. The sky above was blue, without a hint of a cloud. A huge flock of what seened to be geese could be seen above. Wherever she was, it was hotter and more humid than Greece.

She could now clearly see the steps on the hill, there were a good many steps, and she saw that eventually they led up to a building, a building of a design that she had never seen. It was a Temple of some kind, a strange Temple in the sand. She started to climb the steps, and they seemed to be almost endless. Stopping to rest, she looked up at the sky once more. The flight of the birds finally ended, and the last of them receded into the distance. When she arrived at the top of the stairway, she saw that the Temple seemed to be made of crystal triangular shapes fitted together

Chapter Eighteen...Another dream

to produce a huge dome. Turning to the right she saw a mountain in the far distance that seemed to be a volcano of some kind. Looking back at the dome, she saw that many of the triangular shapes were windows. She walked through what seemed to be a portal, and found herself in a Great Hall. To the right and left of the portal separated by about 15 feet were two large crystal columns about 7 feet high, and two feet wide. The only light in the room came from the many triangular shaped windows, and the room was bright. There were three columns in the center of the Great Hall, all about 15 feet from each other, and they stretched upward, but did not touch the roof of the dome. They too seemed to be of an intricately complex design, that Theoclea had never seen, and they were about three or four feet wide. Each one seemed to be cut or made from one giant crystal.

At the center point of the triangle that the columns suggested, there was a crystal throne, and someone was sitting in it. Theoclea could only see the back of the throne. As she approached the throne slowly, she saw that smoke was coming up from the floor, under the throne, but Theoclea could not detect any smell in the room. Slowly the figure on the throne stood up, turned, and gazed at Theoclea. She looked somewhat like Theoclea.

She stood silently beside the throne, facing Theoclea. She wore the red, gold and black colors of the Delphic Oracle, but the shape of the headdress was different. It was gold-colored and of a very different design. The material had a shimmering metallic texture to it. The robe was red, and seemed to be made from the same shimmering material. The collar and sleeves, and all edges of the robe were fringed in black. There was a symbol on the robe and the design was intriguing, a design of three interlocking crystals within a circle, a design that Theoclea had never seen. The robed figure cocked her head to one side and there was a look of astonishment on her face that gave way to a smile. She took her time as she looked at Theoclea ...assessing her from head to to foot in an intensely maternal way. A lone tear appeared in one eye, followed by more tears. They were tears of joy, a glorious joy, the kind of joy that accompanies a great discovery, perhaps a moment of enlightenment. Then the figure spoke—

"Theoclea my name is Axcelotl, and you are, you are..." she struggled for the right words. Theoclea had trouble making out some of the words. "In a future

Chapter Eighteen...Another dream

time...you are...you are.... I am..." The figure walked forward a few steps, and then didn't seem to be able to walk further, as if she had reached a barrier of some kind. She reached out her hand into empty space. Her tears continued to flow.

Her words started to crackle. She said—"Law of One...Mother...children..." Her image started to fade as two other figures emerged from behind the two nearest columns. One was a woman with short dark hair dressed in black, the other was a gray haired woman dressed in a golden robe. The robes had that same strange symbol of the interlocking crystals on them, and were of a strange design that Theoclea had never seen or imagined. The two women took their places on either side of the woman who called herself Axcelotl. All three figures then started to fade slightly...The woman with the headdress looked at the two others and nodded toward Theoclea. Axcelotl seemed to be saying,

"Theoclea! Look...she is...she is..."

The others seemed to be looking into empty space, a look of awe mixed with wonder, and a hint of suspicion showed on their faces as they assessed the space where Theoclea stood, then looked at each other, and finally at the woman with the headdress. For a split second it seemed as if a man appeared from behind the far Middle Pillar. He was dressed in black, white and purple, and he had something in his hand. All of the images then faded, and the Temple in the sand disappeared. Theoclea was alone in the misty white cloud, and sleep once more embraced her.

Chapter Nineteen...
Theoclea, Morain, and Panelle

Theoclea sat in a chair in her chamber, it was three days later, and she had summoned Morain and Panelle to the chamber. In a short time they entered, and sat down on the couch facing her.

"We have certainly had our adventures here of late. This may not be the time to reveal this…but after all, most of our guests have left, except for Pythagoras, and I was expecting that the Temple would go back to our usual routine," Theoclea said. She sighed, and continued.

"Something has been happening to me that you should know about. I've had a recurrent dream over the years, only…last night was the first time that the 'other one', as I call her, spoke to me." She related the dream to Morain and Panelle. Morain spoke first.

"Axcelotl, as she calls herself in the dream, mentions 'children', and 'Law of One'." Morain sighed, and said, "After the incident with Davros, I began speaking of Atlantis with Vorios and Pythagoras. I believe that 'The Children of the Law of One' were one of the groups that lived on Atlantis. We are speaking, of course of a time that may have been almost 10,000 years ago. Pythagoras calls it 'the time when the ice receded'. What we have seen during the past few weeks gives us a hint of what may have gone on with the two warring factions of Atlantis. The trouble is that when Pythagoras and Vorios speak of these things, they veil them in words like theory, supposition, legend and myth." She paused, choosing her woreds carefully.

"Unlike the 'Sons of Belial', the 'Children of the Law of One' were not arrogant and aggressive. At different times one or another of the factions became the leader in this constant battle between the two. The 'Children of the Law of One' used the technology of the crystal energy in many ways, all of them peaceful. There was also another group...the Crystal Ones, and they guarded the secret of the crystal energy. Both of

Chapter Nineteen...Theoclea, Morain, and Panelle

the other groups had to work through them. That's a part of the legend." She paused once more and recalled that Pythagoras told her to be careful in discussing this with Theoclea.

"The Atlanteans mainly used the Crystal Energy as a source for communications, to heat, light and power their homes, and ships, perhaps. Atlantis was the homeland for a worldwide seafaring civilization with ports all over the world. Pythagoras told me that their maps showed that the Atlanteans were well aware that the Earth was a sphere. Pythagoras and Vorios can probably fill in more of the details, after what we've all been through lately, we must once again call on them for their knowledge of magic and history. I'm very concerned about the other two figures in your dream...it seems to suggest that Axcelotl, as she calls herself is surrounded by two people who resemble Panelle and myself. This concerns me because dreams are often symbolic." Theoclea was perturbed at what Morain had revealed to her.

"Why was I never taught about Atlantis during my training?" asked Theoclea. Morain looked at Panelle. They were silent and looked down at the floor, then Panelle spoke.

"We didn't want to complicate your training with anything that we thought would not be useful to you in your position. Pythagoras, Vorios, and all of the Priests and Priestesses of the Temple, including, of course myself and Panelle all agreed on the course of your instruction. The subject of Atlantis came up in our conversations from time to time."

Theoclea shot a troubled glance at Morain.

"Why do I still feel that you both know more about this, and are not telling me?" Panelle and Morain were silent. Theoclea gazed expectantly at both of them. Morain finally broke the silence. She glanced at Pythagoras and Vorios guardedly–

"I was once told that Children of the Law of One were able to counter the technological arrogance of the "Belial' group with their understanding of the spiritual realm. Their understanding of magic and the various planes of mythos existence, especially what was called 'the Akashic record' was their power. Perhaps we saw a hint of how this could have played out this week, with Davros, and his men, but I believe that there is much more. Your dream seems to imply something else, something that could be of profound significance. I am having trouble focusing on just what that may be. The Atlantean understanding

Chapter Nineteen...Theoclea, Morain, and Panelle

of all of this was much more advanced than what we know of today. A great deal of knowledge supposedly died under the waves that engulphed Atlantis. With the destruction of their homeland, the ports that were visited by the Atlanteans lost their power as well. Remember...what I'm telling you is myth and legend. It seems as if a crystal power and communications network was destroyed. Pythagoras and Vorios have told us, Panelle and I, of this. It was one of the many topics that used to be of interest to us when you were being trained."

Theoclea thought about this and said, indignantly, "Well, is there more? In the end I will have to know all of it...ALL of it!" Morain and Panelle had never seen her like this. They were baffled...where was this coming from?

Morain answered—"We never thought that it would come up again during your reign as the Pythia, that's why we never discussed it with you. There is one more thing—there are many Greeks who believe that we, the citizens of Delphi, and other cities, and many other Greek people with spiritual gifts, especially the Oracles, Sybils, and other diviners, are the descendents of The Children of the Law of One."

Chapter Twenty...
The Discussion

They all sat in Vorios' chamber—Pythagoras, Vorios, Morain, Panelle and Theoclea. The contents of the dream were discussed, along with the discussion between Theoclea, Morain and Panelle. Pythagoras knew that more had to be said, but as always, he was careful with his words.

"There is more...much more. I learned much when I was in Egypt." Pythagoras said. "I believe, and mind you, this is just a theory... that there were crystal power stations all over the world. Their power was greatest when the ice receded, about 10,000 years ago. They were not accidentally or randomly placed. Their placement in the world corresponded to the inner energies of the earth, magnetic and otherwise.

The homeland continent of Atlantis was far from here through the strait of Hercules where the great stone pillars are, if you are looking to the west of here. If the Earth is a sphere, then one might consider that it was east of Greece...very far to the east."

"To the west, there is a great expanse of ocean, I don't believe that there are any islands or other continents in between, but it is a vast distance to the place where Atlantis may have been. I believe that looking East of here is a more practical route *if*, and I say once again—*if* the legends are true. Legend says that there were two pillars there, called the Pillars of Atlas. Atlantis may have been on the other side of the Earth...but where...perhaps... it's hard to know trhe truth, so much knowledge has been lost."

He glanced at Theoclea...he knew from the look on her face that he had to say more. He sighed and continued.

"It has been said that there was a main Crystal Power station on Atlantis, and others around the world. There is a theory that the placement of the crystal power stations in relation to the main power station on the homeland of Atlantis was like the divination that some of our people do with crystals and stones. They measure the distance between different colored stones to the main crystal stone, much in the same way that Theoclea's friend, Anka uses stones for divination. The placement of the crystal power stations was in accordance with the energies of the Earth and the abstract sacred geometry that the Atlanteans were well aware of." He looked down at the floor, not daring to look at Theoclea and how she was reacting to all of this. Pythagoras continued.

"I must say at this point that what I have been speaking of is shrouded in *myth, legend, supposition, and theory.* For instance, some of this may account for the Triangle-shaped Temples that are found all over the world…it may account for the shape of the buildings called 'Pyramids' in Egypt, for instance, or it may simply be that the Atlanteans shared their architectural expertise when they established contact with the native peoples of the ports that they visited. It might simply be explained in the 'Diaspora' of the Atlanteans in the years preceding the mythical destruction of Atlantis. It's hard for me to believe that they didn't know that Atlantis would be destroyed again."

"Again?" asked Theoclea.

"Yes," replied Pythagoras. "There are legends that there were similar destructions of Atlantis about 50,000 years ago, and about 25,000 years ago. It may have been that after the first destruction they rebuilt their civilization. One of their books contained a history of that time, a kind of 'Genesis' or Renewal, but I've never read it, or seen it. The same thing may have happened at the time of the second destruction, a 'Renewal' or 'Regeneration' occurred. It was recorded in one way or another by all of the people of that region. The final destruction is said to have occurred 9000 years ago. It was said to be caused by a mighty volcano, said to have the power of more than 100,000 volcanoes the size of Thera. A volcano like that could easily have wiped out the entire earth." Theoclea was stunned. She gazed deeply at each of the others in turn. Vorios gazed at Pythagoras, surprised that he had revealed so much. He knew that at least part of it was true.

"Remember," Vorios said, glancing at Pythagoras—"there are many myths of what Atlantis represents, and where it might have been located...let's be careful not to come to hasty conclusions."

"Is all of this knowledge lost?" she asked.

"Not necessarily," replied Pythagoras, "remember, I spent eleven years learning of all kinds of things in Egypt. The Egyptians have books about all of this. The language of the Atlanteans is so ancient that the books

Chapter Twenty...The Discussion

can't be read. The books may contain many secrets yet to be revealed. There is one thing, Theoclea, that you can be sure of..."

"What's that?" Theoclea said.

"You can be sure that you will have more dreams of this kind."

They all fell silent. They needed to contemplate what had been said. There was a rectangular- shaped window in Vorios' chamber room. Vorios was dressed in the black, white and purple of his position. He was thinking of the man who came out from behind the middle Pillar, the one dressed in black, white and purple. A cloud approached the sun, and the light in the room dimmed visibly. Vorios stood up and walked to the window.

He saw the cloud, then returned to where he was sitting.

"You said that the man who appeared briefly in the dream wore my colors, right?"

"Yes," Theoclea said.

Vorios pondered this. After a few minutes the cloud dissipated and the sun shone brightly. The light in the room came back, but there were sounds outside...the sounds that are made by a flock of birds.

Vorios walked to the window again. He motioned to Pythagoras to join him.

"Geese, he said. "Pythagoras, is this their season of migration, should they be flying in that direction?"

Pythagoras followed the flight of the geese.

"I would say that the answer is no to both of your questions, Vorios." The room darkened again as the geese continued to fly across the Sun. It was a huge flock of geese, a sight that had not been seen in Greece for many hundreds, perhaps thousands of years.

Chapter Twenty-One...
The Next Dream

That night, Theoclea dreamed the dream again, but this time it was different. Theoclea was surrounded by the cloudy white mist, and the mist was coalescing into shapes, more quickly than before. The vision of the scene that she was viewing quickly became sharper and sharper. Finally, she saw that she was standing on sand once again. She was there. She looked behind her and saw that there was once again, a vast sea, stretching out into the distance. She turned back and looked ahead of her and there was the hill with steps. Once again, the sky above was blue, without a hint of a cloud. No geese could be seen above. It seemed to be hotter and more humid than Greece.

She could now clearly see the steps on the hill. Once again, she looked up at the top of the steps, and saw the Temple in the sand. She started to climb the steps, and they seemed to be almost endless. She looked up at the sky once more, and there were still no geese.

When she arrived at the top of the stairway, as before, she noted that the Temple seemed to be made of crystal triangular shapes fitted together to produce a huge dome. Once again, she saw the mountain in the far distance that seemed to be a volcano of some kind. Looking at the dome, she noted that many of the triangular shapes were windows.

She walked through the portal, and once again found herself in the Great Hall. To the right and left were two large crystal columns. The only light in the room came from the many triangular shaped windows, and the room once again was bright. There were the three columns, or pillars, in the center of the Great Hall, and once again, at the center point of the triangle that the columns suggested, there was a throne, and Axcelotl was sitting in it. This time, she was facing Theoclea. The throne was decorated with all kinds of symbols, one of which was the knife going through the crescent moon—without the red drop of

Chapter Twenty-One...The Next Dream

blood below it. All of the symbols seemed to be in perfect balance. Next to Axcelotl there was an elaborate altar table with stones of various sizes and colors, and candles that were also of various sizes and colors.

There was a crystal knife on the right side of the table with gemstones embedded in it. Axcelotl stood up and there there was a broad smile on her face. She walked a few paces, and stood in front of throne, facing Theoclea. She wore the red, gold and black colors of the Delphic Oracle, and, as always, her robe had a design of three interlocking crystals within a circle. She continued to smile warmly at Theoclea, and finally spoke.

"Theoclea, you must set up an altar table in this way." She pointed to the altar table set up beside the throne. She took the knife and pointed to other stones. She showed Theoclea a pouch and said, "You must bring your Rose Medallion, and I'll have mine." She pointed to the different colored candles, showing exactly where they went. "The directions must be set up this way."

She pointed to the various stones, telling Theoclea exactly what they were, and where they were to be facing. There was to be a large crystal in the center, and various stones set between the East, South, West and North stones. There were also to be other stones that led to the center crystal, making a pattern of 4 directional crystals of various colors, and the center crystal, making five crystals. The knife was to be on the right side of the table. "You must charge everything in your own way with the crystal knife."

At this point, as in the other dream, the two other figures emerged from behind the two far columns of the triangle. There was the woman with short dark hair dressed in black, and the gray haired woman dressed in a golden robe. Once again, the robes had that same strange symbol of the interlocking crystals on them. The two women took their places on either side of Axcelotl. A man now appeared from behind the Middle Pillar. Once again, he was dressed in black, white and purple and he had something in his hand. The two women then each pointed to the candles, and the stones, noting the positions of every object on the altar. The man continued to stand beside the Middle Pillar.

Finally, Axcelotl said, "You must do this, Theoclea, and they must all be there, Morain, Panelle, Vorios and Pythagoras." Theoclea was told exactly how to call directions, cast a circle with the crystal knife, and attend to the proprieties in an ancient way that seemed somewhat unfamiliar in some ways.

Chapter Twenty-One...The Next Dream

She heard Axcelotl's voice say "...touch the large crystal...say the chant over and over. Vorios must have one of his magical tools. He will know what to bring." All of the images faded, and the Temple in the sand disappeared. Theoclea was alone in the misty white cloud, and sleep once more embraced her. When she awoke, the crystal knife was on her bedside table.

Chapter Twenty-Two...
On Atlantis

The next day, Theoclea related her latest dream to Morain, Panelle, Vorios, and Pythagoras—all agreed that an altar had to be set up. She showed them the crystal knife embedded with the gemstones. Vorios said, "There must be a way for them to send solid objects, my God, I never imagined..." He suddenly became silent, preferring not to say any more, deep in thought.

"Vorios, Axcelotl told me to tell you to bring one of your magical tools. She said that you would know which one."

"Yes," said Vorios, "I think that I know what she's referring to. I'll start to gather some of the other items that we will need. Let's meet tomorrow morning, and conclude the preparations for the altar."

The next morning, they all met in the part of the Temple that most resembled the Great Hall in the dream. It was the room where the concert was held, the room where Davros met his death. They spent the day gathering the remaining stones and crystals that would be needed.

"How I wish that Anka were still with us, her power over stones might have been helpful," Theoclea said.

By the evening, all was set up on an altar in the way that Axcelotl had suggested. Theoclea had been told how to use the knife. They all gathered in a circle, around the altar. They were told exactly how to call directions, cast a circle with the crystal knife, and attend to the proprieties in an ancient way that seemed somewhat familiar in many ways. Theoclea heard Axcelotl's voice in her head, *'touch the large crystal...say the chant over and over'*.

The others joined in the chant, raising immense energy with their voices. They all knew how to do that! Suddenly, the altar, and the Great Hall of the Temple of Delphi disappeared, and they all were standing on the sandy beach. Theoclea looked behind her and saw that there was once again, a vast sea, stretching out

Chapter Twenty-Two...On Atlantis

into the distance. They were all looking around at the steps, the sky, and the vast sea. Vorios looked up at the sky, and there was a huge flock of geese approaching the Sun. He pointed up at them, so that everyone could see them. Theoclea turned back, looked ahead of her and there was the hill with steps.

Everyone felt that it was hotter and more humid than Greece, the sun seemed unusually bright, and there were auroral effects in the air, even though it was daylight. Theoclea pointed to the steps on the hill. The sky became darker as, once again, a huge flock of geese flew across the sun. She pointed to the top of the steps, at the Temple in the Sand, and motioned to everyone to climb the steps. The light became brighter, they all looked up at the sky, and the geese were gone.

When they arrived at the top of the stairway, once more, she noted that the Temple seemed to be made of crystal triangular shapes fitted together to produce a huge dome. They all saw the mountain in the far distance that seemed to be a volcano of some kind. Smoke was rising from the volcano. Vorios noted the volcano and the Temple, and said, "I've been here before."

Theoclea smiled, gazed at Vorios, and said,

"Yes, I know." Vorios looked back at Theoclea with a questioning glance. Turning to the dome, she pointed to the triangular shapes that were windows.

She motioned to everyone to walk through the portal. Everyone was looking at Vorios, because of his remark, but they followed Theoclea's direction and entered the Great Hall. To the right and left were the two large crystal columns. The only light in the room came from the many triangular-shaped windows, and the room once again was bright. There were the three columns in the center of the Great Hall.

As in the other dreams, at the center point of the triangle that the columns suggested, there was a throne, and Axcelotl was sitting in it. Next to Axcelotl was the elaborate altar table with stones of various sizes and colors, and candles that were also of many dimensions and hues. There was no crystal knife on the table. Axcelotl smiled, stood up and faced them. She wore the red, gold and black colors of the Delphic Oracle, and, as always, her robe had a design of three interlocking crystals within a circle. She smiled warmly at Theoclea.

Axcelotl assessed everyone, somehow showing an awareness of why they were there. They were there to *see*, and *know*. She turned, and gazed at one of the

Chapter Twenty-Two...On Atlantis

two front columns. She said, "Aura," and the woman in black came forward and stood directly across from Morain.

Morain said, "I am Morain."

The woman in black responded with a quick succession of hand gestures, and executed a complex dance step.

"Aura is mute, she communicates through hand gestures, mental images, and dance-like body movements," Axcelotl said. Morain had a quick mental picture that conveyed an aura to her.

Both stood for a minute in silence a look of awe on their faces. Morain felt a warm surge of empathy coming from the other woman, who looked very much like her, and promptly returned the greeting. Axcelotl nodded to the other column and said, "Sonja." The woman in gold came out and stood across from Panelle. She had a crystal wand attached to a red belt. There was a look of caution on her face and she glanced at each one of the visitors, finally resting her gaze on Panelle. Panelle suddenly felt a protective ward of a kind that was expanding—she had never felt anything like it before, it was powerful yet vigilant.

When it settled on her, she returned the gesture, placing a protective ward around the woman in gold.

They both looked at each other with satisfaction, acknowledging the craftsmanship.

"I am Panelle."

"Sonja," the other woman said. Then Axcelotl looked directly at Theoclea, and a wordless exchange occurred.

Axcelotl reached into a bag that she had placed on the altar table, and took out a Rose Medallion that was about the same size as Theoclea's. All eyes were on Axcelotl's Medallion. On the face side, it showed Axcelotl wearing a crown of three interlocking crystals.

"This is one of the three Medallions that The Grandfather made for us," she said. She held it out so that Theoclea and the others could see it, then gazed at Theoclea, obviously expecting something. Theoclea had her pouch with her, and reached into it. She took out her Medallion, and showed it to all.

"The face on my Medallion is the face of a Sumerian Goddess, Inanna," Theoclea said.

Axcelotl spoke—

"The face on your Medallion is not known to us, it was made sometime between *our* future and *your* past. It was obviously made by someone who was familiar with the Grandfather's Art, or perhaps it is to be made by a reincarnation of the Grandfather

Chapter Twenty-Two...On Atlantis

sometime in *our* future." They held their Medallions firmly in front of them, and almost immediately there was a fast, sharp lightning flash that proceeded from Axcelotl's medallion to Theoclea's. Obviously, a bond between the Medallions was formed. There were two more similar flashes.

Theoclea put the Medallion away, reached into the pocket of her robe and took out the crystal knife. She held it out to Axcelotl. The knife rose into the air, and circled about Theoclea's head three times, then made a fuller circle and rose higher, as it turned and started in the direction of Axcelotl. When it reached a certain midway point it seemed to pass through a barrier, faded for a second, and flew around Axcelotl's head, circling above her head three times, then it slowly settled on the right side of the altar table.

Axcelotl approached the midway point, looking in her maternal way at Theoclea, and reached into her pocket. She produced a Red Key from her pocket. Theoclea reached into her pouch and withdrew her Red Key. Axcelotl nodded, tears in her eyes. There were tears also in Theoclea's eyes and she wavered for a second. Morain reached over and propped her up, sending a wave of calmness to Theoclea. Theoclea regained her balance and motioned to Morain that it was okay.

The other woman in black looked at Morain with admiration. Theoclea placed her hands together and made the Gesture of the gates of Eleusis and Axcelotl returned the gesture. Then, Panelle and the woman in gold, Sonja, strengthened the Wards and Spells that had been created—for they sensed something—some kind of faltering. For a few minutes they all stood there with various emotions and magic passing between the two groups.

"Theoclea, you have known that hand gesture since childhood, Vorios told me. Soon you will meet one who may explain it to you."

"I thought that it was the 'Gate of Eleusis'," Theoclea said.

"It is that and much more, my child," Axcelotl said.

Vorios stood back all the while standing about 5 feet in front of the columns near the portal, out of the way. His eyes were now on the middle pillar in the back. Axcelotl nodded at the middle pillar. The man in black, white and purple came out from behind the pillar and took his place next to Axcelotl. Vorios stepped forward and did likewise, standing next to Theoclea.

Chapter Twenty-Two...On Atlantis

Pythagoras stepped behind and to the right of Vorios, sensing that the two men had something important to accomplish. Neither man smiled, a look of the utmost seriousness on each face. They gazed directly at each other. They had met before.

"Hermeticus," Vorios said.

"Vorios," the man replied, with a smile of recognition. He reached into his pocket and withdrew a red clay medallion, about three inches wide. It resembled the Rose Medallion, but it had the face of a man on it, his face surrounded by all kinds of triangular shapes.

All eyes were now on Vorios. He closed his eyes for a few moments in deep concentration. He reached into his pocket and pulled out his red clay medallion. He moved the medallion in such a way so that all could see it. Everyone gasped. His medallion also had the face of a man but the face was different, and the man was bearded, and surrounded by leaves. The Medallions seemed to be the same shade of red, but the men on the face sides were different. The man next to Axcelotl turned to her and nodded. Vorios turned to Theoclea. Theoclea smiled at Vorios, and said—

"I knew that you had another medallion." Vorios smiled at her.

"Yes, I thought so," he said. *The thought came to Vorios' mind that perhaps thousands of years would go by before these four medallions would be together in the same room at the same time, whether in dream, vision, or reality.*

The two men held the medallions out, the image sides facing each other. At first nothing happened. Then slowly a beam of light emanated from the medallion of 'Hermeticus'. It widened and strengthened in brightness as it reached farther, aimed at the midpoint between the two medallions. It struck the middle point and went beyond it, becoming smaller and smaller until it touched Vorios' medallion. Both men held the medallions firmly. The man next to Axcelotl then whispered something, and small black objects started to appear in the beam of his medallion, they moved forward and got larger. One could see that they were tiny geese, a flock of tiny geese.

The flock continued to grow, moving past the midpoint, then growing smaller and smaller as they moved toward Vorios' medallion, finally touching it.

The flying geese continued for a couple of minutes more, moving from one medallion to another. Finally, the last of the geese appeared in the first medallion, flew slowly across, and settled in the point of light at

Chapter Twenty-Two...On Atlantis

Vorios' medallion. Everyone looked around in awe at each other.

Pythagoras had been standing away from the others, a few feet to the left and behind Vorios. Suddenly, a flash of white light emanated from Hermeticus' medallion aimed at Pythagoras. It touched him, but didn't hurt him in any way. Everyone saw this and gazed back at Axcelotl's magician. Twice more the same thing happened, a beam of light aimed at Pythagoras. Hermeticus noted this, stared at Pythagoras, closed his eyes, then opened them. He showed a slight smile of recognition, as if he had seen a glimpse of the future.

Axcelotl gazed once more at Theoclea and a lone tear appeared in one eye, followed by more tears in both eyes. She looked at everyone, taking her time—it was a moment of remembrance and enlightenment. Then she slowly said, for all to hear *"It's starting."* The giant crystal column to the left of Axcelotl started to hum, and it slowly lit up, as if from a source deep within. Again, this time louder, she said, "It's Starting!" The column to the right of her started to hum, and became lit with a bright light as well.

Once again, this time much louder, joyously, Axcelotl said, *"It's starting!"* the middle pillar in the back started to hum and its' light appeared as well.

There was a swirling of sound and an interlocking of light patterns that mingled and flowed for about three minutes, all the while gaining in intensity.

High up at the top of the dome, it seemed as if a circular opening was slowly appearing in the dome. Light beams emerged from the tops of all three columns, and slowly moved upward, merging below the opening. When they met, a great surge of power shot up through the hole in the dome and was dispersed in all directions. Power was moving out in every direction, like an explosion of lava. There were lights all over the sky, and explosive popping sounds. A tidal wave of light and sound swirled all about the sky and then dispersed all over the Earth in every direction. The event continued to build and build in intensity until the sound was almost deafening. Suddenly the Great Hall vanished, and Theoclea, Morain, Panelle, Pythagoras, and Vorios were standing on a vast plain. The entire scene was in black and white, the sky was black and there were washes of white light flowing all around them.

Chapter Twenty-Three...
The Plain of Atlantis

A morphous lights appeared and disappeared in the sky, like silent fireworks, and there was the sound of drumming in the distance. The sounds and lights slowly diminished, and color started to appear in the scene. The sky was a wash of shades of blue. The ground slowly contained a wash of yellow-brown...a vast plain appeared before them, and it was middle of the day. Everyone looked around. Theoclea gazed at Vorios.

"Vorios, you've been here before, what can you tell us?" Vorios surveyed the scene, sighed, and finally answered.

"Let's sit in a circle, for I have much to tell you." They all sat down, formed a circle, and held hands.

"We are on the interior plain of Atlantis, and it is about 9000 years before our time. As a magician, I am like you in some ways, Theoclea. I know of the past, and I know of the future, and I've been to these places, times and realms. This time and place is special for me. It is the place of my...birth." Everyone was respectfully silent. Vorios glanced at Pythagoras for a moment, then he looked into the distance.

"This was a fertile plain. Many crops were grown and harvested here, but the main crop was rice. The soil was so fertile that there were three rice crops a year! To my knowledge there has never been or will be another place on the Earth that could produce three rice crops a year!" He pointed in a certain direction.

"Not far from here is a part of the Atlantean Continent that will be called Java some time in the future. The name 'Java', and words that sound very similar to it come from the most ancient languages of South India, and the words and names all mean 'rice'.

"Do you see that grove of trees over there? Most likely we would find coconuts there, other tropical fruits, and scented woods only found in this part of the world. It is temperate here now, but after the ice melts the average temperature will go up perhaps 15 degrees, and this will be more of an equatorial place."

Chapter Twenty-Three...The Plain of Atlantis

He gazed at the grove of trees. "I wouldn't venture there now...we would see large extinct elephants called Mammoths, and dangerous animals called Saber-toothed tigers. There are also Cave bears in there! All manner of rare metals and minerals were here in abundance; gold; silver; tin, and the rarest—orichalcum were dug up in large quantities. The statue of Athena in Athens is made of ivory and gold, most likely it came from the remnants of this part of the world! There were legumes; fruits; plants for ointments; chestnuts; and manner of things to drink. It was a place of infinite abundance that brought forth magnificent Temples, Palaces, harbors and docks. The Capital city, also called Atlantis was designed in circles, so that there were canals, and bridges, that connected the habitable circles, where there were homes, stadiums for sports, and even a racecourse, for horses! Yes, horses were abundant here as well."

"Homes were capped with brass, tin and orichalcum on their roofs. Three colors of stone were mined from the quarries to produce the monumental buildings...and the stones were of three colors, red, black and gold. That may have a connection to the colors that Theoclea wears. The abundance of gold and silver and other precious things led to world-wide trade...and the Atlanteans had great ships. In addition to the great capital city, where the ten kings met, there were other cities, and the city closest to the Pillars of Atlas contained power stations that supplied energy. I could continue to tell you stories of wars and conquests, of Gods and Goddesses that were revered, of entire pantheons of spirits....of magic...and more, but we must move on. I think that we should move in that direction." He pointed straight ahead, and stood up.

"One thing, one question I must ask of you Vorios, before we move on." Theoclea said.

"Yes," Vorios said, sensing what the question would be.

"Why have you not told us of this before? Why have you been so...reluctant to give us answers about Atlantis?"

Vorios sighed, looked at the ground and the gazed at Pythagoras. He alsmost whispered the answer.

"I am not The One to answer your question, Theoclea. Ultimately it will fall upon another to give you the final knowledge that you seek." He smiled at Pythagoras and then looked all around at everyone fondly.

"We should get going now." The others all followed him. They moved ahead, trying to keep up with Vorios. He looked all about as he walked quickly, then,

Chapter Twenty-Three...The Plain of Atlantis

he finally stopped to rest, and the others caught up with him. He pointed all around the plain, and said—

"Far ahead of us there were two pillars in the ocean, in our language they might be called the Pillars of Atlas. That's the direction that we must follow."

He suddenly looked up, and shouted "Get down, down to the ground, everyone, as low as you can!" Then he shouted "Panelle!" Panelle was way ahead of him as she immediately put up a protective Ward all about them. Just in time, for a dark swarm of gray and black shapes, somewhat resembling a swarm of bees came up over the horizon and almost instantly encircled them. It was like being in the eye of a hurricane, with inquisitive buzzing and swirling of air happening all around them. The storm continued for a few minutes, and then abated. Just as suddenly as the swarm had come up, it departed back over the horizon. One by one the visitors all stood up.

"What was that?" asked Pythagoras.

"We have just been visited by the Wraiths of the Sons of Belial. They now know that we're here! We must move on quickly!"

"Where are we going, Vorios?" asked Theoclea.

"We are going to visit 'The Grandfather' Theoclea, and I hope that he is still here!"

They walked on, continuing on the Great Plain. Obviously the harvest was over, nothing was growing, but there were the remains of a great harvest.

"Over there!" Vorios said. "Yes, he's still here, look!" They saw a canvas house made from several large triangular panels, joined together by what seemed to be leather catches. At the top, the panels were all held together by five lengthy sticks that were bound together at the top.

Chapter Twenty-Four...
The Grandfather

Vorios approached the tent, motioned to the others to stand back, opened the flap, said something, and went in. About a minute later, he emerged, and said—

"The Grandfather will see you now." He motioned to them to come in one at a time. They entered the tent, and found that it was surprisingly spacious.

There was a table in the center, and there were crystals and other stones placed on the circular table in the design of what will be called in the future, a Lakota medicine wheel. There was also the smell of sage and sandalwood. The canvas panels were decorated with images of dragons, elephants, gryphons, saber-toothed tigers, mammoths, and other mythological, real and 'extinct' animals. Sitting at the center of the table in the back was an old man.

He looked ancient, his face told the story of a mixed heritage, one might see in him the mixture of both Ethiopian races of Atlantis and Africa, of Australia, of the Dravidian speaking people, of the people of the Americas, yet to be discovered, and other races. He was blind, and his eyes didn't register the vision of the voyagers, but his ears heard much. They all sat down, with Pythagoras on one side of him and Theoclea on the other side, facing him at the opposite side of the table was Vorios, with Panelle, and Morain on each side of him. When all were seated, the Grandfather spoke.

"Vorios, where is the teacher?"

"He is sitting to the left of you, Grandfather." The Grandfather held out his hand to the left, and Pythagoras grasped the hand gently.

"You are the teacher—you have done well my son. You must be very proud," The Grandfather said.

He meditated for about a minute, shook his head and said, "The Counselor is here—where are you, my dear?"

"I am here Grandfather," Morain said, and

Chapter Twenty-Four...The Grandfather

she sent out a wave of empathy to all.

"Accepted with my blessings," the Grandfather said,

"The Protector is here, where are you?"

"I am here Grandfather," Panelle said, and she placed a protective Ward around the tent. He felt it and studied it for a couple of minutes.

"Fine work, you are to be commended. We shall need it. There are those who know that we are here, and they will stop at nothing. You have met them, I know." The Grandfather meditated for a minute or two. Then he said—

"Vorios, the child, she is here!" Tears started to appear in his blind eyes.

"Yes, Grandfather, she is sitting next to you," Vorios said.

Grandfather reached out his hand, it was trembling.

Theoclea gently placed her hand in his.

"I am Theoclea, Grandfather." He tried to hold back his tears,

"Theoclea...yes, Theoclea!"

"Axcelotl's child. You and Axcelotl are one! It was foretold. She is the Ancient Mother, and you are the child from the future...Axcelotl's child. My dear, do you remember? Do you remember the first vision that you had...of the gate, the tree, your hands, the lights, your friends, the Oracle's room, the Tripod chair, the smell?" Theoclea was astounded.

"Yes, Grandfather, that was my first vision of the future, when I was a child, and I saved my friends from the falling of the tree. I told Pythagoras and others about it. It's a well-known story in Greece, but how could you know?"

"Vorios told me, and I told him to keep his eyes on you. He followed your progress. It was he that recommended that Pythagoras teach you. I was younger, we all felt that you were a distant child of Atlantis, a true child of the future...of...Axcelotl! Through Vorios we were able to follow you. What interested me the most was that you *knew* the sign, the hand gesture." He placed his right hand on his left, palms up. He linked three middle fingers, so that only the thumbs and little fingers were touching. He raised his fingers and showed everyone the sign. Theoclea gasped.

"I thought that I made that up, in my vision!" The Grandfather turned in Theoclea's direction.

"No, Theoclea, it is an Ancient sign, a sign with which one Atlantean, no matter how far he or she is from the homeland can recognize another. It is also a sign that can summon up magical energy as well.

Chapter Twenty-Four...The Grandfather

But its' most important role is to symbolically show that whoever makes it has a knowledge of the relationship between the Pillars of Atlas, on Atlantis, and the Pillars of Herakles or Hercules in the sea where your homeland Greece resides."

"It is not just a recognition of geography, it has the power of truth and shows that whether the person knows this or not the maker of that sign is a truth seeker, and is possessed of extraordinary gifts. When Vorios told us that you instinctively knew the sign, or that it had appeared to you in a vision, we were very excited!"

"As a truth seeker, Theoclea, you will learn that we live on an unstable planet, a sphere, the Earth. The likelihood of our ever leaving the earth and exploring the other realms of the cosmos can only be done in our visions and dreams. Even technologies of the present and future may not allow us to go further than the moon, and even there our visions and poetry serve us best. Perhaps there will be machines that will be our eyes and ears, perhaps not. Our visions and our poetry serve us well in this regard. There have been times when the earth was frozen, times when it was unbearably hot, times of great annihilations and the complete destruction of life. These destructions came from without and within the planet. They came from the Macrocosm and the Microcosm, from the space without and the space within. Knowledge of the Nature of Nature is essential for the survival of the human race, its' history must be known, or many shall perish." The Grandfather paused, and looked with wonder at all of them, as if sharing an ancient secret.

"The truth of all of this is written on the Akashic record…the spiritual record of life on this unstable planet. It can never be erased, and is available to all who search for truth on every level, and with all of the means at their disposal. In my youth, I could see, dear child. I am old now…I am your distant Grandfather… and you have been chosen. My son Vorios has followed you all along! Vorios, the Magician, and my son, is very old. He and the Pythagoras, the teacher, are Chosen Ones, they will live long, and go through many lives, each in their own way. I am tired, and it is not safe for you to stay here any longer. Theoclea, make the sign for me." Theoclea made the sign. He grasped her hands and kissed them.

"You all must go now or you will be in grave danger." He smiled as they all said their goobyes to the old man. As they left the tent the Grandfather had

Chapter Twenty-Four...The Grandfather

one more thing to say—"Vorios come here, the others can wait outside."

"Yes, Grandfather," Vorios said. When everyone had left, the Grandfather spoke:

"Vorios, there are others that she must meet, Princess Aurora, the Gryphon, and others."

"Yes, Grandfather, I understand"

Vorios joined the others outside. As they all waited, a white misty cloud started to surround them...and in a matter of moments they were back in Greece, standing together before their altar table.

Chapter Twenty-Five...
The Gryphon

They were all back in the great Hall of the Temple of Delphi, the altar table was in front of them. The table looked the same as before, except that the knife was gone. Vorios was the first one to speak.

"I suggest that we meditate on what has happened for a week. We shall all meet here in week. The Temple has to settle down to its' usual routine. In a week we shall all feel more clarity about what has happened."

Theoclea went to bed, and slept. The night was devoid of dreams. This persisted for two more nights, and then she had one more dream. In the dream she was sitting on the Tripod chair down in the subterranean chamber, inhaling the Dragon's Breath. No question seems to have been asked of her...perhaps it was her turn to ask the question...perhaps the question would be asked later. Suddenly the scene shifted and she was back on Atlantis—she saw The Grandfather. He was sitting outside of his Triangular canvas and wood tent. He looked at her with blind eyes and said—

"My child I know one who will take you to see the light of the Gods and Goddesses, for your name 'Theoclea' means 'The Glory of the Gods and Goddesses, you have touched the Gate, and now you will see the LIGHT." He stood up, and said, "All of the Gods and Goddesses are One," then he chanted something three times. Suddenly he turned into a magnificent Gryphon, with feathers of all of the colors of the rainbow.

The Rainbow Gryphon spoke to her, in a voice that sounded vaguely familiar to her. He looked at her with eyes that could *see*!

"To gaze properly into the light, you must visit the source of the light. Get on my back and I'll take you there," the Gryphon said. Theoclea hopped onto the Gryphon's back, and with a great flapping of wings, the Gryphon flew upward.

The air currents swirled taking Theoclea and the Gryphon this way and that way. They were rising through the dust of the clouds, and a faint melody was

Chapter Twenty-Five...The Gryphon

heard. They were now high enough to see the currents of the sea. A flock of hundreds of birds was seen below, and the birds were riding on the currents of air. The Gryphon and Theoclea were high enough to see the Earth as a sphere, spinning slowly in a regular rhythm. Theoclea could see the clouds moving across the face of the earth, as the melody got louder. It was the 'Song of the Earth', and it was plaintive, and sweet. They could see the moon coming out from behind the earth, with its glow of reflected sunlight. The Gryphon said—

"Theoclea , an ancient wise one called the moon the first star, the first sphere. For your people it is the place of Artemis, the Moon Goddess….a place where promises are fulfilled, and even though the Will may be tested, vows are kept here, and the Earth sings to the Moon." They flew beyond the moon, and the Gryphon spoke again.

"We are flying toward what the Ancients considered the second sphere of Mercury. According to the people of your time, it is the abode of Hermes, the God of the unexpected, of synchronicities, the God that creates a bridge between mind and body, reason and imagination. Mercury, quicksilver, the spirit of matter, unites opposites, shifting across levels, crossing boundaries. He teaches us to discern the true nature of things, to see the magic within us. Do you hear the Earth singing to Mercury?"

"Yes, I do!" Theoclea replied.

The Gryphon whirled around, and headed for yet another sphere. When they were much closer, Theoclea said—

"What is the name of the sphere that we are approaching? For some reason I feel younger, more alive, my senses seem to be keener!"

The Gryphon spoke—

"We are in the sphere of Venus, the place of your Goddess, Aphrodite, the third sphere. Aphrodite tells us to add love and beauty into our lives. The third sphere is the place of sensuality, of beauty. It is also a place where one learns of one's own nature, and the nature of the outer universe. Can you hear the Earth singing to Venus?" the Gryphon said.

"Yes," said Theoclea.

"We must now move on to the fourth sphere," the Gryphon said. "The fourth sphere is the sphere of the Sun, said to be the abode of your patron Gods, Apollo, and Dionysus. Look, you can see that within the Sun a dark five pointed star is appearing. There is singing and dancing here. Here we may meet the wise ones

Chapter Twenty-Five...The Gryphon

who sought eternal truths. Here we are cautioned to not judge too quickly. There is a place for wildness here, as well as truth-seeking. This is a place where one learns not to make rash decisions and opinions formed in haste. It is a place where we learn to be accepting of others who are different from us, and a place to strengthen the courage of our convictions. The Earth sings to the Sun."

"We are rising again, are we moving on to the fifth sphere?" Theoclea said.

"Yes, Theoclea, we are approaching the Sphere of Mars. Notice that our vision is becoming clouded. Do you see the rays of light crisscrossing its' surface?"

"Yes," Theoclea said. "There are flames crisscrossing this way and that!"

"As our vision clears we will see that the flames form a Pentacle from top to base, particles of matter, like harp strings are leaping from side to side. One point of the Pentacle contains the power of the East Wind, another the power of the South, a third the power of the West, and the fourth the power of the North wind. The top point contains the Spirit. Creative tension all in balance, held together, connected and united in one place by Love. Do you hear the Earth singing to Mars?"

"Yes," said Theoclea, "but what is that sphere in the distance, the one with the swirling colors?"

"That is the sixth sphere, the sphere of Jupiter, a place of Higher Justice." The Gryphon passed the sphere of Mars, and moved on to Jupiter. He spoke again. "The swirling colors of its' surface collect to form the first words of the Book of Wisdom, 'Know Thyself'. To these, I add the words of one of our ancient ones—'Dance the Dance of Polarities, the Union of Opposites, may the Earth always sing to Jupiter." They moved quickly to the silvery seventh sphere of Saturn.

"Theoclea, do you hear the whispers? Saturn whispers to us, telling us not to presume to know more than Nature does. Saturn whispers—*'Let go, and watch for the Synchronicities, let them happen, let them reveal the Universal Form that fuses all things'.*"

Theoclea listened. "I hear the whispers, yes I can hear them!" The Rings of Saturn then rearranged themselves to form a ladder. The Gryphon flew up, all the while following the rungs of the ladder, and proceeded to climb up, beside the ladder with great speed, through the constellations, past the stars, through the dust and dark matter. They looked down, and their vision traveled through the seven spheres,

Chapter Twenty-Five...The Gryphon

seeing how the Moon, Mercury, the Sun, Venus, Mars, Jupiter and Saturn were all connected.

"We have now reached the eighth sphere, the sphere of the fixed stars, the abode of all of the Gods and the Goddesses, do you see the Red Key, the key to all of the altar rooms?"

"Yes," Theoclea said, "I see it!" There was a huge Red Key that exploded in a vision of rose petals, a shower of rose petals, like shooting stars. "My mind is buzzing with old questions and new answers," Theoclea said. Suddenly Theoclea lost her vision and couldn't see anything. The Gryphon spoke to her.

"The God and the Goddess will transform your sight so that you can see the Vision of Balance and Truth." The blindness receded, and slowly things that Theoclea thought were separate seemed to be more connected and united. Finally they ascended to the ninth sphere.

The Gryphon said—

"This sphere was called the 'Primum Mobile' by an Ancient One. Here we can see the entire Milky Way Galaxy. It gives all of the stars their movement."

"The stars are like snow flakes!" Theoclea said.

"All the spheres dance their movement by the power of the Galaxy," the Gryphon said. "Their very existence depends on this dance."

"How is this all of this bound together?" Theoclea said.

"Theoclea—listen as the Earth sings to the Moon, Mercury, the Sun, Venus, Mars, and to all of the spheres. We are seeing pure form, pure matter, form and matter connected, all coming forth at the same time like the arrows from a three stringed bow. They are all pointing to the center, the final sphere, the tenth Sphere, the Empyrean! Look, Theoclea, we are moving to the center of the Galaxy, a massive black hole ringed with an endless sea of light, and in the black hole can you see it—there appears to be the image of a Rose. When one of our ancestors saw this vision she said, 'Embrace the tension, Let Go and Dance'."

Theoclea watched as the rose turned into the image of a pentacle—The Pentacle of Transformation. The pentacle then became a rose again—the pentacle of transformation and the rose of rebirth were woven into each other, and back and forth they danced... the rose...the pentacle...the rose...the pentacle... the rose, the pentacle. The Gryphon spoke once again.

Chapter Twenty-Five...The Gryphon

"Theoclea, we have traveled across vast distances, and it is now time to return. We can move through all ten spheres quickly, through the dust and dark matter to the Earth."

The spheres flew swiftly past them—the Empyrean, the Primum Mobile, The Fixed Stars, Saturn, Jupiter, Mars, Venus, the Sun, Mercury, the Moon, and finally the Earth. They descended through the currents and waves of the air to the earth below, and slowly Theoclea felt the dance of the rhythms of her body and mind.

Chapter Twenty-Six...
Aurora

The Rainbow Gryphon landed in front of the Grandfather's tent. In an instant, the Gryphon changed back into the Grandfather.

"There is one more that you shall meet. She is over in that tent over there," the Grandfather said. Theoclea saw a tent about thirty feet away. It was exactly like the Grandfather's, but there was a design on the outside of children of many colors, all holding hands, a rising sun in the middle of the pattern. He approached the tent, and opened the flap. A woman dressed in brown buckskin, with fringe on the arms appeared from inside of the tent. She smiled at Theoclea, as if she knew all about her.

"I am Princess Aurora…and you are…Theoclea! I've heard all about you from Axcelotl and the Grandfather." Grandfather then embraced Theoclea, and said his goodbyes to her.

"It has been a blessing to me to see you…Axcelotl's daughter…in my mind. Aurora will answer more of your questions…and perhaps lead you on to new ones, for ultimately the Gate waits for you." The Grandfather sighed, and thought silently about the future. He was sure that he would meet her again in another incarnation. "Theoclea, I have some things that I must attend to, in my tent. I place you in the hands of Princess Aurora. We shall meet again…on some windswept plain in the future perhaps." Theoclea embraced the Grandfather, and kissed his cheek. He walked back to his tent and turned once again.

"Yes, Theoclea, we will meet again…on a windswept plain." His voice trailed off…he waved and entered his tent.

The woman dressed in the brown buckskin stood in front of her tent and said—

"So, you are Theoclea…we've all been waiting for you, you must have questions, my dear, and the questions will lead to more questions…so what can I say to help you?"

Chapter Twenty-Six...Aurora

"Aurora, who is the Grandfather?" Theoclea asked.

Aurora replied, "Grandfather, is... grandfather. He is the leader of 'The Children of the Law of One'. You'll learn about more of this later. But first, you must be purified." She wore a headband. On it was a symbol. There were children of all different colors holding hands all the way around the band and in the center of the headband above her forehead was a rising sun. She pointed to her headband and said, "This is the symbol of The Children of the Law of One."

Aurora opened the flap to her tent, and told Theoclea that she could bathe in the tent and that there would be new clothes for her inside.

Axcelotl picked them out for you, they are in red, gold and black—your colors. They are also Axcelotl's colors. You'll see—there they are, hanging up for you."

"There's also a tub with hot water. Bathe in the tub and it will purify you."

Theoclea walked inside. Aurora waited outside, the sun streaming down on her face and headband. Theoclea did as she was told. She went in and took off her clothes, saw the tub and slowly sat down in the hot water. The water swirled about her. There was an incense smell, and incense was burning. There was a window, and a wide ray of sunlight was shining through the window. She looked at the ray and could see the tendrils of incense smoke, dancing in the light. She looked around the tent, and saw the same symbol of the children of different colors all holding hands with the rising sun in the center.

The symbol was depicted in various ways on the wall of the tent. Sometimes there seemed to be two pillars on either side of the rising sun. She sat back in the water, and visions and thoughts danced around in her head. She saw her two children dancing in the huge paws of a human-faced lion in front of two triangular buildings like the ones in Egypt that Pythagoras told her about when she was his student. She saw books with strange writing in them, on tables in a great library. She saw shadows that looked like arrows on the ceiling of a room.

These things and much more she saw as she sat in the tub, and dreamed, on and on. After a while, feeling refreshed, she then got out of the tub, put on her new clothes, and opened the flap of the tent. Aurora was standing there, but it was nighttime. How long had she been in the tent?

Aurora turned to her and said—

Chapter Twenty-Six...Aurora

"Feel better? Those colors, red black and gold suit you. They are your colors." She looked kindly at Theoclea.

"The headband and the symbols in the tent—I'm sure that you must have noticed them. They're the symbols that we wear. We are 'The Children of the Law of One'. We are the peaceful ones who worship, respect, and try to understand the Sun, and its' many cycles—both long and short. This is not a peaceful time. All throughout Atlantis' history there have been two factions, 'The Sons of Belial', who are warlike and aggressive, and 'The Children of the Law of One'."

"We've had peaceful times when there has been tolerance, wisdom and balance. The troubled times come when one or another group becomes too powerful. Then imbalance occurs. At all times, there are the others, like Axcelotl . They're the ones who guard the secrets of the Crystals. They worship the Goddess, and have the Rose Medallion. Their meetings are shrouded in secrecy...they guard 'the Mysteries' of our time. The Crystal ones are always needed to bring peace between the Sons of Belial and The Children of the Law of One. Come with me, Theoclea, there are two others that you must meet." She held Theoclea's hand and raised her other hand high, moving it from left to right.

Suddenly they were on a windy cliff, about ten feet from the edge. They walked a little closer, and Theoclea could see a city of glistening white, with huge triangular shaped spires that seemed to be made of shining white crystal. Crystal lanterns floated in the air like snowflakes, thousands and thousands of them. Here and there Theoclea could hear explosive sounds, and saw smoke.

Aurora pointed to the city and said—

"We can't go down there, it's dangerous. The factions are fighting, and the Crystal Ones are trying to stop it. They have even threatened to turn off the Crystal Power, although that has never been done, and would probably accomplish nothing."

"I understand," said Theoclea. "It's like me. I understand those who follow Apollo, and those who follow Dionysus, but Inanna and her Rose Medallion are needed to keep the true peace and wisdom."

"Yes," said Aurora. "Axcelotl told me that you were the one from the future, the one with the Rose Medallion."

Chapter Twenty-Six...Aurora

"Aurora, what is that Crystal Spire in the center of the city? It dominates the landscape, the one with all of the windows?"

"That is the Main Crystal Power Station. It is the center of the crystal energy. The buildings to the left and right of it are the headquarters of 'The Sons of Belial', and 'The Children of the Law of One'."

Theoclea looked at the spires and marveled at their design. Then she sighed, remembering the destruction in her visions.

"Aurora, I see two Pillars beyond the Power Station out in the sea. They remind me of the Pillars of Hercules that exist in my own time and place." Theoclea knew the answer, but she wanted to be sure.

"Those are the Pillars of Atlas. They are both volcanoes that have been dormant for thousands of years."

"Aurora, I see smoke coming out of the larger Pillar."

"Yes, Theoclea, of late, smoke has been rising from the larger pillar. It is between those Pillars that the sun rises, and the sun….sets in your land, between the pillars of Hercules, far beyond the Great Sea."

"Aurora, what time are we in?"

"It is exactly 9000 years before your time, Theoclea, and we are perhaps half way around the world."

"Vorios said that 9000 years ago…there was, perhaps…"and her voice trailed off. What could she say?

Theoclea looked at the larger of the Pillars. More smoke was coming from it. She heard more loud explosive sounds from the great city below.

"There, look down there," Theoclea said. What is that statue?"

"The one showing the warrior with the symbol of the Sons of Belial on his shield?" Aurora asked.

"Yes," Theoclea said with a trembling voice.

"It is the symbol of the 'Sons of Belial', it stands to one side of the Power station tower. Look at the spire to the right of the Power station. Do you see that huge sign? That is the sign of my people, the children all holding hands, and in the middle is the sun rising between the two pillars. The middle building— the Power station is controlled by the Crystal Ones. It's controlled by Axcelotl and the people from the Crystal Temple. You can see the sign of the Three Crystals on that building."

The wind started to whip up, strong gust of wind here and there. Theoclea could see an aurora borealis, shimmering shapes seen against the backdrop of the night sky. She saw the constellation of Leo, in an

Chapter Twenty-Six...Aurora

unfamiliar location. Clouds were appearing in the sky here and there obscuring the stars and the moon.

"A storm may be brewing," Theoclea said.

"There are two others that you must meet, Theoclea, and I must go. Aurora embraced Theoclea, and then said—"Look over there. The Dancer, the Woman in White is waiting for you." She pointed to the right, and Theoclea looked in that direction.

Chapter Twenty-Seven...
The Lady in White

There was a woman dressed in a white loose fitting dress, and in front of her was a ballet practice bar. Her right leg was all the way up on the bar. She wore ballet shoes, and was stretching on the bar. Theoclea looked back and Aurora was gone. She approached the dancer—The Lady in White. The woman looked back at Theoclea and smiled a painful smile.

"This used to be so much easier when I was young," she said. She took her leg off of the bar and steadied herself.

"Once more, the other leg, then I'll be with you." She raised the other leg to the bar and stretched once again.

"I haven't done this in a while," the Lady in White said. "That's why it's so painful.' She continued to stretch.

Suddenly, Theoclea felt a stabbing pain on her left shoulder. She lifted up her sleeve and saw a gash—and bleeding.

"Oh no," she started to cry. "Not again!" She cried out in pain and gazed at the gash remembering Eleusis, and the gash on her right shoulder. "No, not again." she whispered.

The Lady in White, The Dancer, stopped her stretching, put her leg down and rushed over to Theoclea.

"My child," she said. "What has happened?" Theoclea raised her sleeve and showed the bloody gash, and the Dancer examined it.

"Theoclea—that is your name—right child?" Theoclea tearfully nodded her head.

"Theoclea, has this ever happened to you before?" Theoclea looked into the distance as if remembering...all of it.

"Yes, when I gave my speech at Eleusis—it happened when I approached the end of my speech—I felt it, but I hid it from Panelle and Morain. I saw the blood and felt the pain. I saw the gash. When I got

Chapter Twenty-Seven...The Lady in White

back to my tent and was alone, I raised my sleeve and it was gone!" She started to cry again.

"It healed by itself!" She kept on crying. The Lady in White lifted up Theoclea's sleeve. Then, she said—

"The first time it healed itself?" She seemed astounded by what Theoclea had said.

"Amazing, such power! But it rarely heals itself the second time, Theoclea, and we must not take any chances with it, my dear. I am the Lady in White, The Dancer, a healer, the dispenser of wisdom. Now let's take a look at that wound."

She raised Theoclea's sleeve and touched the gash. The blood started to vanish, and within a few moments the wound started to heal. The Dancer continued to touch Theoclea's shoulder until the wound had completely healed. Theoclea felt the warmth of the woman's touch all over her body. It was an aura that lasted perhaps a minute, or two, although time in this place had no meaning.

"It might have healed itself like the last time, my dear, but we can take no chances. There, my dear, you're good as new! You have such power, Theoclea. It healed by itself the first time! Now my child, I must give you this piece of wisdom. I will always be with you. You may not see me, but I will always be there. By touching you and healing The Wound, I have passed some of my healing power on to you. I've healed many people, and sometimes some of my healing power passes on to the one that I have healed. It will grow and be a further blessing to you."

The Dancer took out a knife that was hidden in the white sash that she wore.

"Take this knife, Theoclea." Theoclea took the knife, a look of confused concern on her face. The Dancer extended her right leg. "Now make a small cut on my leg." Theoclea said—

"No, you're a dancer, I don't think that I can do that!"

"Theoclea, do it, you will see." Theoclea bent down and did as she was told. She made a small cut on the Dancer's leg, and blood appeared at the site of the cut.

"Now place your right hand on the cut, Theoclea," the Dancer said. Theoclea did so, and the blood vanished, and in a few seconds the wound had healed completely. She saw this and stood up. She handed the knife back to the Dancer.

"I have added the Gift of the Healer to the many other Gifts that you have." She smiled and once again

Chapter Twenty-Seven...The Lady in White

checked to see if Theoclea's wound had completely healed.

"Theoclea, even though I am a healer, and many say that I have great wisdom to share, I still wear the Black Key. She reached for the thong around her neck and produced the Black Key, and showed it to Theoclea. Theoclea touched the Red Key that was around her own neck, held it up, and showed it to the Lady in White. The Lady in White stared at the Red Key. The words of The Merchant came back to Theoclea.

'Usually, only those who have had the Black Key and the wound can be considered for the Red Key, and the wound has to have been healed. They also must have reached for and attained higher spiritual levels and guidance. Most of all, they must answer the question, and the question changes with each new situation'.

Theoclea felt the stirring of the elements, she saw the twin Pillars...the two volcanoes...and strange aurora borealis shapes forming in the air. Smoke was coming out of one of the volcanoes. She turned to the Lady in White—The Dancer, and said, "I see destruction, death, a cataclysm. What will become of all of this?"

The Dancer sighed, then she replied.

"Atlantis shall be engulphed by fire water, air and earth. There will be a death here of immensity that is unimagineable. Those who escape will be the seeds... they shall travel to the West and the East. And wherever they land, they shall be as seeds. The story of Atlantis' end will be known all over the world. If they place and the time are right, if the conditions are met, then the seeds of Atlantis will grow again, its' Gods and Goddesses, its' Myths, and all else shall be reincarnated, reborn as trees that will share the treasures of Atlantis."

"You have given me the Gift of the Healer," Theoclea said. She took the Red Key and the thong off of her neck and said—

"Take off the Black Key!" The Lady in White looked stunned! She took off the Black Key and let it fall to the ground. She then bowed her head to Theoclea, and Theoclea placed the Red Key around her neck.

"The Red Key opens the doors to all of the altar rooms of all of the religions of the past, present and future. It also unlocks the locks of all of the chains that bind you!" Theoclea said. There were tears in the Dancer's eyes.

"Thank you, Theoclea." They embraced and then wept. "Theoclea, you have given me *your* Key…you're

Chapter Twenty-Seven...The Lady in White

unprotected now. You do you have other Red Keys... am I right?"

"Yes, but they are back in the Oracles' room, near the tripod chair, and in my bedchamber. The..." She hesitated before speaking again.

"The *others*...they only make a certain number of keys each year. I am oath bound not to say more." The Dancer seemed to understand.

"I'll always be with you, Theoclea, but I can only use this Red Key to protect you and myself. No others will be protected, unless you are wearing your own. I can protect you now, even though you may not see me." She embraced Theoclea, then they parted.

The Lady in White said—

"He is waiting for you, Theoclea, look over there...!"

Theoclea turned in the direction that the Dancer was pointing in. She was momentarily shocked at what she saw. There, a short distance away was the Gate of Eleusis, with its Crystal Lanterns flowing away from the Gate. She heard a voice...the Dancer's voice, whispering to her—

"The Guardian of the Gate is waiting for you, Theoclea."

"Nor shall he then be vanquished in the fight-by which the spirit-portals are flung wide,
If eye to eye undaunted, he shall brave The Guardian of the Threshold of that realm"

    Rudolph Steiner- "The Soul's Probation"

Chapter Twenty-Eight...
The Guardian

Theoclea looked back and the Dancer was gone. She turned, and there was a ramp, like the one at Eleusis—that led to the Gate—the Gate was lower down and away from the cliff. As before, at Eleusis, she walked to the ramp and descended. There were Crystal Lanterns on either side of the ramp. As she approached the Gate with the trailing Crystal Lanterns, she could see the Watchman's face—he was the same man—the Guardian of the Gate of Eleusis.

She sighed, and nodded to him, for he had a grave responsibility. He smiled back at her, bowed his head to her, and gestured to the pole that held the lights. His hair was waving in the breeze as the wind continued to whirl and stir. With a worried expression on his face, he turned and walked away. Suddenly, he stopped, folded his arms and looked up at the stars. He saw wavering plasma-like shapes of different colors wavering in the air, like a magnificent Aurora Borealis. He noted the movement of the clouds, as if an army was moving in. He didn't like what he saw.

Theoclea looked at the crystal lights, and once again admired the way that they trailed down, forming the hair of a headdress. She remembered that, at Eleusis, it was her tribute to Inanna. She bowed her head, and with her hand trembling, once again, she slowly reached forward and touched the Gate. As before the same feeling of 'giving of herself' filled her, and she took one step forward, touching the side of her head, and a shoulder to the Gate. Her trembling ceased, and she felt something. Once again a quiet strength flowed through her, but this time it grew, building upon itself, for now there was a new power, the power of a healer added to the mix of her gifts. She felt an energy coming through the ground up to the root of her spine, and around, up, through her, through her heart. She let out a cry, not of pain, but of *joy* she *saw* with a new Vision, and the power streamed through and out of her head, and through the Crystal Lanterns. They slowly brightened until it

Chapter Twenty-Eight...The Guardian

was almost impossible to look at them and she had to turn her face away. Then slowly the lanterns dimmed back to their normal luminosity, and slowly she felt the warm aura that she felt the last time. She lingered at the lamp pole for a few more moments, then stood back and bowed her head.

The Guardian turned around and watched her for a few seconds, then slowly, he walked forward. When he was near the Gate, he smiled at her and bowed his head, but this time, instead of remaining silent, he spoke:

"Theoclea, you are a survivor...a witness to the Dark Night of the Soul. You have wandered through the Soul's Probation, and survived its Wounds. Now you have reached the Second Gate." He looked around with a look of concern on his face. There were more storm clouds and the air was whirling at a faster pace. He took Theoclea's hand.

"We must walk back up the hill to the cliff again. Something is happening in the city." He held her hand as they both walked back up the ramp, and then to the edge of the cliff. The air was whirling and howling all about them. His hair was long and flowed around his face. Theoclea felt an aura surrounding her.

"I can protect you, but I cannot extend the aura to him," she heard the Dancer whisper in her mind.

They were in the center of a storm, and the wind was now approaching from the South. Indeed, the South wind entered with its' passionate fire...an explosion of fire, the fire of a giant volcano spewing its' lava hundreds of feet into the air. It was an eruption that was heard thousands of miles away, said to be the loudest sound ever heard on the earth. On islands half way around the world, the sight of the plasma-like Aurora Borealis and the sound of the event was recorded on tablets that have yet to see the light of day. An event of horrific proportions was occurring. Lightning flashed everywhere. She could see the sea slowly receding...revealing a sea floor that had not seen the light of day in thousands of years, and even then it had been encrusted with a thick coating of ice.

Theoclea and the Guardian held on to each other. She had given the Red Key to the dancer. Theoclea felt its' protective aura, but he was not protected. There was a lull in the storm, but things were slowly starting to fly about them. A large crystal suddenly flew by and hit the Guardian on the forehead. Another one hit him in the chest. He fell and was within inches

Chapter Twenty-Eight...The Guardian

of the edge of the cliff, his head and chest bleeding profusely.

Theoclea kneeled before him and saw the blood oozing from both wounds. She hadn't noticed the black key around his neck, for he wore a Guardian's medallion in front of the Key.

She placed her right hand on his forehead, and the left hand on his chest. In about thirty seconds the blood vanished, and the wounds healed. The Guardian regained consciousness. He was momentarily stunned, then realized what had happened as he touched his forehead, and saw one of the crystals lying on the ground.

"Theoclea , I must go. You are protected, but not for long. You must go too." He made the sign of the Gate of Eleusis with both hands. She tearfully returned the gesture. He touched his forehead and smiled—

"Theoclea, now a Healer. We shall meet again, perhaps near a pond in a different time and place, perhaps in Egypt. Maybe there you will learn the complete meaning of the sign." That having been said, he vanished into the air. Theoclea looked over at the Gate, and it had vanished as well. She stood up and looked once more at the city, and the Pillars of Atlas.

The sounds of the Volcano gave way to the crackle of the shifting magnetism in the air. There was sudden movement of the earth that she stood on. The sea was receding quickly and could be seen to be miles and miles away. Then all died down to a dull roar.

Theoclea looked at the two pillars, and saw a lightning flash cross the sky in the direction of the larger pillar that was spewing its' lava. An instant later from the opposite direction another lightning flash could be seen, heading toward the smaller pillar. The lightning flashes met in the center of the sky. The second flash hit the smaller volcano, and a small cloud emerged from the smaller pillar and quickly rose to the spot above the place where the lightning bolts had crossed. It was her sign, **the SIGN OF THE DELPHIC ORACLE!**

Suddenly, all sound ceased, and everything was frozen. Theoclea could see into the immediate future. She saw that the smaller Volcano would explode, sending rocks and debris everywhere. She saw that the winds would enter from the west and north and the water would mix with the rocks. She saw that the wave would approach...a wave of horrific size. She started to hear sounds, a whispered hiss...and the wave approached. Somehow she felt that she was in

Chapter Twenty-Eight...The Guardian

two places...part of her was still on the cliff and part of her was in the chamber sitting on the Tripod chair.

The wave approached, a wave of a magnitude that had never been seen on the earth. A wave of horrific size, a mile high, and it was approaching the land. She smelled the smell of the dragon's breath, and felt the chair beneath her. The whirling got faster. The West wind entered ...the air was moist with water...but not healing water...all was flying about and whirling. The wave rose higher as it approached the land. The hiss of steam could be heard as the volcano instantly turned the water in the air to steam. The wave rose higher and higher, approaching the shore faster and faster. She could barely see the top of the wave. For a second she saw the Oomphalos stone, ten feet away from the Tripod chair, the dragon's breath seeping from it. Suddenly the wave came crashing down!

All was chaos as the North wind entered , with its' rocks and soil...the very earth was shaking around her. The land was sinking into the sea in a huge landslide. The rocks were flying, there were flying sacred crystals of a multitude of shapes...the Power Station was destroyed in a matter of seconds! So many crystals of different shapes and sizes...There was a smell of pumice in the air...the smell that comes when lava hits the sea, cools and floats on it. The air was full of ash, or was it? She felt the chair below her.

There were screams that were drowned out by the cacophony of the chaos.Whispers abounded...downward, upward, inward, outward—all was a mass, a blur, a whirling. Pieces of columns were flying upward—parts of roofs flying downward. Theoclea's hands reached down, she felt the chair and grasped it. There was a flash of light and a whirling of whispered words...

Antilia, Antipodes,
antoechi, antichthon,
Attal-anti, and others.

A colossal statue of a man holding a shield with the gold crescent moon and the black arrow through it flew by, and smashed into the huge sign showing the children of many colors holding hands, with the rising sun and pillars in the middle. The Dragon's breath enveloped her, its' tendrils grasping her, holding her. Bodies of people drowned by the water, or burned by the fire were whirled upward...inward...outward... whirling crystals, a mass of crystals, water, air and fire. She saw the central crystal building, with the symbol of the three crystals on it, melting from the heat.

Slowly, she slipped from the Tripod chair as the building melted, she slowly slipped down, off of the

Chapter Twenty-Eight...The Guardian

chair. She fell slowly to the ground her face met the ground slowly and her head nestled in the spot where the fault lines met...the 'Hearth at the Navel of the Earth.' The Dragon's breath continued to seep out of the ground. and suddenly all was darkness. She groped around in the darkness, and found it—an extra Red Key. It was hidden under the Tripod chair. She pulled on it, and its' thong seemed to be stuck. She gave it one more pull with the little strength that she had. It was stuck to the bottom of the chair. As she slipped from consciousness she heard The Dancer, The Lady in White, The Healer say—

"I am with you."

She was found the next morning, an alarm was sounded and they searched all over the Temple. She was in the subterranean chamber, where the Prophecies were made, and she was barely alive, barely breathing. Someone saw that she was clutching the Red Key, but the thong was stuck to one of the feet of the chair. They quickly freed it and placed it around her neck. Pythagoras and Vorios were there, as well as Morain and Panelle.

"My God, said Pythagoras. "Why did she come here? It was not her time. The Oracle can only be here for two days a month...she could have...should have died. How did she survive? Why did she take the Key off? Why was it tangled in the leg of the chair?" asked Pythagoras. The others just shook her heads in disbelief.

Vorios turned away. He *knew*. It had to be the Dancer, The Lady in White, the giver of wisdom. He *knew* that the healer was with her.

He knew!

"The Powers of Destiny have granted me
The vision which can penetrate the past; Already too
have I received the signs
So to direct my free-will sacrifice
That good may pour therefrom for every soul
Whose thread of life shall have to twine with mine."

Rudolph Steiner 'The Soul's Probation'

Chapter Twenty-Nine...
Theoclea Returns

Theoclea opened her eyes. She was alone, in her bedchamber. How long had she been there? She slowly remembered the vision, it came back to her, or was it a vision? If it was, she realized that she may have had the strongest dream, or vision of her life, and in the end, she vaguely remembered some words—part of a poem. She thought about the vision for awhile, and heard the Guardian's words whispered to her... *'We shall meet again, perhaps near a pond in a different time and place, perhaps in Egypt'.* Then she drifted off to sleep once more. The next time, when she awoke her eyes remained closed. She heard voices, and felt Morain's touch. Pythagoras, Vorios, Panelle and Morain were in the bedchamber. Morain touched

Theoclea's forehead. She bent over her. No one spoke. Morain closed her eyes and continued to touch Theoclea's forehead. That went on for a few more minutes, then Morain opened her eyes and there were tears streaming down her face. The other three looked at her with questioning looks on their faces.

"She's coming back to us, she's awake, but can only hear us, I suspect. Only the Goddesses know how long she breathed the Dragon's breath. Her face was directly on the Hearth, at the point where the cracks in the earth meet. Anyone else would be dead. She must rest, it will take many days for her to recover from this." She looked at the others, and her eyes continued to fill with tears. "She reached the second Gate, she touched it and spoke to the Guardian, and he spoke to her as well. More than this I cannot tell you. You will all have to see with your own eyes whether she has changed. I am oath bound not to reveal any more."

She wiped the tears from her eyes and they left the chamber. As she walked down the hallway, Morain thought, *'She has changed, she's evolving...in a process of becoming..."*

Chapter Thirty...
Theoclea Healed

About a week later, they were all once again in Theoclea's bedchamber. She was sitting up and the color had come back to her face. She had just finished a hearty breakfast. In front of her was another tray with a book on it, a pen, and an inkwell.

Theoclea spoke first-

"I feel much better. I'm writing a book called 'More Whispers', it's another book of my sayings, verses, stories, song lyrics, and bits of wisdom. The book will be distributed to the Greek people and others, like my first book, 'Whispers'. I thought about including all of the events of the past couple of weeks in the book, but I've decided against that. I may depict some of what happened, but I'll present it in a fictional, poetic, mystical way."

Vorios spoke—

"A wise decision, Theoclea, You must fully regain your health. I think that we can all agree that no one would believe us anyway." They all agreed not to make the events public, for various reasons.

"I must tell you all, that when you found me in the Oracle's chamber, I had an extraordinary dream, or vision. It was so powerful that I've decided for now, to keep it to myself, and ponder the meaning of it." There was an audible sigh of relief in the room when she said that!

"My gifts, you know, can be both a curse or a blessing. They have been, in fact, growing in power, I can *see* back, into the past, as well as forward into the future in my visions. And now…there is…" her voice trailed off. She paused, and chose her words carefully. "The gift of the Oracle's sight has been growing, ever since I was a child, ever since the first time, when I saw that the tree was about to fall, and I saved Troyana and Anka. I shall include many things in my new book, 'More Whispers'. People of the present and future will know of me. They will know of you too. You're my guides and counselors…Morain, Panelle, Vorios, and

Chapter Thirty...Theoclea Healed

Pythagoras. I shall rely on all of you to tell me the true nature of things. The people of the future must *know*."

"They must *know* about some of the things that the Grandfather spoke of. They must know about the Earth, and the history of the Earth that is all about them, written in the stones, the Akashic Record…written in the Earth itself. Trust me, it is the right path." There was silent agreement on that. Morain, Panelle, and Vorios stood up said their goodbyes, and left Theocleas' chamber. Pythagoras stayed with her.

When they were far enough away from the bedchamber, Panelle said—"It will take her some time to recover from this." She shook her head. "I wonder if she had more to say."

"I wouldn't know, Panelle, may I remind you that we are *oath bound*! We cannot reveal any of the important conversations that we hear at Delphi!"

"Yes," Panelle sighed, "I suppose that we must keep this one, as always, to ourselves. That's the trouble, there's never any good gossip around here. I guess that now we'll go back to the old routines of the Temple, right?"

"Right," Morain said, with assurance.

Panelle paused, then spoke again. "The Red Key, she always had it with her when she sat on the Tripod

Chair. The Key—the Key that unlocks all of the chains that bind you, the Key that opens the doors of all of the altar rooms of all of the religions of the past, present, and future! Why did she take it off? Why was it stuck under the chair? Morain, you must know more..."

Morain turned to Panelle and said,

"What Theoclea *sees*, and what she *knows* shall remain—a mystery!"

They walked along in silence. They came to an archway, and gazed at the words on the arch.

'*Know thyself*'. They bowed their heads, and walked on through. '*She is becoming...more than I could ever have imagined...*' Morain thought.

Chapter Thirty-One...
'Seeing and 'Knowing'

The *seeing* and the *knowing* happened a few days later. Theoclea was sitting in bed, writing her new book, 'More Whispers'. Pythagoras was sitting in a chair, and momentarily he had fallen asleep. The last few weeks had been difficult for him.

Theoclea's cat jumped up in the bed. She petted the cat. "Where have you been? I've missed you so much," she said to the cat. The cat licked its' right paw and Theoclea noticed that there was a thorn in the cat's paw. There was blood all around the thorn. She said, "This may hurt for a second." She reached forward, and quickly removed the thorn with her right hand.

The cat winced, and the wound continued to bleed. Theoclea held the cat's paw. The blood started to vanish, and in a matter of seconds the wound was healed. "There, you're good as new." The cat licked its' paw and settled in to sleep beside Theoclea.

Theoclea's mind went back to all of the conversations about Atlantis. She had *seen* Atlantis. The others had *seen* Atlantis as well...as if in a shared vision, a dream, perhaps a reality of a kind. But whenever she asked them for the facts, they often used words like conjecture; theory; supposition; legend; stories; beliefs; indications. At least Vorios, the magician was forthcoming with the details of life on Atlantis in their joint 'vision'. The time had come. She had to *know*.

Pythagoras suddenly woke up from his nap and walked over to Theoclea. She was writing. He sat on the edge of the bed, she looked up at him, and said—

"Pythagoras in the last part of my vision there was a flash of light and a whirling of whispered words. I seem to remember many of those words, and can be somewhat sure of some of the meanings, but the other words puzzle me. I must know the meanings of all of the words that I heard in that vision. You know of course, Pythagoras, that words are very important to me."

Chapter Thirty-One...'Seeing and 'Knowing'

Somehow, Pythagoras *knew* that this was coming.

"What are the words, Theoclea?"

"Let's start with four words, Pythagoras—*antilia, antipodes, antoechi, and antichthon*—what is their meaning? I must *know* the exact meaning!"

Pythagoras sighed, and said—

"Antipodes refer to a place, or places on the Earth where people are standing with their feet on the ground, but in the exact opposite direction that we stand in. Some say that the Earth is round. All of the words that you have given me mean the same thing, antipodal, the opposite place, usually shown on our maps surrounded by the one great ocean."

"...and what would Attal-anti mean?" Theoclea said. "I want the truth...no legends; conjecture; theory; suppositions or beliefs...I want to *know* the truth!"

Pythagoras gazed at her, he had never seen her like this.

He pondered his reply, then said,

"Attal- anti is the derivation of our word 'Atlantis'. It comes from the most ancient languages of southern India. It literally means 'having the feet opposite'."

Theoclea looked down at her book, then gazed deeply into his eyes.

"Pythagoras, I have studied a map of the known world. I saw to the very left, the strait of Gibraltar and the Pillars of Hercules. I saw Libya, Arabia, Asia, India and Scythia.

It all seems to be one continent, with various smaller seas here and there surrounded by the one great ocean. To the far right at the bottom of the map, I saw what appeared to be an island called Taprobane, then another island, and a name, Sundaland—with a strait between them. I know nothing of these lands. Must I forever be kept in the dark about these matters? Pythagoras, it's time...I want to *see* and *know* the truth of it, all of it."

He sighed. He *knew*. He *knew* from the very beginning that it would fall upon him to describe all of the events, all of the truth. She would settle for nothing less than that. She deserved to *know*...to *know*...all of it, and, in fact, almost all of it was *known* to him. Pythagoras paused, trying to form his words carefully...

"Yes, Theoclea, I'll try my best. I am like Vorios, the magician in some ways. I *know* of many things... things of the past, and, yes...things of the future. In those lands that you spoke of there are now many islands. Taprobane is but a remnant—an island in Indonesia...some call it Sumatra. Taprobane, and

Chapter Thirty-One... 'Seeing and 'Knowing'

Sundaland are the old names for Atlantis. There is a strait there called the Sunda strait and there are two Pillars. One is the mightiest volcano in our *known* world, Krakatoa, and the other is its' sister volcano, Dempo. They form the Pillars of Atlas. There is an old saying amongst our people—'The sun rises between the Pillars of Atlas, and sets between the Pillars of Hercules'. The Sun itself was a part of what happened! The Sun has its' own cycles, and occasionally sheds some of its substance in order to remain balanced. That occurs once every ten thousand to twelve thousand years or more. When that happens, there may be beautiful Aurora Borealis shapes all over the world caused by plasma, a substance from the sun. The Aurora Borealis is beautiful, but deadly. That was the moment and cause of the awakening of the spirits of the Pillars. The Pillars of Atlas are the two volcanoes that most certainly caused the rapid melting of the ice, the end of the Ice Age, the floods, and the destruction of the continent of Atlantis. Yes, Atlantis was a large continent, not an island.There were tsunamis caused by mile-high waves, the ash in the air, the raining pumice and heated rocks caused countless deaths of people, animals, other creatures, and plant life. I myself *know* that the Cave bear, the Mammoth, the Saber-toothed Tiger and many more species vanished from the Earth. It all happened in one day."

"In one day?" Theoclea said. "How many people are we talking about here, Pythagoras?"

Pythagoras sighed and closed his eyes. He *knew*. He was visibly shaken by the thought of it. She had to *know*...all of it.

"Taprobane, Sundaland, the continent that we now call Atlantis was the size of Libya and Asia Minor combined, before the sea rose up and engulfed it. It has been estimated that...over twenty to forty million people died that day, and that doesn't include people on the Earth who died in other places."

"Twenty to forty million people...and more?" Theoclea said, as tears ran down her cheeks. She grasped the thong around her neck, and the Red Key. Pythagoras whispered,

"Yes." Theoclea stared into the distance.

"I *see*. Yes, I *see*...the flood...Atlantis engulphed by the sea...I have *seen* it, Pythagoras...and now, I *know*... the *seeing* and the *knowing* can be both a curse and a blessing." Tears continued to run down her face. She closed her eyes and the words on the arch came to her, '*know thyself*'.

Chapter Thirty-One...'Seeing and 'Knowing'

She took out her handkerchief and tried to dry her eyes, but the tears kept coming. 'More than twenty million people...' she thought. He comforted her, but it took a while before she calmed down enough to do what she had to do, and say what had to be said. "Twenty to forty million people...and more—and we don't even honor...commemorate...remember... the memory of them, their deeds, their hopes, their dreams, is all lost to us? The least that we can do is to acknowledge that Dark Night of their Souls."

She stood up and walked over to an altar...her own personal altar. She kneeled, and touched the Red Key again. There was a white candle on the altar, and she lit it. Pythagoras walked over, kneeled and joined her. They both gazed at the candle, then she spoke.

"I'm crying in remembrance of those millions of people, and the other creatures that died on Atlantis, and elsewhere on that tragic day, and night thousands upon thousands of years ago. All that may remain of the Atlanteans may be buried in the sea. Atlantis was destroyed by Air, Fire, Water and Earth, but I feel...I *know* that the Spirit of Atlantis lives on. The blood of the Atlanteans flows in each of us, and perhaps if everyone sheds a tear for the Atlanteans, then Atlantis may once again rise up from the depths of the sea. Our tears contain drops of that ancient sea...that I *know*." She closed her eyes, and when she opened them she saw the seed from Eleusis—she always kept it on the plate with the images of Demeter and Persephone. She picked it up, stared at it, and then put it back on the plate. She stood up and walked over to the edge of the bed, and he followed her.

They both sat down, Theoclea sighed, then looked at Pythagoras, and reached for his hand. Her hand was trembling. They held hands...after several moments, she released his hand, turned and saw the book.

"Pythagoras, I've written a poem. I started it a few days ago, and finished it yesterday. I would like you to read it...out loud for me. I...didn't quite understand the poem when I was writing it, but now, I *see* and I *know*."

She handed him the book that she had been writing in, and he started to read.

Atlantis Rising

> We were on the deck,
> the day was done—
> Atlantis was ablaze,
> the sea was rising—

Chapter Thirty-One...'Seeing and 'Knowing'

and no one else would leave alive.
We were the last to leave.
Our parting thought was—
would we ever see the Sun
rise between
the Pillars again?
That was the One Day and the
Dark Night of our Souls.
We sang to the Sun, the Pillars,
and the Sea.
The Ancient Mother, the Earth said—
"This, my children, this must be!
The Nature of Nature is what
you must *know*.
You cannot avoid that,
you *see*, it is...simply so."

We sailed for parts unknown to man
we heard the seagull's cry.
We crossed the strait
and headed west.
The others sailed toward
The Isles of the Blessed
in the East, and beyond.
Would we ever *see* them again?

...and if so, how would we *know* them,
and how would they *know* us...
...after so many millennia?

***

Yes, it was the One Day,
and Dark Night of their Souls
and I thought of the words...
the words...engraved
on the Sacred Arch for all to *see*...
for all of time,
for eternity—

'*Know Thyself*'

As the Oracle of the Temple of Delphi,
The Pythian Priestess, the Pythia,
The Dragon Priestess of the Earth,
as I am known in *this* life—
I Theoclea, *see*, and
now, I *know*...
*of the One Day and
the Dark Night of their Souls...*
and I say this—

Chapter Thirty-One... 'Seeing and 'Knowing'

If their
legends spoke of a flood,
of pillars that spread fires
of smoke and of blood—
If their buildings were monuments
to the grand design of the heavens—
If they spoke words that are in our language,
and we spoke words of theirs,
then the meeting and the truth
would come down to legends, symbols,
art, architecture, and words...
words from many languages...
Those words I, Theoclea, have heard
whispered to me in a vision.
words like...
Atlantis,
Atlan, Atlas, Aztlan, Attal-anti
antipodes, antoechi, antichthon
Antilia, Aztatlan, Azteca, Tolan...Aztec

Those words should show all of us that
we are them, and they are us,
and in the moment of that meeting,
after so many millennia,
and the loss of so many lives

on Atlantis...
on that One Day and Dark Night...
in the moment of that revelation—

We shall all
'Know Ourselves'
and we shall all *See*
Atlantis rise again.

Pythagoras' eyes were full of tears. There was nothing more that he could say. She reached for her handkerchief once again and dried her tears, and his. For about a minute they stared into the distance to honor their ancestors. Theoclea turned to Pythagoras—*there was a question that had to be answered.*

"Pythagoras, why was everyone so reluctant to discuss Atlantis with me?" He carefully considered *the answer.*

"Theoclea, there is a reluctance to discuss Atlantis in the altar rooms of all religions of the past, present, and future—you see—one question that comes up is what kind of a deity, or group of deities would allow more than twenty to forty million... to die in one day? There is also a question of whether the altar rooms of science or mathematics of the past, present, or future would have been, or would be...able to predict

Chapter Thirty-One...'Seeing and 'Knowing'

or prevent the cataclysmic events of an Atlantis. How much evidence is needed to simply state that something is *seen* and *known* as truth? We must all be able to speak freely on these subjects, no matter how many additional questions come up. Ultimately, we must *see* and *know* the the truth...the Nature of Nature! No subject should be considered to be outside of the realm of true scientific or religious discussion. All of this might be considered to be one question, one answer viewed from many perspectives. Sometimes questions lead to answers that suggest other questions. Maybe the deities, the spirits, the immortals, the ancients, the scientists, magicians, and mathematicians have been trying to tell us of these things, and maybe we just haven't been listening."

Theoclea thought about what he had said. The words of the Merchant came back to her once again— *'Usually, only those who have had the Black Key and the wound can be considered for the Red Key, and the wound has to have been healed. They also must have reached for and attained higher spiritual levels and guidance. Most of all, they must answer the question, and the question changes with each new situation'.*

"Is there anything more that you need to *know?*" Pythagoras asked.

"No, Pythagoras, I *see* the complete picture, but there is something that you need." She pointed to the black key on a thong around his neck. "Take off the black key, Pythagoras." He took the key on the thong off of his neck. He was speechless. Theoclea reached behind a pillow for something.

"When I was a young girl, playing with my friends I was so sure of myself—there was one thing that I knew from the very beginning. I knew that I was on the *right path*." She found what she was looking for behind the pillow. She took it out and showed it to him. It was a Red Key on a leather thong.

"Pythagoras, I have a feeling that we will be together for a much longer time than either of us can possibly imagine, perhaps in realms, times and places that have not been revealed to us yet. There will be things that I will see, and things that you will *know*. There will be new adventures and challenges for both of us."

She placed the Red Key on its thong around his neck, and smiled fondly. Theoclea gazed into his eyes, kissed him, and whispered to him.

"Pythagoras, wherever we go, whatever paths we take, you're going to need a Red Key."

Chapter Thirty-One...'Seeing and 'Knowing'

He gazed at the Red Key—then looked back at her. *'No one could have survived what she went through without...changing'*, he thought. He felt as if he was changing as well—that he could believe what she was about to tell him.

"What kind of adventures do you foresee, Theoclea, what does the future hold for us?"

"I see us being together, past this life—I see us going through many gates in many times and realms—I see us in a process of becoming...and evolving."

"Of becoming what, Theoclea? As a scientist, I've never been sure of incarnations, reincarnations, other realms and times. I know nothing of these things."

Theoclea gazed into the distance...she saw a great city...she heard a strange music.

"What will I become, Theoclea, and who will you be? What do you see?"

"We may not always be together, Pythagoras. There may be adventures that we will have together and apart—as we have had in this life. We will continue to have adventures on the Earthly realm. When we pass on—things will continue as they have on the Earthly realm in other realms and times, there will be more Gates to pass through in those places. Whatever entities we may evolve into...we will have children...of a kind...just as we've had in this life. We will rise and evolve...past our own imaginings. I will continue on the right path just as I imagined it as a child playing with my friends in the woods, and you will be with me."

She continued to gaze into the distance...finally she saw a fiery desert and a cold wasteland. She closed her eyes

"What do you see, Theoclea?"

"We will become..."

Slowly she opened her eyes...and once more stared into the distance. There was a look of awe on her face, as if she herself could not believe it.

"Yes...Theoclea...what will we become?"

She stopped looking into the distance and gazed at him once again. A new light was shining in her eyes.

"You and I will become...The Mage...and The Source!"

*Author's Note—If you have enjoyed this book, please leave a review. Reviews can be given at:
http://**www.amazon.com/heo-clea-Pythagoras-Eleusis-Atlantis/product-reviews/1482052229/**
Just click on the 'Create a review' button.

Chapter Thirty-One...'Seeing and 'Knowing'

You can also search other retail sites:
www.createspace.com
and my own website
www.delphic-oracle-books.com

Here are some of the KeyRose images and poems that are mentioned in the book

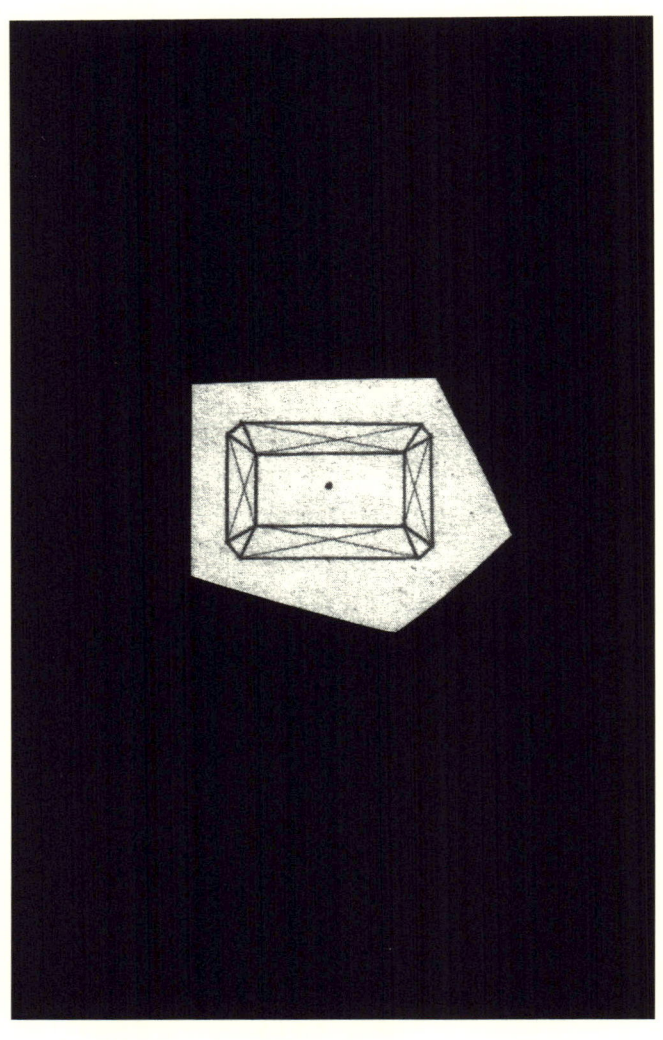

A RIGID STRUCTURE

A rigid structure,
but what of the dot?
Don't tell anyone who
you are,
tell them
who you are not.
Oh, I'm not this
and I'm not that,
and certainly, I'm not
them,
for they're all wrong, and we're all right,
for we're in the rectangular gem!
Yet others see a trampoline,
a telescope, perhaps.
a telescope that finds the dot,
the place where other life exists,
we're not alone,
there's other life,
what's it like?
does it look like us?
very unlikely,
that planet is smaller,
it's star is larger,

and what might we find when we zoom right in,
perhaps a world of purple plants,
perhaps a world devoid of SIN.
Ah, those folks who dream
those others who see,
look what happens
if we listen to them,
if we extend our hand
if we see what they see
that there's so much more
that's under the sun…
Oh my!
Our
rhyme may come undone.

ANCIENT MOTHER

Ancient Mother,
what do you see,
moon-lit mirth,
infinity?
The past, the future,
the shore at night,
all are part of your
luminous sight.
The verdant plain,
the lake of gloom,
the perfumed garden,
where roses bloom.
The risen sun,
The sunbeams' motes
the foam-born singer
with the sweet-scented notes?
Ancient mother, I hear your song,
a song of hope, for all day long
it calls to me
when I'm alone
the heart-gladdened-notes ,
from the incense-throne.
They speak of Eleusis

what a joyful scene
when Demeter the mother
met Proserpine.

you sing of that joy
you sing of that place
you sing of a time when the Human Race
shall seize the thunder
and forget the shame
and sing joyful songs
that honor your name.
Ancient Mother we hear your song
calling all of us together
in a joyful throng.
Our voices will rise in a
Candle-lit swoon,
and the sound will be heard
by the Stars and the Moon.

THE DANCE

As we grow old,
the dance lives on
'tis the same ancient dance that met the dawn
in a time when all the maidens and men
would dance with abandon in some shade-laden glen,
then run with each other to lie in the field
in the soft-dewy grass
where all wounds are healed.
Yes, they danced with each other, for they did not know
that their dance would end
with the soft-falling snow
and the wint'ry cold that would chill every heart.
So, with age and change the dancers would part.

Now, as we grow old
The dance lives on
'tis the same ancient dance
that met the dawn
in a time when all the women and men
would dance with each other in some shade-laden glen.
Now the glen in its gladness sheds its

wintry-silver Moon
and the stillness is broken by the song of a loon.
The moonlight is fading,
the Rose awaits the morn.
The dawn is rising, and no longer forlorn,
The dancers return,
but 'tis not them!
'tis their children,
who'll start the dance
once again.

The Pentacle Man

To bring back Spirit to Earth
to become complete
and feel rebirth
we first need fire
the passion within.
From without comes air
and our voices begin.
There are forces that bind us to the Earth
and the God and the Goddess that gave us birth.
from the water within
that shapes our tears
to the water without
to the sea of our fears.
We look up to Spirit
our heads held high
we do not fear it
we hear its' cry.
The Goddess protects us
in a circle of light!
as Spirit ascends
What a glorious sight!

The Rose

In the Elysian Fields
a flower grows,
its' shape, its' scent is
like a Rose
but it's pale and wan
as Roses go,
the Rose of Hades is white as snow.
It's lost its' life and redness here
it longs for the Earth,
it sheds a tear.
On the plain of Eleusis
there is a Rose.
Each spring and summer
its' redness glows.
It tells the story
we hold so dear
of how—
Persephone escaped from fear,
and Demeter joined her
in joyful song.
A chant was sung by the
heaven-sent throng

The Gods and Goddesses clapped as they sang and the High world rejoiced, as the morning bells rang!
(Thanks to Edward Carpenter)

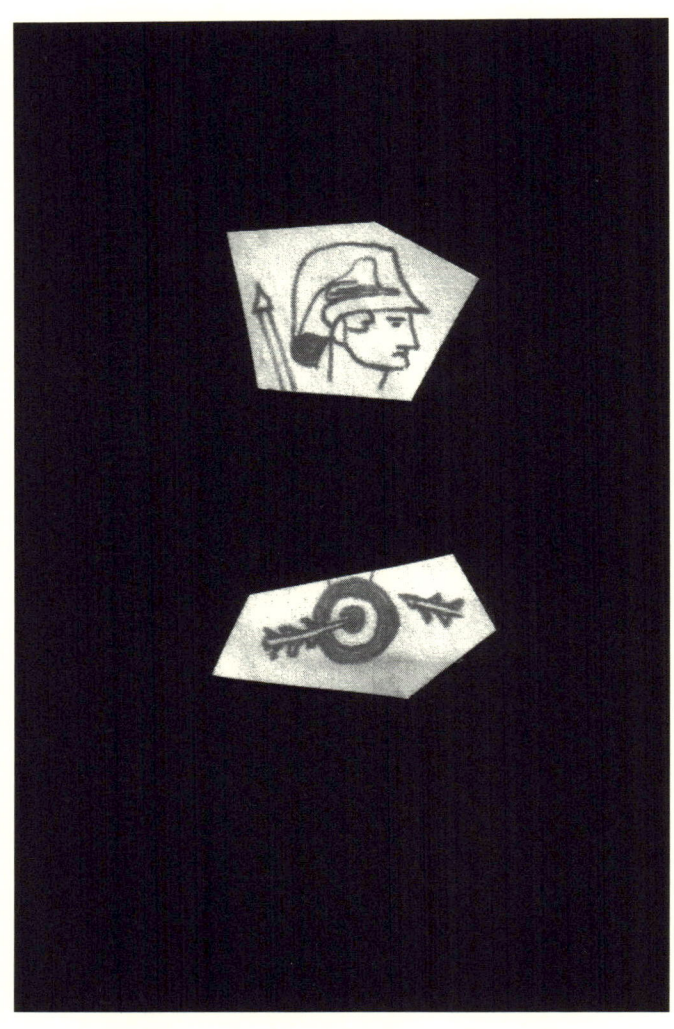

THE GUARDIAN AND THE BULLSEYE

"What are you aiming for?"
(the Guardian seeks an answer)
...and I reply
"A truer arm,
a steady gaze
with no alarm,
a focused mind, a fuller heart,
protection from
life's chance-laden dart.
The Guardian thinks
and then replies-
"I see the truth, it's in your eyes
your heart is good,
you seek the cause,
to be yourself,
obey YOUR laws,
to be complete,
your task to meet."
(Then I reply)
"I seek an answer to this question—
How can this be done?"

(He thinks a moment,

then reflects)
"To reach the Gate before life's end
to see the reborn YOU
'tis better to miss
again and again
In the end your aim will be true!

THE FINGERPRINT

She left a fingerprint
on the Gate,
it took so long to get so near,
now YOU are here,
why hesitate?
for most of us the path is clear.
Now why stand still when you've come so far?
your strength and will
tell us who you are

Ah, yes this Gate may be your last,
and you are filled with fear, of course!
GO THROUGH!
The stones have all been cast,
this Gate will lead you to the Source!

There is a poem that forms

One of the central themes and final action

of the sequel to this book,

'Theoclea (The Delphic Oracle)

and Pythagoras in Egypt'

I have reprinted the poem,

"Summer Light, the Tree and the Pond".

A year after writing the poem, a companion

poem revealed itself to me,

"A Time of a Prophecy Fulfilled!"

and so here they are

for the first time, published together!

Summer Light, The Tree, And The Pond

I sat on a bench at the
edge of a cliff,
overlooking a pond
that had been created
by the overflowing of the Nile.
In the distance, I saw fishermen
at the edge of the pond—
their nets revealed a meager catch
for the day.
Slowly they went home.

Then, I saw something that I had never seen before.
To the left of me was a great tree
that grew on the edge of the cliff.
Suddenly, I saw bands of light
flowing inward towards the trunk!
They started at the right from the very edge
of the smallest branches, and flowed inward.
They reached the trunk and then flowed outward
toward the very smallest branches to the left.
Each band could not have been more
than six inches in length.

There was a continuous movement
of these bands and then they vanished.
What was causing this?
I noticed that a young boy had
thrown stones into the pond.
I watched him pass by, and then disappear out of
sight.
I threw two stones into the pond,
and watched the waves that were created
when the stones hit the water.
Then, I witnessed
a solemn procession of Priests and Priestesses.
They could not see me sitting on the bench near the
tree.
I smelled their incense,
and heard their chanting.
I sensed that
It was possible that they were an illusion,
and that they could not see me,
the tree, or the bench.
None of them looked in my direction
They were looking at another tree,
another bench, in another time.
My attention was brought back to
the waves in the pond

The motion of the waves moving away
from the two central points,
the interference caused by the waves,
all of this was being
reflected by the tree in its' entirety.
A seemingly chance coming together
of events of this particular day
at this place and time
had created a magical tree!
I have long felt that light and sound are created by
waves
that appear to us as something else.
On that particular day, at that particular moment,
something had been created.
I looked at the bands of light, and noticed
that they were all not the same size!
There was a minute difference in size and luminosity.
They were self-similar, and yet different.
I decided to climb
down the cliff to the pond.
When I reached the pond,
I sat on a rock.
I looked toward my left
and saw the dappled sunlight.
The sunlight reflected

a multitude of self-similar
repeated patterns of leaves,
creating sparkling lights that
were hovering over the water.
Under the water, there seemed to be
A procession of green lights moving,
moving toward me,
yet never reaching me,
an army moving in, and then vanishing.

I was in Egypt for eleven years.
Every year on that day at that same time,
I returned to the same spot.
For eleven years I witnessed the
same illusions.
I smelled the same incense, I heard the same
chanting.
It was only on that day, at that time,
that I saw it all…for I returned
to the spot at various other times during
those years.
Finally, in my eleventh year,
it was all once again the same,
the fisherman with their meager catch,
the solemn procession that could not see me,

the bands of light moving across the tree.
The sparkling lights on the water
I didn't realize something—
that would be my last year in Egypt,
and I would never see any of it again.
I knew that for the rest of my life,
I would ponder those events,
especially on that day,
at that time,
every year.

A Time of a Prophecy Fulfilled!
Some time ago, I wrote a poem about summer light,
a tree, and a pond.
In the poem, I sat and reflected upon
events and a vision that I saw from a bench that
overlooked a pond
that was formed by the inundation
of the Nile.
I was a student of the Mysteries of Egypt—
The Prophecies were of
special interest to me.
There was a stone stairway that led down to the pond.
As part of the vision in the poem, I looked behind
me
and saw a ghostly procession of Priests and Priestesses
walking and chanting.
They didn't even see me,
sitting on the bench.
It was as if they were in another time
where there was the bench, the tree
and the pond,
but in their time, the bench was empty,
there was no one sitting on it.
***
Recently, I attended the

Mysteries of Egypt once again.
The culmination was to be a ritual—
I didn't realize until I looked at the program
that the ritual was to take place near the bench,
the tree, and the pond.
It all started at midnight
on the full moon.
We gathered, and had already learned a chant—
I stood there, waiting for the ritual to begin,
and then had a realization—
a revelation—
I was to be a part of a
procession of Priests and Priestesses!
I looked over at the bench and the tree.
I knew that Nature had demolished the stone steps
that led down to the pond!
I was in the same place, but in another time,
and I was to be a part
of the ghostly procession!
I stood back and leaned against another tree.
Oh my God—was this a dream?
Perhaps I was asleep...
we were all to be part of a procession of souls...
following the Sun God Ra...
through the underworld.

I closed my eyes,
Blessed Goddesses, how could this be?
I was stunned, and then the moment of truth,
the moment of a profound awakening
came to me like a sudden inundation of the Nile!
Suddenly, I opened my eyes—
I knew that there would be others—
and that there had been others
who sat on the bench
in a number of possible times—
in an infinite number of possibilities
of the past and the future...
and the time that I was in...
Praise be to the Gods and the Goddesses—
for this gift...
a revelation that
the time that I found myself in...
praise be...
...was a time of...

***

A Time of a Prophecy Fulfilled!

Printed in Great Britain
by Amazon.co.uk, Ltd.,
Marston Gate.